Molly s _____ ___ng toward her, holding out his hand.

He led her into the actual ballroom and Molly realized that now she was one of the crowd, enjoying herself like everyone else on the dance floor. A good feeling, yet odd for someone who'd always yearned to stand out. To stand above. To be the best...

Her world had shrunk in the past few years. Now Molly felt it begin to grow again. Tempting her with infinite possibilities.

The music changed to a slow waltz, and Sam's arm tightened gently around her. She couldn't resist laying her head on his shoulder, relishing the strength of his broad chest, powerful arms and the total masculine entity that was Sam. She stroked his back where her hand rested, feeling the hard muscle beneath and enjoying it.

She felt a brief kiss on her temple, and tears threatened to fall. She felt so normal! Totally feminine and desirable. Just like other women. Just the way she used to feel before the accident changed everything.

Now she knew differently. Now she understood that she had the power to change her life yet again.

Dear Friends,

Finding love is such a quirky thing. It can happen when we least expect it or don't even want it. There are no rules as to when, where, or how our hearts will be given to another. But one truth I do know: Love can change everything!

Molly Porter's life has literally turned upside down after a disabling fall while skiing a practice run for the U.S. Olympic team. Her professional and personal dreams are over.

Sam Kincaid has lost three dotcom companies as well as his girlfriend and is left with nothing except his car.

Their opinions of each other are not high when they meet. In fact, they're downright low. But throw them together with a common goal in an historic hotel, and watch how two people can grow on each other. And grow up at the same time.

By the way, you've met Molly before. She's Amanda Shaw's little sister (Superromance #971) who's had to age quickly in order to star in her own story! Forgive me for playing with the passage of time.

Happy reading!

Linda Barrett

P.S. I'd love to hear from you! Stay in touch through my Web site at www.superauthors.com or write to me at P.O. Box 841934, Houston TX, 77284-1934.

The Inn at Oak Creek
Linda Barrett

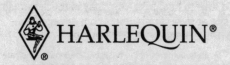

TORONTO • NEW YORK • LONDON
AMSTERDAM • PARIS • SYDNEY • HAMBURG
STOCKHOLM • ATHENS • TOKYO • MILAN • MADRID
PRAGUE • WARSAW • BUDAPEST • AUCKLAND

ISBN 0-373-71115-8

THE INN AT OAK CREEK

Copyright © 2003 by Linda Barrett.

This edition published by arrangement with Harlequin Books S.A.

® and TM are trademarks of the publisher. Trademarks indicated with
® are registered in the United States Patent and Trademark Office, the
Canadian Trade Marks Office and in other countries.

Visit us at www.eHarlequin.com

Printed in U.S.A.

This book is for Zilla Soriano,
editor, teacher, partner and friend.

Thank you for always wanting the best book possible and
for possessing the intelligence and talent to light my way.

I'm so glad THE CALL came from you!

PROLOGUE

HEAVEN.

On her skis at the three-thousand-foot mark, Molly Porter paused beyond the lift station, pushed her goggles to her forehead and scanned the horizon in her usual deliberate manner. First to the left, then to the right, her eyes absorbed what Mother Nature had provided. A smile tugged at Molly's mouth. Beauty. Today she was surrounded by beauty.

Snow-covered mountains glistened in the bright winter sun. Virgin snow mostly, pristine white blankets barely marred by skiers' tracks. Overhead in the never-ending sky, small, fluffy clouds were scattered across the field of blue. Molly blinked back incipient tears. No artist could reproduce this panorama that so touched her soul.

She sighed with pleasure as she snapped a mental picture of the view, then tucked the memory away and shifted her attention to the challenge ahead. No, not this slope. The run down this mountainside would be for sheer pleasure, a time-out to mentally prepare herself to win the gold. Olympic gold. For her country, for her family, for herself.

She dug her poles into the hard-packed snow,

shifted her weight and started her run, dreaming of what the medal would mean to Diamond Ridge, her family's ski resort in Vermont. Mom and Dad would burst with pride, but her sister and brother-in-law would couple their cheers with an advertising campaign to grow the business yet again.

At the base of the mountain Molly checked her watch and quickly caught up with the rest of her teammates. Respect, affection and loyalty had already bonded them into a unit. An American unit, seeking a medal sweep for the United States. They were competitors, every last one of them. They were athletes, healthy and strong, both physically and mentally.

She grinned at her friend Julie, who jabbed repeatedly at her watch. "Sorry," said Molly. "I needed my own space for a minute."

"Find your own space later," Julie replied. "Now get ready for a timed run." Julie inclined her head toward the rest of the group as they made their way to the lifts.

"Not to worry, Jules," said Molly. "I *am* ready. I've been ready for twenty-two years, my whole life. Centered and focused. Even have my number on." Molly pointed at her vest, where the number six stood a foot and a half tall.

"Jeez, I don't know why I worry about you," Julie grumbled. "You've already posted the fastest time during our trial runs so far. And you're always in total control."

"Is that a polite way of saying I'm a control

freak?'' Molly laughed, unconcerned about the answer. Control was the name of the game when the
game was played at seventy miles an hour or more.

"Nah," said Julie. "Maybe I wish I had a little
extra."

Molly glanced at her friend and squeezed her
shoulder. "There's nothing wrong with you or your
skiing. In fact, I've never seen you in better form."

A moment passed before Julie answered.
"Thanks, Molly. Coming from you, it means a great
deal."

Coming from her? Molly shrugged. She wasn't
the captain of the Olympic team as she'd been of
her high-school team. And Julie had only known her
since they'd met at the nationals two years ago. But
Molly was used to leadership, of taking the initia-
tive. If she could inject a fraction more confidence
in the other girl, so much the better for everyone.

"Our turn," Molly said, slipping onto the chairlift
and leaving room for Julie. "Look," she said seconds later, pointing at some men with video equipment riding the big cats partway up the hill. "Seems
like we're being filmed today."

"Does it bother you?" asked Julie.

"Of course not," Molly replied, a little surprised
at the question. "I'm so focused on my skiing I
don't even notice. And besides," she added with a
grin, "I like to study myself later. If I can increase
my speed even a fraction of a second by doing
something a little differently, I'll do it."

"I know, Molly," Julie said. "We *all* know."

Then Julie grinned. "And we all do the same thing."

Molly returned her friend's smile. Skiing at top form was their job. It was definitely *her* goal. She was at one with the mountain, in Vermont, in Colorado or here in Lake Placid, New York, at the Olympic Training Center. In every season of the year she ran to the mountains—climbing, hiking or skiing. During every school break from college during the past two years, she would first visit her family and then head to the sky-high summits. She craved that time, that space. Her older sister, Amanda, understood it best because she'd run to the mountains, too, years ago, when she'd needed solitude.

Now Molly slid from the chair, skied into the start house and waited for her turn, after Julie. She spoke to no one. Instead, she stood near the entrance, goggles in place, and studied the terrain. Little by little, the people and noise around her faded until she was in her own world, concentrating only on the mountain, on what she was born to do.

"Porter, get ready."

Molly nodded, stepped to the start gate and leaned forward into position.

"Ready...set...go!"

She shot down the slope, legs pumping, skis gliding, picking up speed with every stroke against the snow. The wind whipped her cheeks as she banked into each turn, pushing and pushing, hoping her skill, along with gravity, would take a second or more off her time.

She hit sixty miles an hour, sixty-five, then seventy by the halfway point. She was on! Might even establish a new personal best. Shifting her weight, she took a turn, then headed straight downhill again.

Faster, faster and into another turn. *What the...?* *Ice. Hidden ice.* Her skis chattered and slid. Applying pressure to catch an edge, Molly leaned over hard. And then everything happened at once.

Her skis slipped out from under her, catapulting her into a backward somersault. Her shoulder slammed into the slope, the skis now above her head. Ice tore at her cheek as she continued to slide down the mountain. *Roll with it! Roll with it!* She twisted to get control. Too fast. She was spinning too fast. Head over heels, she pinwheeled. Her legs tangled. One ski off, one ski still on. She couldn't breathe. Over and over, cartwheeling, banging her head against the hard-packed snow. Her vision dimmed, blackened. *Inhale!* Blinking as she hurtled down the hill like an out-of-control missile, she glimpsed the orange safety fence looming in front of her, a virtual brick wall.

Good-bye, family. I love you.

CHAPTER ONE

Four years later

HELL.

Sam Kincaid stood in front of a room filled with his employees and knew what hell felt like. A powerful heat. A powerful sweat. But most of all, a powerful sorrow.

He cleared his throat, hating what he had to do, hating himself for having caused the bankruptcy. He glanced at his watch. One o'clock. By five after, they'd all know. The telling would be over.

"Good afternoon, everyone," he began, "and thank you for being so prompt." He hoped his voice wouldn't crack as it did so often when he was an adolescent. Funny how at twenty-nine, he didn't seem so far removed from his younger self.

The room had become quiet, all eyes studying him. He tried to smile, but his effort fell short. Just like his efforts to capitalize on the dot-com revolution.

He gazed at the large group in front of him. These were people he had recruited, people who had believed in him. They'd use him for spitball target practice when he was through.

"There's not a man or woman in this room I don't respect," he began. His voice was steady enough, but dang, if his Texas drawl hadn't reappeared to keep his nerves company. A Southern twang in a Silicon Valley crowd.

"You've worked hard to build a business with me," he continued. "Toys-2-Go.com required creative energy, technical skill and an old-fashioned work ethic. And you've come through with them all."

He wished he could stop right there and turn the funeral into a celebration. But folks don't celebrate when they lose their jobs.

"The company should have succeeded," he said. "But it hasn't."

Now he heard a murmur go through the room. He waited. "The bottom line is that our assets are being liquidated. Capital equipment, inventory, everything. Toys-2-Go.com no longer exists, and we are all out of jobs. Including me."

Deafening silence greeted his announcement. He'd expected it, but the intensity contained an element of drama he wasn't used to.

Then came the questions. Yes, they'd be eligible for unemployment. No, there was no outplacement service. Couldn't afford it. What about Sam's other two online companies?

Sam met their collective gaze and swallowed

hard. "This is my first go-round." His voice did break now, but he quickly coughed to cover it up. "When I leave here, I'll be visiting Groceries-2-Go.com and then Books-2-Go.com and delivering the same news." He spoke the words, he heard the words, but he couldn't believe he was saying the words. Perspiration trickled down his back, and he shivered in the warm room.

The day was, without a doubt, the worst day of his life. "Three years ago," he said, almost ruminating, "we thought the world was ours."

"Then why?" asked Fred Marks, a customer-service supervisor and one of Sam's most loyal employees. "Why have the companies gone under?"

Sam's thoughts raced. How should he answer? He could be flippant. He could go with the economic theories of supply and demand and simply admit they had too much supply and not enough demand. But that would be only part of it. They'd gone under for the same reasons that ninety-one other dot-coms had closed their doors since the "revolution" began.

The big hype. The limitless possibilities online. The excitement of the new economy. Greed. Investors had hopes of fast money, and venture capitalists had lowered their standards. Sam hadn't seen that his companies, as well as many other failed companies, were built on a foundation of sand.

But blaming others had never been his style. His folks hadn't brought him up that way. He took a deep breath. "We went under because I made mistakes."

He'd been the CEO—still was—at least until the filings were completed. The bottom line was his responsibility. He should have taken more time to analyze. He should have known better. He'd earned two degrees, one in computer technology, the other an MBA from Stanford. He should have known better!

His friends at the software-design company he'd worked at after his second graduation had backed him in these online ventures. Buddies from school had invested, as well. And now, not only were almost a thousand good people out of work, his friends had lost everything.

And so had he.

SAM'S SHIRT was totally damp when he returned to his upscale duplex that evening. With impatient fingers, he managed to pull the buttons through the holes, and by the time he opened the door, the shirt had become a crumpled ball in his fist. He tossed it on the floor and pushed his hair out of his eyes for the millionth time that day. His straight hair always seemed to be too long, falling down his forehead even a day after it was cut. Next time he'd opt for a military style.

He finally closed the door behind him and basked in the familiarity of home, like an injured wolf returning to his lair. A safe place to lick his wide-open

wounds. But was his home safe? He studied his surroundings—the parquet floors, the soft leather
couch, the beautiful cherry desk in his office—and
he had his answer. No. This home was no longer
safe because soon it would no longer be his. Another
month. Two, at best. He rented the apartment at an
exorbitant rate, always too busy managing his companies to take the time to invest in a permanent
home.

In the beginning the money flowed like cham-
pagne on New Year's Eve. Each day was a holiday.
There was no rush to buy a condo or a house. That
would come later like so many other dreams....

Sam leaned against the door and started to laugh.
Not a happy sound. The three-year roll had been too
good to be true. Suddenly his dad's plainspoken
voice echoed in his mind. *If something seems too
good to be true, then it probably is.* His hardworking, common-sense dad had been right again.

His heart lurched as he pictured his folks back in
Texas. He'd grown up just outside of Austin, where
his parents still lived. Sam was their only child, their
"miracle baby," and he'd dreamed of providing
miracles for them each time he visited. Money for
their retirement, for trips, for whatever they wanted.

He kicked his shirt along the hall toward the bedroom, not gaining any satisfaction in its light weight
and weak resistance to his foot. He'd rather be kicking ass. Or a least a football. Instead, he donned a
pair of shorts, a T-shirt and running shoes, eager to

escape the depression that stalked him. A beautiful April evening beckoned.

He jogged toward the kitchen for a quick drink of water, hoping that Adrienne would stop over that night, then sniffed the air. Adrienne's perfume. A bold aroma for a bold contemporary woman. His girlfriend had a key to his apartment, a convenient arrangement. He must have just missed her. Too bad. He could have used her support today. God knew, he'd tried to provide all-out support to her this past month regarding a totally different problem. He amended the thought. His ambitious girlfriend considered it a problem. For him, her unplanned pregnancy, while a definite accident, was still classified as a miracle in his mind.

Sam stopped in his tracks at the threshold to the kitchen when he spotted the array of items on the table. He frowned. He hadn't left anything cluttering the place. He walked closer.

A key, a tie, a plastic supermarket bag with… underwear—his underwear—and two pairs of socks… What the…? And then he noticed a cassette tape with a note in Adrienne's block-style print. "Play the cassette," it read, "and you'll understand my decision."

He jammed the tiny tape into his answering machine and pushed the "play" button.

I wish you the best, Sam, but I'm flying solo now. There's too much negative energy around you, and I can't afford to be surrounded by failure when I'm on a fast track straight up. I'm leaving town tonight and taking care of our little—shall we say—problem. You're off the hook. I won't be back. My promotion came through and I'm relocating out of the country. Please don't try to track me down. Don't contact me. I'm doing what I want. Good luck. No hard feelings.

He stared at the machine, dumbfounded, watching the cassette turn until it shut itself off. Would this day never end? Was he having a nightmare or an out-of-body experience? Maybe he was acting in a play?

Self-deprecating laughter threatened to erupt in his throat. Unshed tears pressed behind his eyes, and pain throbbed throughout his body. On what scale would he measure losing the promise of a child? Losing a connected human being? And losing Adrienne? Beautiful, sensuous, violet-eyed Adrienne? A yearning traveled through him, but stopped just short of his heart. He drew a breath. Was his loss for what might have been rather than for what they had actually shared?

Sam walked to the window, needing to see the sun, needing to know it still shone. The park beckoned through the glass with its familiar mile-long, tree-shaded track. He needed the track tonight just as he needed to feel the sun before it faded from the sky. But instead of running his usual five laps, he'd walk them. He couldn't run on empty.

A MONTH LATER Sam had lost count of the number of meetings he'd had with accountants and lawyers, how many papers he'd signed or how many phone calls he'd made to arrange for the liquidation of inventory. On the last day of May, he visited that inventory in the graveyard of dot-coms. A warehouse the size of eight football fields, it housed the remains of not only his products, but the inventory of hundreds of companies that had closed their doors. Legally his visit wasn't mandated, but he wanted to go. He wanted to see the process through to the end. And then maybe he could walk away with some of his conscience salved.

As therapy, it wasn't great, he admitted to himself when he left the warehouse behind him that evening. Like going through nicotine withdrawal or a last goodbye. But at least the visit was over. The meetings were over. The bankruptcy filings were over. Everything was finished. He hadn't run away; instead, he'd seen it through. He was exhausted.

And now he had to begin all over again.

As he drove back to his apartment, he sorted his priorities. First, he needed money. And second, he needed time. His financial situation was serious, because he'd plowed all his profit back into his companies. He considered his best plan of action. While his first love was software—hell, he could write the stuff blindfolded—he craved the challenge of managing a complete entity. He needed to reestablish himself in order to run a high-tech business again, and that would take time.

He pounded the steering wheel in frustration. Who was he kidding? He didn't have time. He needed an income now! Any reasonable job would do. He was still young—he still had time to make his mark. He'd start an all-out job search tomorrow.

Third priority, he needed a cheap place to live until he got back on top. He'd grown up living plain. He could do it again. He'd start looking for apartments tomorrow.

And fourth, he had to finally accept Adrienne's defection. He hadn't heard from her. Rumor had it that she'd relocated to Europe, maybe the French division of her corporation. He'd had virtually no time to do any detective work—and judging from her parting message, she wouldn't have appreciated it if he had.

Adrienne was who she was, and she was going her own way. He could deal with that. Their relationship had certainly been affectionate and sexually intimate. But was there love? True love? He didn't think so. It wasn't Adrienne, or her departure, that caused a hard knot to form in his middle. It was the other matter that made him wince, the other matter that he doubted he'd ever forget.

By the time he walked into his kitchen, his mind was clear. His priorities were clear. He was calm and ready to act. Ready for a good night's sleep, tomorrow couldn't come soon enough for him.

The blinking light on his answering machine caught his attention, and he pushed the button quickly. Maybe one of his buddies had come through with a job lead. But it was his dad's voice he heard, the words coming slowly, with pauses for breaths: "Uncle John passed away today, Sam. Totally unexpected. Call when you get in."

His hand shook as he punched the familiar Texas number. His heart raced, his mind refusing to believe. His dad's brother was like a second father to him. He loved the man. Admired him, too. His uncle ran an historic hotel twenty miles west of his folks' place, in the scenic and popular hill country. When his aunt died several years ago, the family thought his uncle would sell, since he and his aunt Ruth had no children. But Uncle John had surprised them. He needed to keep busy and the Bluebonnet Hotel helped him fulfill that goal.

"Hello?"

His heart cringed at his mom's pain-filled tone. "Hello, Mom. I got Dad's message. What happened?"

"Oh, Sam. I'm so glad you called. We're all so upset. The poor man. There was no warning, nothing. A heart attack. And poof! He was gone." Her voice broke. "Can you come home for a few days, son? We'll plan the funeral around your schedule."

"I'll fly tomorrow," he replied before slapping

his forehead. His funds were too low to afford a last-minute flight. "Never mind, Mom. I'll drive down and stay as long as you need me."

"You will? You can? But what about your job?"

"I can get away," he said. "Don't worry about it."

"I'll be glad to see you, Sam. Very glad. Your dad and I miss you."

"And I miss you, too." A comfortable silence filled the wire for a moment, until Sam thought about practicalities.

"What about the Bluebonnet, Mom? With you and Dad working your own jobs, is there anyone who can run it until we figure out what to do?"

"Yes, thank God. That's all taken care of. Your uncle hired an assistant about two weeks ago. What timing! She's young. Just graduated from hotel-management school in the East. Maybe," his mother said thoughtfully, "John was feeling poorly and needed someone to help him."

"And didn't tell you?"

"Your uncle wouldn't have told me if he had a hangnail! Stubborn man." Strong affection mixed with frustration in his mother's voice.

"No," said Sam. "Not stubborn. He just didn't want you to worry."

"And look what happened!"

Sam chuckled. Couldn't help it. His mom always wanted to protect her family and fix whatever was wrong. She always thought she could make "it" better, whatever "it" happened to be. "You couldn't have prevented this, Mom," said Sam. "Don't even think about it."

"I know you're right, but I wish…"

"Yeah," he whispered. "Me, too."

"Come home, Sam. We're staying at the Bluebonnet in the meantime."

"I'm on my way."

Sam replaced the receiver, rearranging his list of priorities. No job searching, no apartment searching, no time for anything except some quick phone calls to his friends and getting himself back to Oak Creek, Texas, and the Bluebonnet Hotel. He laughed with a measure of irony. He might be broke, but at least he'd arrive in style. His BMW 535i was fully paid off and no one would be the wiser about his finances. Like his uncle John, he didn't want his folks to worry. With a little luck, they'd never have to know about his career, or the lack of it.

"I'M VERY SORRY for your loss, Mr. Kincaid."

Sam nodded at the young woman standing behind the front desk in the lobby of the Bluebonnet Hotel. Although she stood at an angle, reaching for something behind her, the gentleness in her voice reached him, even with its clipped vowels and Northern accent. Not Boston or New York, but somewhere on the East Coast.

"Thank you," Sam replied, nodding briefly before turning to scan the ornately tiled room. He

noted the familiar wrought-iron ceiling fans and wall
sconces as he searched for a familiar face. It was
late afternoon; he'd driven for almost two days nonstop and he needed to crash. But first, he wanted to
say hello to his parents.

"Your folks aren't here," came the quiet voice
again.

He swiveled around, his systems becoming alert.
Was she reading his mind? "And you are…?"

"Molly Porter," she replied, extending her hand
across the desk. "The new assistant manager of the
hotel, at least for now."

She offered a firm handshake, her palm engulfed
in his larger one. He assessed her quickly. Not his
type. Her complexion was too pale, her face bare of
cosmetics. Her honey-blond hair was pulled straight
back, neatly gathered behind her neck with a bar-
rette, and her simple white cotton blouse did nothing
to show off her figure. But when Sam looked into
her eyes, he paused. They were the saddest eyes
he'd ever seen. Or maybe, hopefully, they were just
tired. Maybe *she* was tired. The past two days had
to have been rough at the hotel because of his uncle's death. But sad or tired, those big blue eyes
were looking, rock-steady, back at him.

"The new graduate?" he asked, remembering his
mother's words on the phone.

"That's right. Cornell University School of Hotel
Management."

Great credentials, but she didn't seem like a re-

cent grad. Not with her calm, self-possessed manner
or the patient way she waited for him to reply.

"Well, Ms. Porter," he said, reaching for his suit-
case, "which room is available to me?"

She smiled at him, and he blinked with surprise.
What a difference! Beautiful. The woman was beautiful, and he was speechless. But…how? She had no
style. She was nothing special. But when that smile
appeared…

"I'm told we're informal in Texas," she said.
"Call me Molly."

She turned her head to procure a room key and
he barely controlled his gasp. A jagged scar snaked
from her right temple down the side of her face all
the way to her jaw. He shivered at the possibilities.

"Your parents are at the funeral home making
arrangements," she said, offering him the key. "I'll
let them know you've arrived as soon as they return,
Mr. Kincaid."

"Sam," he replied. "Call me Sam. As you said,
we're informal here. Texas friendly." He took the
key and waited.

"Sorry, only have a third-floor single at the back.
We're full up. I'm sure you know the way."

He grinned. "I certainly do." He hefted his va-
lise.

"Oh! One more thing," Molly said.

Sam paused and turned his head.

"Welcome home."

"Thanks, but it's only a visit."

She offered another smile and waved his remark away. "Just following orders. Your folks asked me to welcome you home, so I have."

"Then consider your mission accomplished."

She nodded. "If you need anything..."

"I know what to do. Thanks." Too impatient to wait for an elevator, he strode to the closest staircase and started to climb while he sorted out his impressions. Interesting woman. A little strange, though, or maybe intriguing. Seemed competent behind the desk, but time would tell.

Curious, he looked back to observe her once more, and froze in place. Molly, in a long, flowing green-and-white-print skirt, was slowly limping her way—long step, short step—across the wide lobby floor. Long step, short step.

He gaped at her uneven progress. Poor woman, but for God's sake! What had his uncle been thinking? She may have the smarts, but certainly not the stamina to manage a busy, successful hotel. He shook his head. Changes would have to be made.

So that was the son Irene and George Kincaid were so proud of. Molly shrugged as she walked back to her office. He hadn't struck her as anything special. Keeping in mind that the Kincaids were the older-than-average, doting parents of an only child, she decided to reserve her judgment. She had to admit, however, that on the outside, Sam was a hunk. A six-foot, broad-shouldered, honest and true male hunk. Under the scruffy beard and shank of black hair that flopped into his intense dark eyes, Sam exemplified the male of the species in the prime of life. She hoped his interior profile was as handsome.

Impulsively Molly glanced over her shoulder toward the staircase. *Gotcha.* Her eyes caught his and in his expression she saw…pity. She felt herself stiffen, her mouth harden and her eyes blaze. She hoped she scorched him with her stare.

With a slow, deliberate motion, she lifted her chin and turned her back, continuing on her way. Self-pity had almost defeated her in the past, and sometimes in the middle of the night, its tentacles still threatened to pull her under. But she'd finally conquered it during the past year—at least she'd made a start—and she wouldn't let an outsider's opinion undo her achievement.

She scanned the lobby as she walked, impressed with the Old World charm John Kincaid had maintained through the years. She would have enjoyed working here with him, a hotelier through and through, concerned about his guests and the quality of service the hotel provided. They had started to forge themselves into a strong management team. A long sigh escaped her. Poor guy. And as for her, well, she'd keep her suitcases half-packed, despite the standard six-month contract she'd signed with John. Who knew what would happen to the hotel now?

She laughed at the irony of her situation. Her family had been totally against her taking this job and leaving Diamond Ridge, their ski resort in Vermont. Not after almost losing her four years ago. And not after going through hell to bring her back to life. They'd nursed her and cajoled her; they'd pushed, they'd pulled, they'd praised, they'd scolded, they'd cried, they'd laughed—in short, they'd fought like demons to make her well after the accident, when all she wanted to do was die. They'd simply refused to let her.

And when she was finally on her feet, they'd pushed her again. "Finish your degree. Go back to school." Deep lines etched her dad's face. He'd aged twenty years in two, and he wasn't a young man anymore. Her mom, also, had more gray hair than Molly cared to acknowledge.

Molly hadn't needed a diploma to work at Diamond Ridge. She hadn't wanted to return to school. But when she looked into the faces of the people she loved and who loved her, and when her sister, Amanda, said, "Make new friends, be around young people, start over," she knew she had to go. Not for her own sake, but for theirs.

Cornell University in upstate New York was close to home, and her family had heaved a collective sigh of relief about her proximity to them. They sure hadn't wanted her to find a job almost two thousand miles away! But Molly wanted out of snow country, away from the mountains, away from the joyful tumult of the busy slopes.

She settled back into the chair behind her desk, her fingertips absently stroking the scar on her cheek. It didn't bother her. She'd trade her fractured bones for a dozen more scars in a heartbeat. For strong legs she'd trade anything. Damn! She'd been an athlete! An Olympian! Even now, the rage of injustice surged through her blood and her hands balled into fists on the desk.

If only she could undo that day. If only, she hadn't skied so fast. If only she could blame someone or something. But it had been an accident. For cripe's sake, a stupid accident. And no *if only*s were going to change the outcome.

Snap out of it. Now! She focused on the paperwork in front of her and felt her tension slowly dissolve. Soon she was absorbed in the weekly reports from each department—Reservations, Catering, Housekeeping, Facilities, Staffing and Public Relations. She and John Kincaid had been reviewing the reports before his death. He'd been eager for her to learn as much as possible, and she'd appreciated his attitude. Work was therapy for her, a weapon against depression. As long as she was on the payroll, she'd continue to do her job at the Bluebonnet Hotel.

TWO DAYS LATER, after the funeral of his uncle, Sam stood next to his parents in the comfortable lobby of the hotel, greeting visitors and accepting condolences. He'd shaken a least a hundred hands so far, and more people were coming in.

"John had so many friends," Irene Kincaid whispered. "After all the years in the same town, his business friends became personal ones."

Sam nodded and wished all the friends would leave quickly. His mother looked tired, and his dad's shoulders were bent with a heavy load of grief. No question, the brothers had been close, and his dad's heart was breaking now.

"Why don't the two of you sit down for a while," he suggested, glancing around the room. Love seats and sofas coordinated with the old-fashioned decor, and he tried steering them toward the closest couch.

Irene shook her head. "No, dear. Molly's set up the grand ballroom for lunch. Just a simple buffet."

Sam nodded, resigned to another couple of hours making polite conversation. With seating for two hundred people, their grand ballroom was the size of a normal party room in a modern hotel. Sam had a feeling that every one of those seats would have an occupant today. With his arm around his father's shoulders, he escorted his parents to the ballroom.

"Oh!" Irene paused at the entrance. "Molly did a wonderful job. I think John would have approved."

Vases of seasonal flowers and a variety of foods covered three long buffet tables, while round dining tables sported pale pink cloths and pitchers of iced tea. In the middle of the room, a table larger than the rest held a reserved sign next to a colorful bouquet. Sam led his parents directly to it.

"My brother took a liking to Molly," said George Kincaid. "And maybe she took a liking to him, too. She once told me that John reminded her of her dad."

Sam grunted. His uncle was gone; Molly's feelings about him didn't matter anymore. But he had to admit, her arrangements for the luncheon would have done John Kincaid proud.

"Sit for awhile," Sam suggested again. "I'll bring you something." Relieved when his parents acquiesced, he made his way to the buffet and filled a plate from the pasta table with tossed salad, garlic bread and penne pasta with house marinara sauce. He filled a second plate with honey-glazed ham, smoked turkey breast, potato salad and two dinner rolls before bringing the selections to his parents. Now they'd be able to choose whatever they wanted. Whatever they could manage to eat.

As he returned to the buffet table to prepare a plate for himself, he saw Molly standing to one side, speaking to a server. The young man nodded and left. Then a woman approached her; they shook hands and soon were in animated conversation.

A long, flowing skirt and short-sleeve blouse tucked in at the waist seemed to be Molly's self-imposed uniform. A pair of sandals adorned her feet, nails polished a bright red. A neat package. Self-contained.

She hadn't noticed him yet. Just as well. For the past two days, he'd wanted to see her in action on the job, but except for brief moments he hadn't run into her. Now he watched. He watched the staff defer to her; he watched visitors chat with her. And he watched her hold on to the back of a chair as she spoke with them.

How in tarnation could she run a business requiring the physical energy a hotel demanded? She should be sitting in one of the chairs, not holding it. And why was he getting so upset?

"Good afternoon," he said when she was alone again, his voice harsher than he intended.

She turned quickly. Recognition, then wariness, crept into her eyes. She didn't smile. "Good afternoon. I'm sorry I wasn't able to attend the memorial service."

"I see you were busy." He nodded in the general direction of the whole room. "Thank you. It looks good. I guess you know how to manage."

She caught his eye. "Yes. Yes, I do." Her voice was quiet but emphatic. He'd have to be a stump of wood not to realize she was sending him a message. But why? And then he remembered the first night he arrived when she saw him watch her cross the lobby.

He winced inwardly. No one appreciated being pitied. Well, it wouldn't be the first apology he'd offered lately. "Have you eaten yet, Molly?"

Her eyes widened, her brows raised. Good. He'd caught her off guard. Maybe he'd have a chance to redeem himself.

"I'll have a meal later."

She stood in front of him tall and proud, her posture as straight as a ruler. He wondered if the effort caused her pain. "Please have lunch with me," he asked.

Now her mouth opened slightly. He'd surprised her again. Must have been the "please."

She stared at him for so long he had to force himself not to squirm. "Why?" she finally asked. "Why do you want to have lunch with me?"

"I owe you an apology."

Now her chin hit the floor and Sam almost laughed. He'd thrown her off balance three times. Then her full mouth curved into a smile, and her somber blue eyes sparkled with mirth.

Stunned at her loveliness, Sam dropped his empty plate. Who had surprised whom? She'd gotten the better of him without even knowing it.

CHAPTER TWO

SAM SNATCHED UP the fallen plate and turned to Molly, who still wore a smile. "Stay, Molly. Join me for a meal." Her blond hair was in its usual style, neatly tied back. If she'd allow it to hang loose and frame her face, he'd bet the scar would be hidden. But he'd also bet she'd never allow tousled hair. It seemed she'd already decided on the straight-and-narrow path, a path she could control. The thought flitted into his mind and stuck there. Instinctively he knew he was right and felt satisfied as he waited for her response.

"As much as I'd like to," Molly began, "I really need to be available to the staff. Without John..." Her voice trailed off and a flash of regret crossed her face. "Maybe later..." She stopped again. "Forget it, I think I'm on round-the-clock duty for a while. At least until we know what happens to the hotel."

"I don't know anything about that," Sam said, "but I do know you have to eat. The wait staff knows where you are. In fact, every employee must know where you are today."

Molly chuckled and looked up at him. "You've got a point, Sam. Let's grab a couple of plates."

"Why don't you sit down? I'll be happy to..." And why couldn't he keep his mouth shut? Her eyes had hardened, and her mouth had pressed into a firm, straight line. If looks could kill, he'd be the proverbial dead man.

"You'll owe me a double apology if you don't stop pandering to what you think are my disabilities."

He wasn't an ex-football player for nothing. Offense scored points. "That was courtesy, ma'am, not pandering. I was minding my manners with a lady, like I've been taught."

Touchdown. He saw the blush rise from her neck to her cheeks, but she met his gaze.

"Then please forgive me. I'm used to taking care of myself. I do understand about fitting in with the customs of where I live. So, I'll wait for you right there." She indicated a nearby empty table and began walking toward it. Short step, long step.

Sam silently apologized to all his female contemporaries south of the Mason-Dixon line. Smarts, ambition and independence were their hallmarks, too. And they wouldn't hesitate to fix their own lunch plates. But Molly wasn't aware of that yet. She'd only been in Texas for a short time, and he thought his small deception would hold up. At least for a while.

He loaded two dishes and made his way back to

their table only to find Molly still standing as she
spoke to a woman Sam didn't know. His shook his
head in exasperation. Would she never sit down?
Instead, Molly waved him over and quickly introduced him to Carla O'Connor, owner of Jewelry by
Carla. "She's got a fabulous shop in the historic
district. Lots of antique and period pieces, and she
creates one-of-a-kind jewelry, as well."

He deposited the plates and shook the woman's
hand. Around his own age, he guessed. She seemed
like an exotic bird, with red hair halfway down her
back, bright lipstick and a long turquoise dress. Silver earrings touched her shoulders and were
matched by a braided silver necklace.

"I knew your uncle through his work with the
Economic Development Association in town. A
wonderful man. We'll miss him."

"Thank you," he replied. "I keep thinking he'll
walk across the lobby at any moment." And that
was true, despite having attended the funeral that
morning.

He turned to Molly. "You've only been here two
weeks or so. How did you meet each other?"

"That's easy," Molly replied. "I walked into her
store."

Carla chuckled. "She walked into every store in
the district. Said she wanted to meet the neighbors."

Sam was lost. Neighbors? The historic district
was five miles away. "Why?" he asked.

"That's what I asked, too," Carla chimed in.

"Isn't it obvious?" asked Molly, her forehead creasing. "How can I act as a good concierge if I don't know the area? The hotel's guests are my responsibility, and repeat business is the name of the game. I can't be very helpful if I don't know what's going on around here." She spoke to them patiently, as though lecturing two inept pupils.

Sam whistled long and low. Sharp. Molly was a real pro. No wonder his uncle had hired her. He couldn't believe, however, that she'd learned all her strategy in a classroom. At least she'd have no trouble getting another job when the time came.

Carla waved goodbye, and Sam stepped toward Molly and pulled out her chair. "Think we can finally have lunch?"

Molly nodded and sat down. Sam took his own seat, looking forward to spending the next few minutes with her.

"So tell me about the financial genius of the Kincaid family," Molly said before taking a bite of potato salad.

Sam's heart plunged to his stomach. Definitely not a topic he wanted to pursue right now. "And who might that be?" he asked.

"According to your family, I'm looking at him. But it's nice to know there's no evidence of a swelled head."

She was teasing him, and ordinarily he would have laughed. But her subject had touched a raw nerve. "Don't believe everything you hear."

Her face became a polite mask at his curt tone of voice, and he could have kicked himself.

"I'm sorry, Molly. I didn't mean it the way it came out."

She put her fork down and studied him for a moment. "You and I," she said, "should be grateful that our time together will be brief. Some people just don't seem to hit it off, and I guess that describes us." She shrugged. "It's no big deal."

Speech deserted him, and Molly made a comment about the warm weather, the universally accepted safe topic when there was nothing else to say.

It seemed he was inept in every part of his life these days.

THE LAST OF THE VISITORS shook Sam's hand two hours later as he sat with his folks at their table in the grand ballroom. His mom and dad hadn't budged from the center of the room since they first arrived. A never-ending cadre of friends surrounded them at all times. Sam downed a glass of iced tea, preparing himself to convince George and Irene to take a nap. His dad's complexion seemed grayish; his mom looked plumb exhausted. It was time for them to rest.

He turned toward Michael Hassett, his uncle's close friend and attorney, who was chatting with them now.

"I knew your brother for almost as many years as you did, George," said the lawyer. "Graduated from high school together. We had some good times way back and all through the years."

His uncle had been highly esteemed in this community, Sam realized as he politely listened to another good-old-boy story. As a child, Sam thought Uncle John was the best. And then Sam went to college in California and stayed, never living as an adult in the area where he grew up. Strange to see all the hometown relationships—personal, business, community—with a grown-up perspective.

Sam stood. "Mr. Hassett," he interjected before the stories continued, "thank you for sharing your memories. We surely appreciate it, sir." He extended his hand and, also standing, the lawyer shook it.

"Then you'd prefer me to return tomorrow to review John's will?" he asked. "That's no problem at all."

"That's fine," Sam began. "My folks need to rest—"

"No, Mike," interrupted George Kincaid. "Might as well hear what John had to say." Sam's father rose to his feet and reached for his wife's hand. "Come, dear. Maybe Molly can find us a private place."

Sam scanned the area. By this time Molly could be anywhere. "For someone who's been here only a couple of weeks or so, Uncle John sure seemed to trust her," he said. "Threw a lot of responsibility her way."

For the first time that day, Sam saw a grin cross his dad's face. "I wish he'd hired her years ago. He might've slowed down a bit then. But at least when he finally decided he needed help, my brother picked a winner. Molly knows her stuff like she was born to it."

Now his mom laughed. "Well, she *was* born to it."

"Tell me," said Sam, his curiosity piqued about the girl who seemed to throw him a curve every time they met.

When Irene's eyes glowed at his interest, he wished he'd kept his mouth shut. He didn't need any matchmaking from his mom.

"Her family has a very successful ski resort in New England. Her schooling provided official credentials, but she could run a hotel three times the size of the Bluebonnet without missing a beat."

That explained her hotel savvy. "So is the Bluebonnet just a diversion for her? Why did she leave her home? How long would she have stayed with Uncle John?" And why was he so suspicious of the woman? She'd done nothing but provide great service and assistance to his parents.

His mom frowned. "I guess you'll have to ask her that yourself, dear. All I know is that after interviewing a number of candidates, Uncle John raved about Molly and offered her a contract. As a new graduate, she was affordable, too."

"Hmm. I guess he got a bargain."

They had arrived at the office his uncle had used. Molly was sitting behind the desk, studying some papers, phone propped to her ear and a pencil in her hand. She waved them in and finished the call, then scribbled some notes on her pad.

"July Fourth," she explained as she rose from the chair. "I guess we're the site of the evening celebration for Oak Creek. Someone from the Chamber of Commerce was just filling me in."

"It's only a month away," Sam remarked.

She turned her head to face him. "Don't be concerned," she said calmly. "Your uncle spoke with me about it just last week. I guarantee we'll be ready."

He'd absolutely keep his mouth shut from now on, he swore to himself. She managed to put him in the wrong every time he spoke to her. And he hadn't been trying to criticize.

"So, how can I help you?" Molly asked, looking at his mom.

"You don't have to do anything, dear," Irene answered. "We just need to use an office for a little while. Can you direct us to somewhere private?"

"That's easy enough," Molly replied with a smile. "Stay here and use John's office. I'll go next door to mine and take this paperwork with me."

She started to gather her materials, but the attorney interrupted. "You might want to remain with us for just a few minutes, Ms. Porter. The disposition of John's property affects you in some small way, too.''

"It does? I only knew him for a month—from the time he first interviewed me.''

Her amazement was genuine. Sam was able to read her clear eyes, her tone of voice, her posture. He'd somehow become familiar with her every nuance of movement.

"Sit down, Molly,'' said Sam, as he arranged several chairs to accommodate the group. "You're officially invited to stay.''

She glared at him. "I'd prefer to stand if you don't mind.'' And she limped to the side of the room.

"Stubborn woman,'' Sam murmured, eyeing her back.

The lawyer walked behind the desk; his mother sat down in front of it. Sam glanced from his dad to Hassett as they stood next to their chairs. Then he walked over to Molly. "We can't get started if you won't take a seat,'' he said softly, nodding toward the other men.

He saw her glance follow his, then turn toward his mom. He saw the moment she understood. "Please, Sam,'' she said sweetly, "would you mind moving that chair closer to me? I don't want to hold up the proceedings. Thanks so much.'' She lowered herself into the seat as though she'd been planning to do so all along.

He had to give her credit for the rebound, but he

wanted to shake some sense into her at the same time. Women!

And then his attention was totally focused on Michael Hassett as the lawyer spread John Kincaid's will on the desk in front of him.

"John visited my office almost three weeks ago to update his will. I'll save the personal items for last, since I know the main concern of everyone here is the hotel itself, the property and the business of running it."

He looked directly at Sam. "You're the son he never had, Sam, and quite simply, the hotel is yours. The building, the ten acres it sits on, and the business."

"Mine?" said Sam, totally taken aback. "I don't know the first thing about running a hotel."

"John knew that, but he believed that your experience in other fields could be applied to the hospitality industry." Hassett looked down at the papers in front of him, then back at Sam. "He may have had a premonition—he joked about not being the man he used to be…." The lawyer dabbed at his eyes. "I say this because we had a conversation about the hotel when we made the changes to his will. He was talking about what a successful businessman you are, Sam, and how, if anything happened to him, he could see you running this hotel with Molly at the helm. He thought the world of Molly. I know that he'd want you to honor her contract."

Sam could barely absorb the news. Run a hotel? He'd just lost his own companies, businesses that he understood, or thought he did. How would he run a company he didn't understand? Sure, he'd spent high-school summers at the Bluebonnet as a bellhop, car hop, gardener and doing whatever odd jobs needed to be done. But that was a far cry from being the CEO.

He looked at the lawyer. "What about my parents? Why didn't he think of them?"

"We don't want such a big responsibility at our age," said George Kincaid. "We've run our own business in the past, but now we're gainfully employed elsewhere, with health benefits and vacation time. Soon we'll be wanting to retire. Son, we think *you'd* be the best one to handle the Bluebonnet."

Too bad no one asked him if he wanted it. He was a high-tech person, not a bricks-and-mortar person.

"But if you don't want it, son, you can always sell it and concentrate on your businesses in California."

Hassett nodded. "That's true. You do have the option of selling it. John didn't want to force you into a business you might not like. The proceeds of a sale would be divided equally among Irene, George and you after you buy out Ms. Porter's contract."

Whew. A way out. He didn't have to accept the Bluebonnet if he didn't want to. His mind raced. On one hand, he was out of work and he needed a job, needed to accumulate cash. The hotel could provide all that. On the other hand, selling the hotel would make him liquid again, also. Even one-third of the sale after commissions would put him on his feet. He could have an interlude in which to think before deciding his next career move.

"Of course," continued the lawyer, "selling it might take a long time. Operating a hotel is a complex business, and the right buyer would have to come along, one who knew the business and had the financing—enough financing to pay off a mortgaged property, plus profit to you and your folks."

"Mortgage? That's a surprise, isn't it?" asked Sam, glancing at his parents. "I thought Uncle John had paid off the mortgage years ago."

Sam's dad shrugged. "I did, too, but I never asked John about his finances, about the details. And he never spoke to me about them."

"In other words," said Sam slowly, "if this property is mortgaged and a buyer is hard to find, I could be running a hotel for a while, maybe a long while, whether I want to or not?"

"That about sums it up."

The interlude he'd imagined suddenly seemed like a never-ending black hole. "Easy for you to say. But it's not what I had in mind for myself at all."

WHAT A JERK Sam was! That's what happened when a person had too much money. A jewel of a business—at least a potential jewel—fell into his lap and he didn't appreciate it. Molly glanced at the man in question. Grim. Furrowed. Intense. His dark eyes burned, his square chin jutted, the planes of his face stood out strong and defined. God, he was gorgeous! And irritating as hell.

But gorgeous did not equate to brains. Still, maybe she wasn't being fair. Sam hadn't asked for a hotel. He liked computer chips better. But jeez, the Bluebonnet was profitable. At least that's what John Kincaid had told her. Not tons of money, but a respectable amount. John knew what he was doing—except when he gave his business to his nephew. With poor management, Sam could easily run the hotel into the ground in no time. And that would be a shame.

Also, working with Sam might be a nightmare. Molly envisioned them arguing about every decision. She absolutely couldn't risk it. Although a second choice by far, her hotel career was the only thing she had left now. She had to preserve her good name in industry circles.

Molly stood up. ''Mr. Hassett,'' she began, ''I'd like to declare my contract null and void. Sam doesn't have to buy it out or think that I have to be part of the deal.''

The lawyer frowned in concern. ''My dear Ms. Porter, in effect, John was protecting you as much as he was looking out for Sam by assuring him of your assistance.'' The lawyer couldn't have been more solicitous, more avuncular. ''John wanted you to feel secure about your job, to feel comfortable about staying on.''

''And I appreciate that,'' replied Molly. ''I respected Mr. Kincaid.'' She glanced at Sam. ''Mr. *John* Kincaid,'' she clarified. ''But Sam should have the freedom to hire whomever he wants to help him. And I should have the freedom to leave.''

''But I'm afraid you don't.'' The lawyer looked at her. ''The contract is between you and the Bluebonnet Hotel, not between you and John Kincaid personally. So your commitment is to the hotel, not the person owning it.''

She grabbed the opening. ''Exactly. It's all about the hotel. Preserving its success and growing it.'' She paused and stared at the lawyer. ''Mr. Hassett, please understand. Hospitality is what I do. Babysitting is not. And I don't want charity, either.''

''That's enough!'' Sam's voice cracked like gunshot. He jumped from his chair and walked toward her, glaring all the way. ''First of all, working hard isn't charity, and second, do I look like the kind of person who needs a baby-sitter?''

Not quite. He was a six-foot example of solid manhood coming at her. Once upon a time, she would have flirted or been outrageous or more sensitive in her relationships with men. Depending on who, what and where. Now men were simply people to be dealt with, other humans with whom she came in contact as allies, adversaries or neutrals. But not as sexy specimens who fired her imagination.

Molly planted her feet firmly on the ground, stretched to every inch of her five foot seven, raised her chin and looked Sam directly in the eye.

"Do I think you need a baby-sitter?" she repeated. "I guess only time will tell."

He barely flinched. "Don't bother watching the clock, Blue Eyes, and don't hold your breath. Just listen up. We can do this hard or we can do it easy. Trust me when I say easy works better." He rocked back on his heels. "The ball's in your court, Ms. Porter. Now what's it going to be?"

IN HER HOTEL APARTMENT that evening, Molly stretched out in her Jacuzzi tub and reveled in the hot water that lapped over her. Her leg ached. She felt tense. And she needed to get Sam Kincaid out of her mind.

"Hard or easy? Hard or easy?" she mimicked as she soaked. As though there was a choice. Hadn't Sam learned that nothing worthwhile came easy? Hmm…maybe not, she concluded. His ambitions seemed to be graced with good fortune while hers…

Don't go there. Look forward, not back.

Oh, the water felt good. She massaged her leg, not that it did any good. An over-the-counter, extra-strength analgesic would help before she got into bed. She flexed her ankles, the one set of leg bones that had been spared.

"See, darling?" her mom had said. "The accident could have been worse."

But Lily Porter was a nurse. She always pounced on any malady that dared to threaten her family. She'd cared for Molly's dad, Ben, some years ago when he'd had a stroke. She'd fought for Ben's life then, and she'd fought for Molly's more recently. Molly wished she hadn't.

And now Molly was soaking under jet-spewed, frothy water, rubbing a leg that looked as if it had gone through a concrete mixer. The rawness had faded, but the scars criss-crossing her thigh and lower leg would always be very visible. The scar on her healed pelvic bone would not. Together, the injuries left her with one leg a full inch shorter than the other, and a pelvis narrower than it was supposed to be. Her leg ached so much now she decided that tomorrow she'd better wear her custom shoe with the lift inside. She wrinkled her nose. She rather wear sandals in sunny Texas.

She regretted insulting Sam earlier. She hadn't meant to be so harsh. She really loved the beautiful hotel. It had an old-fashioned charm all its own, warm and mellow, yet managed to include an oak-paneled, up-to-date pub with a big-screen TV, a nightly gathering place for hotel guests and outside visitors alike.

Her favorite place was on a bench under a live oak beyond the back patio, where she was surrounded by magnificent gardens. She didn't know the name of one flower! But she loved the color they provided. After agonizing about leaving home, she couldn't have picked a better place to begin her second career. She really wanted to run this beauty, and now everything depended on Sam.

So why had she antagonized him that afternoon? His attitude, for one. That was the easy answer. The hard answer lay within herself. She'd felt threatened, vulnerable, caught in a storm. She'd have to change her tactics in order to regain control. From now on, she'd offer him all her support and as much encouragement as he'd need to run the hotel.

Ten minutes later, she towel-dried her shampooed hair and slipped on a long, cotton nightgown. She automatically reached for the moisturizer on the vanity and started smoothing it on her face. Her fingers paused on her disfigured skin. Like a brand burned on cattle, the long scar marred her appearance.

She'd never bothered with plastic surgery after the original emergency stitching had been done, and she normally didn't pay much attention to the souvenir from a time she'd rather forget. But tonight, she watched her fingers trace the elongated wound. She turned her head so her good side showed in the mirror, then faced front and, pretending to dry her face, raised her towel to cover the scar. She held the position and looked at her reflection.

A pretty girl stared back. Big blue eyes, long lashes, straight nose, nice mouth.

She moaned, surprised at the sight. "Oh…my." She reached her free hand toward the glass, stroked her reflection. "That's me," she whispered, and continued to stare at the familiar stranger.

Suddenly tears began to roll down her cheeks. A sob escaped, followed by another and then another until her throat hurt. She turned away and closed her eyes, burying her face in the towel.

Why? Why was she thinking about her damn scar tonight? Why was it bothering her now when for four long years she refused to think about it?

The answer came quickly, and on its heels, her groan of disbelief. There was only one new element in her life that could have caused this awareness. A male human being who should have barely made a dent in her conscious mind.

Sam Kincaid.

SAM DRUMMED his fingers on his uncle's desk at eight-thirty the next morning, impatient for the bank to open. He'd just spent an hour glancing through the hotel's monthly statements and now had a clearer picture of the type of expenditures the Bluebonnet incurred. He still had one big question. Why had his uncle been making hefty mortgage payments for the past three years? He was sure John had paid off that debt a long time ago when Aunt Ruth was still alive. Now Sam needed an appointment with the loan officer to end the mystery.

He glanced out the window at another sunny day.

Then he looked at his watch again. He'd use the time to talk with Molly. He walked next door and waited until she hung up the phone. She wore navy blue today with white trim on her blouse. A thick blue ribbon tied her hair back in its usual ponytail. Round earrings finished the picture. She looked good. Different somehow. He studied her, searching for the change. What was it?

She hung up the phone, tipped her head back and smiled. "Good morning."

Her smile dazzled. Words stuck in his throat. The woman was beautiful.

"Good morning," he finally said. "Why are you so happy this early?"

"A piece of good business. We just got confirmation of a family reunion scheduled for this fall. They're reserving two floors of the hotel for a week in October." Folding her hands behind her head, she leaned back in her chair. "Business could be very good here, Sam. The hotel and grounds are beautiful. The location is wonderful, too, with so many things for tourists to do and see…"

He nodded, allowing her voice to wash over him as he continued to look at her. Suddenly he knew what was different. The scar wasn't as noticeable today. Either Molly had covered it in some way or it was affected by some outside element like air-conditioning.

"…and if you'll give yourself a little time, I'll help you in every way. We can work toward excellence. I'm sure in a short while, you'll appreciate what this hotel can offer you.'' Molly leaned forward in her chair now, eagerly looking at him, hope shining in her eyes.

He had to crush it. He wasn't making any promises. For a moment he hesitated. She'd made a couple of good points, but he had to get on with his real life.

"I'm not a hotelier, Molly," he said, pulling his chair closer. "And I wanted to let you know immediately—because as assistant manager, you have the right to know—that if I find a qualified buyer, I will sell the Bluebonnet."

"Oh." Her voice was flat. The smile disappeared. And the light went out of those big blue eyes.

Because of him. He hardly knew her, but a sharp pain stabbed his gut, and he wanted to take back his words. It seemed he'd recently developed a knack for destroying everything he touched, for disappointing everyone in his life.

CHAPTER THREE

THE OAK CREEK SAVINGS and Loan sat square in the middle of the business district on Main Street, the two-story, redbrick building flanked by drive-through windows on one side and customer parking spaces on the other. It looked as solid and steady as a ship in safe harbor. And it looked a lot busier than Sam remembered. In fact, the whole town showed signs of growth. He'd noticed some new-home construction on the way in.

Sam pulled into the bank's driveway and shook his head at his narrow focus. Had he thought nothing would change since he'd gone off to college? The town's economy was based on tourism. There was plenty to do and see, from amusement parks to museums, art galleries, pubs, water sports and parks, craft shops, a dance hall and who knew what else. And if the amount of today's early summer traffic was any indication, visitors were coming to partake of everything available.

Oak Creek was now a significant resort area on the Texas map. No wonder Molly Porter was enthusiastic about the hotel, regardless of her less-than-enthusiastic opinion of him.

Shrugging his shoulders and banning a vision of her sparkling blue eyes from his memory, Sam entered the bank ready for his appointment with Sean Callan, the loan officer who'd worked with his uncle.

Ten minutes later Sam could only stare at the banker and stutter, "How much on the mortgage?"

The man waited before repeating the number. "Three million, Sam. That was the original amount. The hotel was A-plus collateral for us three years ago. I'm talking about both the facility and your uncle. There wasn't anything John Kincaid didn't know about the hotel business. There was no reason to deny a new mortgage on it. Now, of course, the economy is not as good. Business has been off recently. Even in the beautiful Texas hill country, we're affected by world events. So I'm not sure we would have loaned him the whole three mil now."

Three million! A lightning bolt of pain pierced Sam's gut. Then he calmed down. He could handle it, he told himself.

"The bank takes pride in being progressive and in supporting local businesses," continued the banker. "And like I said about John, he was one of a kind."

Sam was beginning to understand that, but to what end? "I haven't had much time to go through my uncle's papers yet, but so far, I haven't found any new expenses at the hotel that the money was used for. So I'll ask again. Do you know why he took out the mortgage?"

"Actually, no. But like I said, there was no reason to deny him. In the past, his repayments were always on time and in full. We examined the revenues and expenses of the hotel and found nothing unusual."

Sean Callan sat back in his seat, his brow creasing in thought. "People do different things with mortgage money, like pay their children's college tuition." He looked at Sam, a question in his eyes.

Sam gestured impatiently. "No way. I paid half my college expenses and my folks paid the other half. Uncle John had no children."

"All right, then. Just let me think a minute."

The bank officer could take as much time as he needed, as far as Sam was concerned. Anything to get to the bottom of this mystery.

But Callan's ruminations didn't take long. "I seem to remember John saying something about investments." The older man snapped his fingers. "That's right. John joked about keeping up with the times, investing in the future. Something about the Internet. Internet companies."

Internet companies? He meant dot-coms. And in a heartbeat, Sam understood. He couldn't move. He couldn't breathe. His fingers clung to the arms of the chair and his legs wouldn't support him if he tried to stand. Heat raged through his body followed by arctic cold. He knew exactly what he would find when he examined his uncle's papers.

Three million big ones invested through a venture-capital company in three dot-coms owned by his nephew, Sam Kincaid. Three million dollars disappearing into thin air. A nightmare to haunt Sam again.

Somehow Sam managed to nod, smile and shake the banker's hand. Somehow he walked to his car and got in. Somehow he drove toward the Bluebonnet—passed it by. He couldn't go in yet. Couldn't put on a normal face, couldn't pretend that life was normal. What was normal anymore for him?

He pulled into a lay-by and stared out the window but saw nothing. There was a small chance that he was wrong about the money, that John had used it for something else, another investment, hopefully a safe, diversified portfolio. But he didn't think so. Not in his heart, not in his gut.

He'd let his uncle down. He'd let so many people down. Now he had to get the hotel out of debt— back on sound footing—no matter what it took. Now the goal was about more than money. Much more.

If a man couldn't look at himself in the mirror, what kind of a man was he?

By the time he drove back to the hotel, he knew what he had to do to satisfy his honor—increase revenues for the hotel and preserve whatever career in technology he had left. But first, he had to confirm his suspicions about his uncle's investments.

He found nothing in John's office pertaining to investments of any kind. Molly flitted in and out while he searched, ignoring him for the most part, concentrating on her own responsibilities. He did the same.

It wasn't until Sam searched John Kincaid's private apartment later that afternoon that he found meticulous records of John's investment. On the letterhead stationery of a prominent venture-capital firm, in clear black and white, were instructions to provide three million dollars to Toys-2-Go.com, Groceries-2-Go.com and Books-2-Go.com. If he'd had any doubt before, even a smithereen of doubt, it was gone now. His uncle, in essence, had invested in him.

Sam took the papers from the desk in his uncle's bedroom and sat on the side of the bed, staring at them, almost in a stupor. He'd known what to expect; it was simply a matter of finding the actual records. And now he held them, proof of John's love and faith and trust in his only nephew.

The aftershock started to fade and Sam glanced at his watch. Almost dinnertime. He'd allow his folks and Molly to enjoy their meal before gathering them together in John's office. He couldn't keep any secrets now. They all had a right to know the Bluebonnet's financial status and they all had a right to know his plans for the hotel's future, even if those plans were still hazy.

One thing he knew for sure. Working with Molly would be a challenge. Amazingly, his mouth curved into a smile.

So SAM WAS BROKE. His companies were gone. She had to give him credit for admitting it; it took guts to admit you tried your best and failed. As Molly looked over to where Sam sat talking quietly with his parents, she had a feeling that he wasn't finished with this impromptu meeting yet and that there was more to come. She waited, her mind kicking into gear. She needed information before she could figure out a plan. How much was the monthly mortgage payment? Would the hotel be able to continue covering it? Would they need to increase the advertising budget? Would they need to reduce staff?

And perhaps, most important of all, would Sam be willing to follow her lead? She glanced at him from where she stood on the other side of the office, trying to give the family the pretense of privacy now. She was surprised Sam had wanted her in on this *mea culpa* get together. There was really no need for him to confess his sins to her.

She watched him speak with his parents. He leaned forward in his chair, no desk between them, each of his hands clasping one of theirs as he spoke. His dark-brown eyes openly met their inquiring ones as he explained what happened to his companies in more detail.

Molly didn't need to know the details of Sam's fiasco. She understood the principles of investing well enough and was familiar with the dot-com phenomenon, which had turned to disaster for so many. In truth, Sam's companies had held out far longer than most. Despite her lack of interest in returning to school two years ago, her brain still functioned, and she'd absorbed the information in her finance and economics classes. As she recalled, investing in dot-com stocks made for a lot of conversation on campus.

But Sam's mistakes were in the past. As the hotel management team, they had to focus on the future. She watched Sam push the hair out of his eyes repeatedly, heard his reassuring tone of voice, if not all the words, saw him pat his mother's arm and shake his dad's hand.

Maybe, despite their initial reservation, his parents would now become involved in running the hotel. Maybe she'd been included in the meeting only because Sam wanted her to understand why he was letting her go.

An interesting theory, but she dismissed it almost immediately. Sam himself said he knew nothing about running a hotel. He needed her. Looking at him now, despite his setbacks, she didn't consider him a fool. Quite the contrary. He was a smart man, energetic and determined. She understood that kind of commitment. He needed her, but he'd never follow like a lost sheep.

"My folks have had another long day," said Sam, walking toward her. "There were more visitors today who couldn't make it yesterday, and they've had little time for themselves just to…to grieve." He glanced back at Irene and George. "Why don't you call it a night?"

"We probably will," said his dad. "Can't remember the last time I've felt so tired."

Molly recognized the expression that crossed Sam's face—anxiety, the same anxiety she had about her own dad from time to time. "Tomorrow's a new day, Mr. Kincaid," she said quickly. "A night's sleep will refresh you."

"I know it will, little lady," Sam's father replied with a touch of Old World gallantry.

Molly tried hard not to smile, but didn't succeed. She liked Sam's parents, just as she'd liked his uncle. They were sweet, good people who cared about each other.

As though they had a silent agreement, Molly and Sam said nothing further until Irene and George had left the office. Then Sam turned to her.

"Are you too tired to cover more ground tonight? And I want the truth."

She stared into his face. He wasn't kidding. "Why wouldn't I tell you the truth? It's no crime to be tired."

"I know that, but do you?" he asked quietly. "You won't be any good around here if you collapse."

So she guessed he wasn't letting her out of the contract. "I'm not tired. And despite what you may think when you watch me walk across a room, I have the stamina of a horse. So stop being concerned. Right now I need to know what your plans are and where I fit in—if I do." She tilted her head back as she looked at him, daring him to comment about her strength again.

He returned her gaze, seemed about to argue, then bit his lip. "You absolutely do fit in here. I may have made mistakes in the past, but recognizing talent isn't one of them." His expression softened. "I can't increase the revenues on this place on my own. And you seem to have all the right qualifications to help me."

So she was right. He needed her. "What did you have in mind?" she asked.

He gestured to a chair. "Sit down. This will take some time."

She sat. And waited.

"Although the Bluebonnet's revenues have covered the monthly mortgage payments, as well as all the other operating expenses since my uncle took the loan, it's been close. Lately we've been barely meeting costs. What's worse is that even if every guest room is booked all year long, the profit to the owner—my family—would be very little." He pulled a chair around and sat facing her. "The loan has twelve more years to run and I don't have that kind of time."

"And I don't have the kind of money to buy it from you," replied Molly with a smile. "So you're stuck with payments for a while."

He pushed his hair out of his eyes, frowning. "Molly, I'm serious. If you know anything about high tech, you know that if I'm away too long, and even a year is too long, I'll never accomplish my goals. I could be interviewing for a dozen jobs right now back in California."

Okay, she wouldn't tease him again. Instead, she nodded. "I hear you, Sam, but we have to be realistic. If it was going to take a while to find a buyer with financing *before* we knew about the mortgage, it will take even longer now. So I don't understand how you aim to be out from under in a year.''

"I may not be, but if I can put my ideas into action, it won't matter too much.''

She waited.

"If I can't go to high-tech, I'm going to bring the industry to me.''

"What?'' She was not only surprised but confused. "I hate to break this to you, Sam, but we already have a computer system. And it's a good one.''

He smiled. "Our system is just a tool we use. That's not what I'm talking about.''

"I'm listening,'' she said.

"How about converting the Bluebonnet into a high-tech conference-and-training center where corporations can get the best of both worlds? The latest in a training facility coupled with every recreational activity the area has to offer. A combination work-and-play retreat. Companies will pay much higher rates than we're getting from individuals now, and we'll pay off the mortgage in half the time, maybe less.''

She stared at him, speechless. "But...but...''

He continued. "We're located close to Austin, which is another high-tech center in the country. I bet many companies will be interested—in fact, will be excited about—a professional, state-of-the-art training facility. And I know the Silicon Valley crowd will go for it. A little California cuisine and they'll feel right at home. What do you think?''

She jumped from her chair, too agitated about Sam's awful idea to sit still.

"What do I think?'' she repeated. "What do I think about taking a gorgeous, historic hotel and turning it into a sleek, modern, dime-a-dozen facility? Are you nuts?''

Her blood surged; she could hardly catch her breath. She couldn't remember the last time she'd felt so passionate about anything. Well, maybe when she won her first downhill medal at the nationals. A lifetime ago.

"I'm not nuts,'' replied Sam. "I'm in business to realize the biggest profit I can, so I'm able to go on from here. I'm not out to rob, cheat or steal from anyone. I just want to provide a different service, and a first-rate one at that.''

She had to use reason, not emotion, to help him understand. "But, Sam, this is a lovely, romantic hotel with atmosphere. Guests want atmosphere. They're paying for it. They want authentic Texas cuisine, not Californian.''

Her thoughts raced one after the other. How could she make her point clearer? "I've just completed one of the top hotel-management programs in the country,'' she said, trying to keep her voice calm, "but since this is my first job, maybe I'm not as credible as you'd like. My brother-in-law, Zach, however, has been in the business for years. He knows *everything* about hotels, and he would think you're going over the deep end, too!''

His raised brow prompted her.

''He's run Diamond Ridge just about forever—that's my family's ski resort—and he's grown it twice over, too. He and my dad. I know he'd never vote for your idea.''

She'd gone too far. She saw it in Sam's closed expression, in his narrowed eyes, in his posture.

''I don't need anyone's approval,'' he said. ''Not yours and not Zach's. He's not in my shoes. Running a hotel may have been *his* lifelong dream and *your* lifelong dream, but it hasn't been mine.''

She grabbed the back of the closest chair, her heart thumping painfully. He'd blindsided her. ''Dreams?'' she asked, as though she'd never heard the word before. ''Dreams?'' She forced herself to inhale. ''What do you know about my dreams? What do you know about me? Or about what might have been? You've only been put on hold, buddy,'' she said. ''Be thankful. And don't talk to me about dreams.''

She'd had enough. Her whole body shook, and she felt as if her legs would collapse under her. Head high, she walked toward the door, one hand clutching the backs of chairs as she went. Her breathing echoed in the room. She didn't care about her clumsiness. She only wanted out. She reached for the doorknob.

''Don't run, Molly. Tell me.''

His voice was low and coaxing, and she turned

her head slowly. "Tell you?" she repeated, her gaze locking with his. "I wouldn't tell you my own name right now."

"I've hurt you," he said. "I didn't mean to do that. I'm sorry."

She remained silent for a moment. "I'm sorry, too," she finally said, her tone matching his quiet one. "I'm sorry the conversation got out of control, but it seems obvious that we have different ideas about what the Bluebonnet is, what it could be. I'm not sure I can work like this."

She was truly regretful. She would have liked to continue at the Bluebonnet, to help it succeed, but not under Sam's new vision. "Find someone else, Sam. Someone who believes in your ideas. Who believes in you." She shook her head. "I'm not that person."

She turned the knob and walked out the door.

SAM COULD HEAR his heart beating in the silence following Molly's departure. The woman packed a wallop with her statements. *Find someone who believes in you.* If he tried to laugh at the irony, he'd choke. Adrienne hadn't believed in him, either. She'd walked out because her disappointment in his business failure wasn't overridden by an underlying confidence in him. She'd walked out on him and on their unborn child. If that wasn't a strong enough message, Molly had just delivered one, too, and hit him right in the solar plexus.

Molly. A paradox. A woman of uninhibited passion hidden inside a woman of total control. She'd surprised him. And unless he'd totally misread her body language, she'd surprised herself, as well. He couldn't possibly have misread—she'd been sublimely clear—her opinion of his proposal for the hotel. So he'd chat with her again tomorrow. Maybe she'd be calmer after a night's sleep. No matter what she thought of him, she still had a contract to honor, and she wasn't the type to break a promise.

He rolled his shoulders and stretched before sitting down behind his uncle's desk. His desk now. He'd have to get used to that. He opened a new file on the computer and began to outline a business plan for the conference-and-training center. He started by formulating a Needs Assessment. If he was to attract investors, he had to do it right. This time, he'd temper his projections with hard data. And if his explorations should prove his idea futile, he'd think of something else. He always did.

He paused, distracted by the thought, and leaned back in his chair. He did have a creative mind, the ability to weave threads together and come up with something new. Although, his ideas were not always good, he reminded himself. But they were usually worth examining.

He looked around the paneled office and grinned. At least he came by his entrepreneurial bent honestly. An uncle with a hotel and a dad with a hardware store—until the big home-improvement chains came to their area and forced its closing. Those had been tough days, but now George managed two departments for the chain, had company health benefits and participated in their retirement plan. His dad was positioned safely now. No wonder he hadn't wanted to take on the big challenge of the Bluebonnet.

Sam focused on the computer screen again. His folks wouldn't have to worry about the hotel. Sam would see the Bluebonnet through to the end, whatever that happened to be.

Two hours later, satisfied with his Internet research on Texas-based conference centers, Sam shut the computer and left the office, locking the door behind him. Glancing at his watch, he strolled toward the front of the hotel.

At ten o'clock on a warm June evening, the lobby was still active with guests mingling and chatting in groups. Sam guessed, however, that many others had congregated in the Brew Pub and Restaurant where his uncle had run not only a top-notch eatery, but a microbrewery offering a variety of handcrafted beers. The pub was a definite profit center of the hotel, which would also fit in with a conference center.

He walked across the main lobby and down a corridor leading to the pub. It seemed quiet as he approached. Too quiet for a busy night. Until he heard the notes of a piano floating through the air toward him. And then a voice intertwining with the music. Female, sensuous, beautiful. The song was unfamiliar, but lush, maybe before his time. Wait—he did know it. The world knew it. Sure. Humphrey Bogart, Ingrid Bergman.

Sam followed the voice. He saw long, dark hair, dangling earrings, a slender figure all in black. She was seated on a stool, one arm casually draped on the granite bar, facing her audience. Young, beautiful and with a musical delivery that had every customer spellbound.

Sam stood in the doorway, loath to disturb the scene. Almost every seat was taken, both at the tables and at the bar. Folks were standing near him and beyond. His gaze traveled the dimly lit room section by section and then stopped at the other end of the bar where Molly sat.

Molly, taking pleasure in the music. Molly, with a soft smile on her face. Molly, totally in tune with the crowd enjoying the show. He hoped she'd chosen to spend her leisure hours there and wasn't on duty now. She'd been putting in more hours on the job than anyone had the right to expect.

The audience showed their approval with applause when the song ended. Sam clapped for the singer but couldn't stop staring at Molly. Her smile broadened as she applauded, and the shadowy lighting of the room set off her high cheekbones. But it was her shining eyes that arrested his movement. She looked happy. Relaxed and happy. A combination he hadn't seen before.

The music picked up tempo and the vocalist transformed herself from a sultry chanteuse into a Shania Twain-like pop star, with hip action and dance steps

to match. As he made his way toward Molly, Sam
watched the performer play to the audience and felt
a niggling sense of familiarity. Where had he seen
this singer before? A crazy thought. He'd have to
be on the far side of a century to have forgotten such
a woman, and maybe not even then.

Woman? He looked carefully when he passed
near her. Examined her face, the clothes and the
glamour. Then he looked swiftly at the glasses on
the bar where the singer had been standing, hoping
the kid hadn't been drinking anything harder than
ginger ale, or they'd all end up in trouble.

"Is she over twenty-one?" he whispered in
Molly's ear as he slipped into the seat beside her.
Molly turned her head, and a subtle fragrance wafted
to him. Light fruit, maybe citrus. A cool, clean
aroma. Nice. Well, Molly was nice. Usually. Head-
strong and smart, as well. And very pretty.

Molly dimpled. "Over twenty-one? Not a chance.
Just graduated high school."

"Holy sh—" He cut his remark as he watched
Molly contain her laughter. Suddenly he felt comfortable. She'd never allow anything to endanger the
hotel. He sat back and enjoyed the rest of the number.

When the applause died down, he wasn't too surprised to see the singer strut—it was the only word
that came to his mind—toward them. Rather, toward
Molly.

"They liked me tonight, didn't they?"

Molly's laugh caused Sam to smile. "They like

you every night you perform, and you know it! Now, say hello to the new boss, Sam Kincaid, John's nephew.''

"Hello,'' said the youngster, looking straight at Sam and extending her hand with a sophistication that belied her age. "I'm Judith Sands.''

Molly rolled her eyes.

"Glad to meet you,'' said Sam, taking the youngster's hand and wondering what was going on. He stared at her, but the niggle didn't go away. Where did he know her from?

"Judith,'' began Molly in a mysteriously comic voice, "masquerades by day as Judy Schneider, our front-desk receptionist. But at night, she emerges as Judith Sands, local celebrity who's headed for Broadway.''

"No wonder you look familiar,'' Sam said to the young woman. "I've seen you a dozen times in the lobby. I thought I was going nuts for a moment.''

"I know,'' said Molly. "I could tell.''

He cocked his head.

"You get a certain expression when you're concentrating. Your forehead crinkles a little, you tap your lips with your pointer finger like this.'' Molly proceeded to demonstrate.

Sam shook his head, knowing she'd mimicked him exactly. "You'll get yours one day, darlin',''￼ he said. "You know what they say about pay-back…''

Molly laughed, her cheeks turning a dusky pink. And Sam could have watched that for hours.

"Isn't she great?" said Judy/Judith, looking at Molly, then addressing Sam. "The first time I sang in here—you know the hotel is just a summer job—Molly said my makeup wasn't right. She said I looked like I was using paint and I thought she was just being an old fuddy-duddy like my mom—"

"An old fuddy-duddy!" interrupted Sam, indignant on Molly's behalf. "Molly's only a few years older than you, I bet."

"I know, I know," said Judy, "but why else would she care about how I looked? I couldn't figure it out."

"Maybe she cared because she didn't want the sheriff's office to close us down," Sam suggested, with a touch of sarcasm.

"She doesn't drink, Sam, just sings." Laughter still flooded Molly's voice.

Judy wasn't finished yet. "Turns out that her sister, Amanda, used to be a model in New York, and Molly knew how I was supposed to look when I'm on stage. Too bad she didn't take any lessons from Amanda. In fact, Molly hardly ever uses makeup, so we had to experiment until we figured it out."

Sam barely blinked, his mind picturing Molly as he'd seen her that morning. She had used cosmetics over her scar today. Interesting.

Judy was still talking nonstop and he refocused on the youngster.

"You see," the girl confided softly, "everything needs to be just right under the lights. Hair, makeup, costumes. The stage is different from real life."

Sam glanced at Molly. The smile had gone.
"Only cosmetically," said Molly. "The people on
the stage may think they're different because of their
talents, but they can still suffer the 'slings and ar-
rows of outrageous fortune,' just like the rest of us."

"No misfortune for me," Judy insisted. "I'm going to New York, and I'm going straight up. I'm not
stopping to breathe until I'm center stage in a smash
musical." She twirled in her excitement. "I'll send
you free tickets!" Then she looked at her watch.
"Oh, it's late. Daddy's waiting!" She waved and
was gone.

Sam stared after the girl, then looked at Molly.
"From sophisticate to Daddy's little girl...I don't
think I was ever that young."

"Sure you were, once." A heartbeat passed.
"And so was I. Once."

"But not anymore?"

She held his gaze. "What do you think?"

"I think—" Sam looked at the strong-willed
woman who took charge as though born to it "—
that your whole life lies ahead and that you can do
anything you set your mind to."

Her travesty of a smile almost broke his heart.
"Should have known you'd be a dreamer with all
your crazy ideas about the hotel," she said, covering
her yawn. "Think I'll turn in. I'm beat. It's been a
long day."

"Good," said Sam. "I'd sleep a lot better myself
if you'd reconsider your decision to leave the Bluebonnet—at least until my plans are in place. And

then, if you still want to leave,'' he waved his hand toward the door, ''the open road is yours.''

''Put your mind to rest,'' Molly replied. ''I don't break contracts. We're stuck with each other for a few months. I just hope we survive the experience.''

''Oh, we'll survive,'' he said, looking at her closely and seeing the fatigue around her eyes. ''As long as you sleep in tomorrow. I know we'll continue to disagree on everything, but life would be dull in the office without you. So do me a favor and stay healthy.''

''Sure,'' she said, reaching for her purse. ''Nice and healthy.'' A note of derision laced her tone. She waved at the bartender and called good-night to him before turning to Sam.

''See you in the morning. Let's try to get through one day without going a few rounds.''

''Not difficult if a certain person would listen to reason,'' Sam teased, and got the response he wanted.

Her eyes flashed, her already straight posture straightened further, and her chest moved in and out rapidly. She was getting ready to argue with him at almost eleven at night. And Sam felt better. An animated Molly was a much lovelier sight than a deflated Molly.

He'd make a point of driving her crazy every day. That shouldn't be too hard. He seemed to have a knack for it.

CHAPTER FOUR

WITHIN A WEEK, George and Irene prepared to return to their own home twenty miles away, and to their own jobs—George to his hardware departments and Irene to her high-school food-service-management position—with the promise to come back for the July Fourth festivities, if not sooner.

"What's twenty miles? It's nothing," George said when they were leaving. "We'll come out for a day if we have time off together."

He looked at his son. "And if you need us for anything at all, you just call. Hear me?"

Sam heard and wrapped his arms around the man who still believed the sun and moon rose over the younger Kincaid—despite Sam's business disaster in California. "I hear you fine, Dad, but it's Molly you should be saying it to. She'll be alone for a few days while I'm tying up loose ends on the West Coast."

His dad turned to Molly as Sam knew he would and made her the same offer.

"I'm sure I'll be fine, Mr. Kincaid. We have a great staff, you know. And without Sam underfoot, the hotel will run like clockwork." She winked at his dad and George roared with a merriment that Sam hadn't expected to hear for a long time. Even his mom couldn't suppress a laugh.

"Can't you two find a way to work well together?" asked Irene.

"But we do, Mom. We just do it loudly." Sam had the satisfaction of hearing his mom laugh again. A sweet sound after a sad week.

TWO DAYS AFTER his parents left, a hotel employee drove Sam to the airport in one of the hotel vans, leaving Molly totally on her own. He'd have to raise her salary when he returned, regardless of their cat-and-dog relationship, and regardless of the profit picture. She'd been forced to take on far more responsibility than an assistant manager would have had working with an experienced hotelier. Thoughts of Molly turned to thoughts of the hotel business, and his mind was occupied until he walked into his old apartment.

After only two weeks away, crossing the threshold was like stepping into another world. The stillness hit him first. The absence of people, the absence of life. Whoa! He was getting fanciful now. But there was his unmade bed just as he'd left it. And a pile of laundry needing to be washed. No fragrance of Adrienne's perfume lingered. No evidence of his former life. Except laundry. How uninspiring.

He let the water run in the kitchen sink and checked the answering machine for messages.

There were more than a dozen since he'd accessed the machine a few days ago. Also, his incoming e-mail was crammed with new messages, along with some duplicated e-mails he'd responded to from the hotel. Bringing a glass of water to the table, he sat down to take notes, tackling his phone messages first. Four friends with job leads for him, a half-dozen ex-employees wanting to touch base and—his hand tightened around his pencil—Adrienne's voice.

She felt badly about leaving him so abruptly and wanted to uncloud the mystery. She'd accepted an assignment with her corporation's French division and was calling from Paris. Was happy and healthy. And going on with her life.

"Well, have a happy one," murmured Sam, fingers now relaxed. Her voice had triggered an automatic response, piquing his curiosity, but nothing more. Strange, after an intimate year together. Intimate, but obviously without the commitment that turned two individuals into a couple. He took stock. His heart wasn't racing...or breaking. His palms weren't sweating. Any regret he felt was for the child who might have been.

After losing his wonderful uncle, a child to love would sure have been a bonus to his family. He shook his head. What a thought! Children weren't born with the responsibility to make families feel better. He knew that, but somehow, babies usually managed it. His mom always did call them miracles.

He put Adrienne out of his mind and listened to

the rest of his messages. Then he picked up the phone and started returning calls.

He arranged to have dinner with two friends in the high-tech industry that evening, as well as a day-time meeting with another pair of friends who'd made their mark in investment financing. Might as well test the waters regarding a full-service, high-tech training center in Texas. Surprisingly he grew somewhat excited at the thought. The Oak Creek location would be different from the competition's. Not only would a first-class hotel be provided, but an abundance of cultural and recreational activities. Client companies could accomplish technical, management and sales training, while offering concurrent social venues to their employees. When Sam returned to the Bluebonnet, he'd have ammunition for his arguments with his favorite nemesis.

He thought of Molly again, and dang, if his heart didn't pick up the beat. Now what was *that* all about? He must be getting addicted to confrontation.

NOTHING COULD REPLACE skiing, not even running a hotel single-handedly at a pace that could challenge even Zach and her dad. Summertime was the biggest season at the Bluebonnet, with autumn a close second, so they were just starting the most demanding time of the year. They weren't fully booked, however, a failure that nagged at Molly.

She had ideas to share with Sam, though, ideas to correct the situation. Marketing campaigns, new suppliers, an inventory-control system, co-op advertising—all aimed to run the Bluebonnet more efficiently and more profitably.

Despite having some empty rooms, her work kept her busy, and Molly wanted that. She fell asleep instantly at night and jumped out of bed each morning ready for the day.

But something was still missing in her life and would always be missing. The frisson of excitement when she awoke each morning. The anticipation. The testing of herself against the mountain. One on one.

Her biggest mountain now was Sam!

She downed a cup of morning coffee in her suite and hurried to her office, her gait almost even because she wore her special shoe. A compromise for speed when she'd rather be barefoot in sandals.

She seemed to be on the run from morning till night since John Kincaid's death. She raced around gladly, however, because she sensed the staff's growing trust and respect for her, which was quite a compliment from a crew that had just lost their beloved leader. John Kincaid had set an example that was tough for anyone to follow.

In truth, she wasn't their real leader. Sam was. And he was returning today to take on the job until he found a buyer. Or until he changed his mind and decided to stay. She wondered how long it would take them to have their next war of words. She sat down behind her desk and as if on cue, her phone rang. From that point, she had no time to wonder about anything.

Arrangements for the July Fourth dance and buffet, sales calls from their laundry and beverage service providers, a question about an overdue invoice, which she referred to Madeline Kay, their full-charge bookkeeper. For goodness' sake, had John handled every business inquiry that came in? Molly wasn't going to do that. If she didn't allow the supervisors to handle their own departments, she'd spend the entire day on the phone and never get her own work done! She hoped Sam agreed with her.

"Hi, Molly."

Startled from her concentration, her head snapped back. Sam lounged in the doorway, grinning and looking good enough to make a girl have crazy thoughts…which she dismissed immediately. But she was glad to see him, at least for now, and couldn't keep from offering a welcoming smile in return.

He walked toward her and clasped her hand. "That bad, huh?"

"What?"

"Life must be rough if you're happy to see me."

Her smile morphed into a broad grin. "Not too rough, nothing I couldn't handle," she said airily, "as you already know from your daily calls."

"If that's true," he said slowly, the corner of his mouth still curved upward, "then you're glad to see me just for the sake of my own sweet self."

Whoa! What was going on here? Better keep it cool. "Of course I'm happy to see your own sweet self," she replied, "for a little while at least."

His expression darkened. Had she hurt his feelings?

"Until the sparks fly again," she explained quickly. "You know darn well a peaceful coexistence between us is just temporary."

His grin returned. "Now I feel like I'm home! Thanks, Molly-girl, for being you. Can you free up some time in about an hour? I've got stuff to tell you. New stuff."

She nodded. "Of course, we have to catch up." She glanced at her watch. "Lord, how did it get so late? I forgot all about lunch, so how about an early business dinner?"

"Fine with me, but you might lose your appetite."

She glanced at him, worried for a moment, until she saw the teasing smirk on his face. Darn! He had something up his sleeve, something he knew she wouldn't like. "I guess I'll have to take my chances," she replied. "How about the pub?"

"Great. In an hour. And bring you best manners," he added. "I like a girl who concedes gracefully!"

He waved and left before she could retort. As she watched him walk away, she found herself wanting the hour to rush by. She felt an emotion she hadn't experienced in longer than she cared to remember. An emotion that seemed foreign to her now.

Anticipation.

SHE HADN'T ANTICIPATED such quick results from Sam's trip. Molly sat across from Sam at a corner table in the pub that evening, listening to the aftermath of his investigations, but also savoring every bite of her grilled London broil smothered in mushrooms and red-wine sauce, with portions of garlic mashed potatoes and steamed veggies on the side. It was her first solid meal of the day.

"Of course," Sam continued, "I still have a lot of research ahead to gather the hard information I need, but frankly, my ideas for conversion are looking good. I've already got backing, or at least, very interested parties."

"Wow! That was fast. You sure act quickly," said Molly, her heart sinking, her appetite vanishing.

"Why shouldn't I? You know where I stand financially. You know my concern about the future. I've been very open with you. As open as I can be."

She nodded. "And I appreciate that, but it doesn't mean I need to feel joyous about your ideas." She had to slow him down so she could present a solid plan, a big plan that would increase revenues without turning the beautiful, historic hotel into cold, bare rooms full of computers for training new users. Think!

"Sam," she said slowly, as a ray of hope started to shine, "the Bluebonnet's listed on the National Register of Historic Places. Have you checked with the Historical Society about what kind of construction you're allowed to perform on the building?"

He sat like a stunned ox, and she surreptitiously covered her mouth to hide her grin. She wasn't down yet! She'd be gracious. Her best manners, just like Sam had requested.

She reached for his hand. "I haven't called them, either," she said, "so you may be all right. It was just a thought…"

"…to keep me from sleeping tonight." He almost glared at her. "Your brain never stops, does it."

Shrugging, she couldn't hide the smile that appeared. "My brain doesn't have time to stop. We've been fairly busy around here. But I have a lot of ideas to save money."

He arched his brows.

She squeezed his fingers, her mind racing. "Give me a little time, Sam. Please. Let me study the figures for the past few years and see if my ideas are feasible. I'm good at analyzing data, but I just haven't had the time to do it. Let me see if there are any holes, any places where I can make improvements, cut costs without cutting quality. Let's see where our advertising dollars pay off. Let me try to increase income without destroying the charm of this place."

A lifetime passed until he answered. "Business has been down recently. You'd have to cut costs and insure a full house every week of the year to increase revenues enough to make a difference."

A full house every week! Even winter. A huge challenge, and her heart sank again. But his fingers remained entwined with hers, and she looked at their hands still clasped on the table. She felt his gentle squeeze as he said, "Nothing's engraved in stone yet, Molly. There's more homework to be done."

But before she could enjoy the small victory of additional time, he added, "But don't get your hopes up. My goal is still to find a buyer, which means increasing profitability so the Bluebonnet's more attractive to one. I'll do what I have to do."

"I understand," she replied, but her heart was lighter and the corners of her mouth turned up again.

"You haven't taken anything I've said seriously, have you," Sam said with a chuckle.

"Sure I have," she replied. "The essence is that I have time to help you see the light!"

Sam remained quiet for a moment, just staring at her. "I'm seeing it right now," he said quietly. "It should be visible more often."

Whew! She avoided his gaze, uncomfortable with a serious compliment or an admiring word. Uncomfortable with flirtation or a hint of romance. She'd blocked all that from her mind in recent years. Now, just as she'd always had female friends, she'd also have male friends. Men as friends only. No intimate relationships.

Love and marriage—and children—were for other women. Not for her. Not for someone who wasn't whole anymore.

She disengaged her hand from his and ignored his leading words. "So, are you ready to put in a full day's work tomorrow?" she asked. Stupid question, but she couldn't think of another topic with which to distract him.

"Darn right I am, and the first item on my agenda is to authorize a raise for you."

"What?" She put her fork down. "I've only been here about a month. I'm not complaining."

"But I am. We need you here and the job's bigger than you bargained for. You've earned a raise and will continue to earn it. The subject's closed."

Just like a man. Or at least the men she was most familiar with. She started to laugh. "Sorry, Sam, but you remind me of my dad. Just because you say the subject's closed, do you really think it is?" Then another thought struck her. "Or are you afraid," she said slowly, "now that you've realized how much you need me—do you think that because we have opposing views about the hotel, I'm going to go back on my word and run out on my contract?"

His mouth thinned, his nostrils flared. "Don't insult me and don't insult yourself."

Heat rose to her cheeks. "Sorry, but I don't really know you that well."

He leaned forward in his chair. "But you will, darlin'. Our relationship has only just begun."

WORKING WITH SAM was not the same as working with his uncle. Definitely not. Molly studied Sam on the other side of her desk the next morning as he perused the reports she gave him. A white short-sleeve jersey, tan jeans and a pair of horn-rimmed reading glasses, which he took off each time he looked up at her.

"Next time, I'll get bifocals," he muttered, pushing the specs back on his nose. "Clear on top, reading on the bottom."

He was the picture of concentration, absorbing the contents of the reports the same way another person might absorb a gripping novel. He asked an occasional question. She answered. He returned to his reading. Either he had a photographic memory or his mind processed information the way his beloved computers did.

The phone rang for the tenth time in as many minutes, and she reached for it, knowing Sam would listen to every word. His eavesdropping didn't bother her. She was on her home turf in a hotel office, the only difference between Texas and Vermont being the cast of characters and the recreational activities. She glanced out the wide picture window. No ski slopes here. She pushed the thought away and spoke to the head chef. When she hung up, Sam looked thoughtfully at her.

"You've fielded five in-house calls in the last few minutes, making a lot of seemingly routine decisions for the various departments. Is that the way you prefer to work?"

It was a loaded question, although neither his voice nor his expression gave anything away. Molly met his gaze.

"Why don't you just ask me if I'm a control freak?" She held up her hand when he went to speak. "I'm kidding you. Micromanaging is not my style at all, but—and I mean no insult to your uncle—I think it was his style. I didn't pick up on it until recently when I was handling everything alone."

"Seems to me you can't focus on anything else except phone calls," he said.

"You've nailed it perfectly." Molly almost cheered, encouraged that Sam's perception matched her own. Maybe they could work as a team, after all.

"All right," Sam said, brow furrowed. "Please send out an e-mail to all department supervisors. We're having a mandatory meeting at ten tomorrow morning." He looked at her. "Where?"

"How about the Houston Room?"

"Fine," he said. "Then see if we have a spreadsheet on occupancy rates for the past five years by month and week. After I call the Historical Society, I'll pull the financial statements for the same period." He grinned. "You wanted a chance to improve revenues, didn't you? Well, start researching!"

His grin was pure Tom Cruise, and so was the gleam in his eye. His wall of chest muscle rippled as he moved, his jersey faithfully clinging to every wave. Molly sucked in air as if breathing was a new skill.

"I'll be happy to," she managed to reply before the phone rang again. This time she grabbed it like a lifeline.

"Hello? Mom! Hi. It's good to hear from you... No, you're not interrupting." She glanced at Sam, who sat back in his chair, looking as if he had all the time in the world and every right to stay put.

"Just meeting with Sam Kincaid, the new owner, who is rudely listening to my end of the conversation... Oh, if you could see him now, stabbing himself in the heart with a pen as though I'd hurt his feelings... Never mind Sam. How's Daddy?... Great."

She listened as Lily filled her in on family matters, content with what she heard. "Yes, Mom. The staff has been very loyal. No one's quit. I still have a job." She glanced at Sam who was mouthing something at her. Oh, yeah, how could she forget? "A job and a raise. For some misguided reason, Sam's upping my salary."

She held the phone away from her ear as Lily's enthusiasm increased in decibel levels. "Thanks, Mom. Yes, everything's fine... You think I sound... Oh-h-h... Well, take care. Love to all."

Molly hung up and turned her chair to the wall. She needed privacy as tears unexpectedly filled her eyes. Tears, when she thought all her tears were behind her. When all her mom had said was, "Sweetheart, do you hear yourself? You actually sound happy. Your voice isn't dead anymore. I have to tell Daddy right away. Oh, Molly. My heart is lighter. Going to Texas was the key, after all."

And for two years while she attended school, she thought she'd been fooling them so well! She shook her head and grabbed for a tissue. Mothers! They always knew. She'd bet her last dollar that the next call would come from her dad no later than tomorrow. She felt more tears roll down her cheeks as she thought how he, side by side with her mom, wouldn't let her give up.

Darn! She hated crying. Now she'd have to face Sam with telling red eyes. She blotted her cheeks and turned around, mentally gearing to get back to work.

He wasn't there.

But the door was slightly open, and she could hear someone, doubtless Sam, pacing the hall. Typical. No guy was comfortable around a crying woman. She'd have to reassure him.

She walked to the door and opened it wide. "It's safe to come back, Sam. Just a wave of homesickness, but I'm over it now. I rarely cry."

She felt his eyes examine her as he stood in the doorway. "Why don't I believe that?" he said, turning quickly toward his own office. "We both have work to do, so I'll see you later."

"Chicken," she called softly, watching him walk away.

"Damn straight," he replied, turning back to her, an unrepentant grin on his face. "And not ashamed."

"Pluck-pluck-pluck," she warbled as she closed the door behind her and laughed at the picture he made escaping a woman's tears.

But she wasn't laughing later that afternoon when Sam tracked her down while she was conferring with Madeline about housekeeping expenses. He held a piece of paper full of handwritten notes and motioned her to join him. She excused herself from the bookkeeper and followed him into his office.

"I guess it was too much too hope for," he began as he paced the floor. "The Historical Society has had the last word."

He shoved the paper at her, but continued talking. "Seems I can improve electrical systems or plumbing, but I can't touch the building's structure. Can't even add a wing to it following the same architectural style, which is what I concluded, erroneously, we could do. It would have solved all the problems. You would have been happy and so would I."

Shocked, Molly stared at him. "Happy? Me? But, Sam, you don't have to make me happy. So what if I've been having a freaking stomachache about all your proposed changes? We've been at odds about the hotel from the beginning. We've had honest differences. Since when does 'happy' have any place here?"

He glared at her. "Since I started to believe your ideas weren't so backward. Since I studied the occupancy rate spreadsheet you pulled earlier. Since I gave some serious thought to your ideas about promotion, like targeting special markets." He stopped pacing and stared at her. "But the bottom line, Molly—and you know this—is that your ideas alone won't do it. We need the income from both ideas—increasing traditional revenues and creating new revenues—in order to make the Bluebonnet an enticing plum."

"Okay, we'll think of something, Sam," replied Molly. "But not today. My brain's shutting down. And Madeline's waiting for me—it's almost her quitting time." She yawned and stretched, and started thinking about a long soak in the Jacuzzi.

She felt Sam's eyes on her. "What?" she asked.

"You need some exercise, Molly-girl. Too much indoors makes a person tired."

Her mind flashed to snow-covered ski slopes. The only exercise she ever wanted or needed. Then Sam spoke again.

"What's wrong, Molly? There's a look on your face." His voice was soft. "What are you thinking?"

She turned away. "You don't want to know."

"Try me."

Not in this lifetime. Not Sam, not anyone. "I don't think so." She waved as she exited the room. "Enjoy your run or whatever you're going to do. Madeline's waiting," she repeated.

"Chicken," he said in a voice so low she almost didn't hear him.

She stiffened. "Touché," she muttered, forcing herself to relax, impatient to leave, impatient to close the conversation. She had an exercise routine she followed in the privacy of her room, exercises learned from years of physical therapy. Discipline to follow them learned from years of being a competitive athlete. And no desire to expose herself to prying eyes.

But she felt Sam's eyes burn into her back as she

walked down the corridor, and had a feeling that the conversation wasn't over. She was beginning to learn about Sam's follow-through ability. Like a dog with a bone, he didn't let go.

She had to make sure she never became his quarry.

SAM WATCHED HER run away. Not literally, of course. He wasn't sure Molly could actually run. But he hadn't a doubt she'd have left him in the proverbial dust if she could.

Interesting how he'd touched a nerve without meaning to. When he'd made his suggestion, he had only a vague idea of taking a walk in mind, not a particular exercise. But now as he changed into jogging shorts and T-shirt, he knew Molly had made a point.

She obviously couldn't jog. But she had a trim athletic body, toned muscles everywhere. Enticing to someone who enjoyed sports as much as he did. So what physical activities *could* Molly participate in?

His mind jumped to the obvious—and just as obvious was his reaction to the thought. He'd have to wait a moment before venturing outside if he didn't want to embarrass himself. But his interest was another surprise. He hadn't thought he viewed Molly in that way.

He pictured her in his mind now, round blue eyes fringed with lashes long enough to sweep a floor, and lips so tempting his breath caught in his throat.

What an incredible mouth! Rosy and full. If only she'd unleash her hair and let it fall naturally down the sides of her face, if she'd use her sister's makeup techniques, she'd be one stunning woman in anyone's eyes. Lord, he'd never be able to leave the suite if he kept up this line of thought. He'd better think about something else. Anything else!

Finally leaving his uncle's first-floor apartment, where he now resided, Sam exited through the back of the hotel on his way to the running track. Not really a track, he acknowledged, more a mile-long meandering trail through the hotel's acreage.

He paused on the flagstone patio, struck as usual by the solid masses of color that met his eyes. Flowers everywhere. Ornamental tubs of yellow and orange marigolds sat next to pots of red and orange cockscomb, all placed strategically among the umbrella-shaded tables and chairs that were available to the guests.

Edging the patio were carpets of pink and scarlet portulaca, and climbing roses covered split-rail fences leading from the terrace to the cultivated lawn and the property beyond.

All good land. Treed land. Stands of live oak provided shade for guests who cared to stroll or rest on the benches under their leafy branches. Hickory and pine trees added a forested appearance.

The place was gorgeous! No wonder his uncle never sold.

Sam began jogging the gently curved path, absorbing the loveliness, appreciating the shady oases as he came upon them. The six-o'clock sun was still quite warm, but the promise of cooler evening air lurked. His gaze swept ahead of him.

Ten acres. The Bluebonnet sat on ten acres of beautiful land, where in the springtime, masses of bluebonnets and other wildflowers blanketed the ground—and could provide fantastic photo-ops for publicity.

Ten acres that, with the exception of the hotel itself, the Historical Society had no control over.

Ten acres that Sam could play with to construct a spanking-new, state-of-the-art high-tech conference-and-training center. His imagination soared!

He'd build the facility in the Bluebonnet's architectural style on the outside. But on the inside, a different story. Networked computers with vast memory and loaded with software and high-speed Internet connections, classrooms for sales and management training, video-teleconferencing capability, VCRs, camcorders for taping training sessions.

They could create a volleyball court for boosting teamwork skills, and there were dozens of potential venues that could be used for discovering leadership qualities. Sam grinned. The guys he knew would rival an Olympic team in enthusiasm at the sight of a volleyball court or a white-water rafting opportunity.

Sam passed the Bluebonnet as he circled around for the second time. She was a beautiful lady in the Spanish Renaissance style, built of yellow brick flecked with the natural color of red clay. He had no problem with the idea of copying her materials and architecture for his project. In fact, her style would add a touch of class to the modern center.

It was time to develop his business plan in more detail. He pounded the corner for a third trip around the path. He had to expend his physical energies before he sat down at his desk again.

He hoped Molly had some kind of exercise routine, because she'd be working harder than ever for the Bluebonnet. But she shouldn't complain, because she'd gotten what she wanted. A big, beautiful hotel to run.

CHAPTER FIVE

"SO, WHO'S THE BOSS?"

The question came from eagle-eyed Gladys Pierce, housekeeping supervisor, known for meticulous linen and a mean game of gin rummy. Sam remembered her well from boyhood summers spent at the hotel.

"Well, Miss Gladys," he replied, a slow grin traveling across his face, "I reckon maybe Molly and I could help *you* with that job!" His answer produced full-throated laughter from the assembled employees at the morning meeting. Sam, as well as everyone in the room, knew that in her heart, Gladys thought she did indeed run the hotel and that John Kincaid couldn't have managed without her.

And maybe that was the secret to his uncle's success. Each department supervisor thought the entire hotel depended on him or her doing a superior job.

Sam looked at the ten employees seated in front of him, delighted that his message today bore no resemblance to the ones he delivered to other groups back in California. There, his staff had lost their jobs; here, they were being given more autonomy in their jobs. But he also knew that any kind of change produced stress. His uncle's death certainly proved that. Gladys's question confirmed it.

"John Kincaid knew the Bluebonnet as well as a parent knows his child," said Sam seriously. "But what about Sam Kincaid?" he asked rhetorically, pointing at himself. "I think we'll consider Sam Kincaid as a parent-in-training who'll be depending on each of you to teach me about your departments. I'll be visiting you all one-on-one to get some private tutoring, so to speak. And, folks," he added, "I'm going after an A in this crash course, so be tough. Don't let me down. Instead, let me have it!"

Sam paused as the group tittered, some whispering to their neighbors. He let his words sink in so he could lead them to his next point. Reaching his arm out to Molly, he invited her to join him in front of the room.

"Getting back to Gladys's question about bosses, I'd like to introduce you to the new Manager of the Bluebonnet." He felt Molly's surprise as her body stiffened, and he whispered, "Nothing's changed but the title. You've been doing the work, anyway."

He watched Molly smile at the group and acknowledge their friendly waves. The meeting was going more smoothly than he'd hoped.

"I see you all know and appreciate this lady," he said. "But perhaps you're not really aware of how deep her understanding of the hotel industry goes."

The staff members sat forward in their chairs at his remark. Perhaps his uncle hadn't explained Molly's full credentials. Sam would do it now. He needed to establish the highest credibility possible for Molly, so he could leave the majority of the hotel's business in her hands while he spent his out-of-training time developing the conference center.

"Molly Porter was born into the hotel business," he began, "and started bossing everyone around as soon as she learned to talk." He winked. "She's a very experienced boss."

Molly laughed this time, along with everyone else. "Why don't you tell everyone about Diamond Ridge?" Sam asked, confident she'd cooperate.

She glared at him and stepped on his foot, instead, then turned and smiled at the assembly. "The interesting fact is that the seasons are turned around," she said. "Winter is the time of big business in Vermont. But to me, each season was beautiful because the Diamond was my home."

Was? Molly had spoken in the past tense. Sam examined Molly's face. She was totally focused on the audience, and he'd bet money she didn't realize the significance of what she'd said.

"It was natural for me to choose hotel management in college, and I graduated from the program with honors. However," she continued, "I don't believe that learning comes only from books. You and I are in a people-oriented industry where success depends on customer service and the ability to change with the times. We need to be competitive. The Bluebonnet's success depends on all of us being professionals in our jobs."

Sam let her roll with what was turning out to be

not only a pep talk but the cementing of a team with a new leader. And Molly was a natural. As he watched her, she continued to enthuse about the hotel, raising spirits, drawing positive pictures of their potential future accomplishments and how to arrive at them. She was the captain of the team. No doubt about it.

He wouldn't have guessed she had it in her. Sure, she was smart, but she didn't show it off. How many times would she surprise him? How many layers would he have to peel away until he understood her? She was like a flower in the middle of the night, its beauty hidden until the sun's rays woke it in the morning.

Spontaneous applause interrupted his musings. Molly flashed her million-dollar smile. Sam raised a brow as she stepped forward and shook the hand of every person in the room. A polished professional.

"Great job, Mol," he said quietly when she returned to his side.

"They're a great bunch," she replied equally quietly. "I wouldn't want to let them down."

"You won't." Sam was convinced of that now. Although he knew Molly still harbored doubts about the conference center, he was beginning to believe she could do anything she set her mind to—including running the hotel with little help from him.

Gladys raised her hand. "I have another question."

"Go for it."

"We heard a rumor about you selling the Bluebonnet. Is that the truth?"

He should have expected a question like that. Rumors had a way of sprouting. He mentally shrugged. He hadn't been president of three companies without learning to handle himself in public. "Selling was discussed, but now we're planning to add to the hotel, not take away from it. So don't believe anything you hear unless it comes from Molly or me. When our new project gets off the ground, you'll all be the first to know."

"*If* it gets off the ground," Molly murmured, casting him a quick glance.

"Atta boy, Sammy," Gladys called out. "Just like your uncle. The Bluebonnet's a family."

Sam nodded and smiled, saying nothing, wondering for a moment if he'd wind up running a hotel until he was ready to retire whether he wanted to or not. It wasn't a happy thought.

A WEEK LATER, Sam's schedule left no time for thinking about anything but hotel business. He spent most mornings with staff "in training," and afternoons developing his plan for the conference center. Most dinner hours, however, were spent with Molly. Sitting across from her each evening had become his favorite activity whether they ate in the office or in the Brew Pub. Tonight was no exception.

He glanced at his watch and lengthened his stride as he headed for the pub. It wasn't Molly, however, but Judy who waved him inside.

"Molly had to cancel," Judy reported. "Said she needed an early night with a hot Jacuzzi."

For a moment a wave of guilt passed through Sam. Had she been working too hard because of him? "Maybe I should take her a meal."

"In her bathtub?" squealed their future Broadway star.

"Then I should send dinner up."

Judy shook her head and poked him. "Boy," she said, "you've got it bad. Forget the dinner. She wasn't hungry, and besides, she can always call room service if her stomach growls."

"You're right," said Sam. "I think I'll order room-service dinner myself and get some more work done in my office. Thanks for Molly's message. Have a good night."

But he couldn't seem to concentrate on work. He paced in front of his desk, then walked into the hall. Why hadn't she called him? Was she sick? He glanced toward her office, a habit he'd developed lately, and noted her half-open door. Dang! Very unusual. She really must have been ill.

As he started to close her door, he peeked inside. Folders neatly stacked and labeled on her desk. Very organized. A trait necessary for running a successful hotel, as Sam was beginning to learn. And every time he learned more about the behind-the-scenes details, he itched to write software for the function. Paper chasing gave him hives.

A videotape protruded over the edge of Molly's desk near her chair, and he pushed it to safety. Then

he glanced at the title. *Training Video, Molly's copy.*
Hmm. Maybe he'd watch a hotel-management class
in action. Must be a good video if Molly wanted to
review it and went to the trouble of having a television brought to her office. He inserted the tape in
the VCR and pushed "play."

He didn't know what to expect, but a vista of
snow-covered mountains with a group of skiers certainly wasn't it. The camera panned to a huge sign
reading Lake Placid. In front and to the right of the
sign stood two flagpoles, one flying the American
flag and the other, the five-ring symbol of the Olympic Games.

Sam dropped into Molly's chair and leaned forward. What the heck was he looking at? Now the
lens focused on an enclosed ski station at the top of
a mountain. A voice announced exactly what was
on the screen.

"This is the December sixteenth taping of the
United States Women's Downhill Ski Team, to be
used for training purposes only. Unauthorized dis-
tribution of this video is prohibited by law."

Sam didn't budge. This was the real thing. But
what was Molly doing with the tape? He watched
as number ten, Julie Martin, emerged from the small
building and threw her weight into her start. He
watched her go faster until her skis chattered on
some ice about halfway down the slope. To his un-
trained eye, the woman looked great.

The announcer noted her timing and then said,

"Next out of the shoot is number six, Molly Ann Porter."

He forgot to breathe. Molly! His Molly. There she was, crouched at the top, in red, white and blue, her long hair pulled back and blowing behind her. She pushed off hard, her face a study in concentration, her goggles unable to hide her intense expression. He recognized the set of her chin, had seen it facing him more than once. He felt her need, her absolute focus, to the point that his own heart started to pound. She pushed harder, then flew into the run, turning with the mountain, then straight down again, then shifting. A smile lurked—a *smile* at that speed. Dang it, she was having fun!

The announcer said, "Porter leads at the halfway mark by 1.5 seconds in a sport that's measured in seconds."

"My God," Sam whispered as he watched Molly chase the wind. "She's fantastic. Absolutely fantastic."

And then, the unthinkable. The backward somersault, the cartwheels, the tangled legs as she sped head over heels down the mountain with nothing to break the fall until she collided with the snow fence.

Sam jumped to his feet, eyes wide, and stared at the scene. He heard the announcer shout in the background, saw people run toward Molly. He couldn't move, just stood in front of the television, fists clenched, throat tight. "Get up, Mol," he rasped. "Get up."

"Not likely, and you can get out of my office."

He whirled around to see Molly in the doorway, glaring at him. "Not a pretty sight, is it," she continued, limping to the television and extracting the offending video. "But you have only yourself to blame. No one invited you to a screening."

"Pretty?" Sam's voice rose, his mind focused only on the one word. "Who cares about pretty? I saw what happened. You could have been killed! Easily."

She tilted her head, chin thrust forward in that familiar manner he was getting to know so well. "Yes, I could have been killed. So, everyone says I'm lucky. Isn't that what I'm supposed to think? That I'm such a lucky woman?" Her voice intoned the exact opposite.

He heard the challenge, saw it in her straight-as-a-post posture, in the hot glow of her eyes. She'd trample him if he gave her a pat answer. The lady didn't want platitudes. The lady wanted a fight.

"Lucky?" he repeated. "You got invited to the most exclusive party in the world and then couldn't show up! You gave how many years of your life to this dream? A dream that most girls—most kids—never come close to realizing. And you...you had it in the palm of your hand...for a moment." His voice fell away. "Am I supposed to tell you that you're lucky after losing the dream of a lifetime? I won't do it."

Her expression softened. "Thank you," she replied quietly. "I don't know why I watch the damn thing anymore. The ending never changes."

He chuckled, wondering if she realized she'd cracked a joke. A glance at her serious face provided the answer. "Maybe," he said, "you're still grieving."

She emitted a hollow laugh. "There's no maybe about it," she agreed. "Grief comes in many forms, but not everyone can watch their own demise over and over again. I'm just one of the lucky ones—like everyone says." Sarcasm overlaid every word.

"How long are you going to enjoy feeling sorry for yourself?" asked Sam with a flash of insight. "You keep watching that tape and thinking your life stopped when you were no longer the girl who was number six. You're still in mourning and you can't get past it. And you're not ready to accept that you really were…lucky."

Her eyes flashed at him.

"How lucky can you be," he pushed, "when not only are you still alive but you've let everyone down? Your country, your team—the women's alpine team lost that year, didn't they? And how about your family? They must have been worried sick about you after the accident. They would have all been better off had you died. Is that the rationale you use to feel sorry for yourself?"

They'd been standing and facing each other, but now Sam leaned into her, over her, until only an inch separated them. "Excuses," he accused. "That's the easy way out, baby, a laundry list of excuses. But Olympians don't choose easy. They seek challenges that we mortals look at in awe."

She didn't speak, but for some reason she was listening. She looked so stricken, however, he had to harden his heart before he went in for the kill.

"It seems to me that the real question is *not,* are you lucky? The real question is, are you an Olympian away from the mountain?"

He thought he'd drown in her beautiful, glistening eyes. In her gasp of breath. He wanted to recall his words and put his arms around her, just let her cry if she wanted to. He stepped toward her.

If she knew his intentions, she didn't let on. Instead, she stood tall and proud before him, not moving, staring into his face, into his eyes.

"Am I an Olympian away from the hill?" she repeated in a soft voice. "No one's ever asked me that before except..." She touched her hand to her own chest. "I've asked myself at least a million times, and now you, in five short minutes..." She continued to study him and in her eyes, he saw a change, a curiosity. An awareness. She looked at him as though for the first time.

"The answer's always been elusive," she continued in a quiet voice, "but maybe it's time to find out." She nodded and before he could move, left the room, video in hand.

Sam watched her retreat—short step, long step— her dancer's posture intact, and couldn't look anywhere else, before collapsing into the chair as though he'd gone ten rounds in a boxing ring. What had he done? Where had he found the audacity to lecture this extraordinary woman as though he had the right? As though he had all the answers?

And then like a bolt of lightning illuminating the sky, awareness flashed in his mind. The lecture he'd given Molly varied only slightly from the ones he'd given himself since his business disaster. Molly had lost her way—and so had he.

MOLLY COLLAPSED on her bed as soon as she was safely inside her suite. She'd put on a good act for Sam. Her body trembled from the effort of walking, smiling and pretending everything was fine. But everything wasn't fine. She wasn't fine.

She was scared. Very, very scared.

Over the years she'd watched that video more times than was healthy for her, but tonight had been different. Because of Sam. He'd voiced what no one else had. Had gone right to the heart of the matter.

Molly got up from the bed and crossed to the dresser to look into the mirror over it. Her skin was so pale that when she turned her head, her scar stood out in stark relief.

Who *was* that girl in the mirror?

Girl? Strange using that word. Was Sam right? Is that how she viewed herself, still as the young girl in the video? The girl she had once been?

Or was there a woman reflected in the glass? A woman who'd been sleepwalking through the past four years, going through the motions of life to make everyone who loved her happy. She didn't know the answer, but for the first time since the accident, she wanted to ask the question. She wanted to go forward for her own sake and no one else's.

A firm knock on the apartment door interrupted her thoughts. Annoyed, not wanting to deal with anyone, she didn't move to answer it. Let Sam handle any staff questions.

"Open up, Molly," came Sam's distinctive baritone.

Shoot. She couldn't take much more tonight.

"Come on, Mol. I know you're in there."

Only Sam could be so stubborn. From the bedroom, she walked through the living room and opened the door. She remained on the threshold, eyes straight ahead. All she saw was chest. Broad, muscular chest in a red jersey. "What?" she asked curtly, with no shred of Texas hospitality in her voice.

"I just wanted to make sure—"

"I'm fine, Sam. Go to bed or to the pub or wherever else you want to go. I'm fine." She started to close the door. He caught the edge with his foot and stopped the movement.

"Then why won't you look at me?"

She glanced up at him and quickly glanced away. "There I've looked at you. Now leave."

"Not good enough," he said quietly, stepping toward her.

She backed up. "What?" she whispered. "What do you want from me? You've already hit the rawest nerve. There's nothing left." Her throat ached as she fought threatening tears.

He took another step forward and she took another step back. "Or maybe," she rasped, jabbing a finger into one of his pecs, "you just want to make sure I'm stronger than steel? That I'm a real Olympian?"

Her voice totally gave out then. She had no energy for more sarcasm, no fight left. Tears ran down her cheeks, the damn tears she'd been controlling ever since she'd walked into her office and saw Sam watching the video.

She turned her back to him.

And felt his hands on her shoulders, pressing, massaging, reversing her position so that she faced him. His arms embraced her, while hers automatically wrapped themselves around his waist. He squeezed her gently, then not so gently. She inhaled his fragrance. Musk and man. When was the last time she'd been held by a pair of strong arms? The last time she'd wanted to wrap herself around someone with a scruffy beard?

He murmured words she didn't hear. She was aware of only the touch of his hands stroking her arms and his mouth kissing the top of her head. She felt herself relax against him and could have stayed forever in that warm cocoon.

What was she thinking! This was Sam holding her. Sam, who argued with her about everything. Who always thought he knew best. Sam...who was making her feel better than her whirlpool bath ever did.

She shivered and stepped out of his embrace,

loneliness immediately wrapping her in its tentacles. She took a deep breath and raised her eyes to meet his, praying for the inner strength to see the conversation through.

His eyes were like hot coals, the perplexity on his face almost comical. Maybe he was as shaken up as she was. He reached for her again and she almost succumbed. But she knew better. Fast sex wasn't the answer for her. An instant fix could never be.

"You need to leave," she said.

"In a minute," he whispered. In slow motion, he brought his hand with fingers trembling and to her mouth and gently stroked her bottom lip. Her heart began to pound. Then he touched her top lip and continued making gentle love to her mouth as surely as if he'd been kissing her.

She moaned, her pulse racing to speeds she hadn't experienced in years and her tongue darting out to lick Sam's finger. He leaned down and kissed her, his lips firm and sure, then more urgent.

She could no more hold back from responding than she could hold back the ocean's tide. Nor did she want to. She gave of herself as though reliving every kiss of her past, and yet this was far better than the vague memories of her youth. Because of Sam? Or because Sleeping Beauty was waking up? At the moment she didn't care. She wanted more. Definitely more. But on the heels of the thought came sudden freedom.

Sam stood in front of her, breathing hard, looking

like a stunned ox. A gorgeous ox. "Mol?" His voice cracked like an adolescent boy's.

"I'm fine," she gasped. "Just fine." Whatever that meant.

"Yeah. Me, too," Sam replied, keeping his distance. "Everything's going to be okay. I don't want to overstep… I didn't mean to hurt you by anything I may have said or done. I just wanted to help."

As her breathing slowed, her mind went into overdrive. "Help?" she echoed, an ugly suspicion taking root. "As in 'help the poor loser become normal again?' Or 'turn the poor frog into a princess with a kiss'?"

"What are you talking about?" Sam asked, his brow furrowing. "What frog?"

But Molly was on a roll. "I'm not some project you need to supervise. I've already been through rehab, months of rehab."

Sam's eyes narrowed. "Well, they didn't do a very good job!"

For a moment Molly couldn't find the words to respond. But only for a moment, and then, "You think, of course, that you could do better." Her tone was scornful. Her index finger jabbed him again. "Well, here's a warning, Sam. Don't you dare try to use me to find salvation for your own mistakes. For all those folks who lost their jobs because of you, for all those investors who lost money because of you." Her breathing tightened, and she thought her heart would jump out of her chest.

"Where do you get your ideas?" he asked.

"None of them have crossed my mind. I had only one goal tonight after you walked into the office. And I've succeeded in reaching it."

"Oh?"

"Yeah," he replied with a nod. "I've got a news flash for you." He paused for a moment. "I've discovered you're still alive, Molly. Whether you want to be or not."

He stared at her, challenging her. "Underneath all your scars—and I don't mean the mark on your face—there's one hell of a woman wanting to emerge." He came toward her. "And you know what?"

She shook her head, unable to form a coherent sentence.

"You don't scare me with your hard talk and accusations. I'm not going to walk on eggshells around you like your family did."

"They did not," she protested.

"Save it," he ordered. "And think of this, instead."

She had no time to protest. His kiss was slow, thoughtful, enticing. It swirled through her like hot chocolate on a cold winter's day. Sweet and warm and delicious. She lifted her face for more.

His lips continued to move over her mouth gently, teasing the corners, then seared a path to her earlobe on her scarred cheek. She quivered. Exhaled. And delighted in the sensations he raised in her. His mouth brushed hers again as he spoke.

"Good night, Molly. All I really wanted to do

was give you something else to think about. But you know what happened?''

She shook her head.

"I outsmarted myself. My idea boomeranged. I've got as much to think about now as you." He hugged her quickly and walked out the door.

Totally befuddled, Molly watched him leave. She laughed at her own confusion. Half of her couldn't wait for him to go, while the other half...well, he was right. She hadn't felt so alive in years! Young and...normal. Desirable. She shook her head. No, she wouldn't go down that path. Dangerous thought. Very dangerous.

But she couldn't deny the electric currents that had charged through the atmosphere all evening. All evening? She glanced at her watch. Only an hour had passed since she'd walked into her office and saw Sam watching her training video. An hour that had turned her well-orchestrated inner world upside down.

But there was no going back, she thought as she changed into her nightgown. She had to move forward. And fifty years from now, when she thought about this summer at the Bluebonnet, she'd remember a guy named Sam Kincaid who wasn't afraid to face the wrath of an Olympian.

She smiled at her imagination and crawled under her sheet, too tired now to take a bath. Her eyes closed and she drifted off immediately.

CHAPTER SIX

MOLLY LOOKED DOWN at her bathroom counter the next morning, amazed at the amount of cosmetics her industrious sister had snuck into her belongings when Molly had packed for her job in Texas. What the heck was she supposed to do with all these bottles of goop?

Shoot! She had never used much makeup, other than lipstick, and even that was used on a casual basis—when she remembered. She did, however, believe in moisturizers. She was an expert in skin care for every atmospheric condition in ski country, which included both North and South America, as well as Europe. Since the accident, she'd also occasionally use some cover-up cream on her scar.

But now, as she looked at the array of bottles in front of her, Molly was overwhelmed and knew only one action to take. She picked up the phone to call her sister. Amanda was the expert; now she'd be Molly's consultant.

"You want to know about the 'goop'? What goop? I gave you the highest-quality stuff... Wait a minute. You really want to use the cosmetics? This is great! Wonderful. What changed your mind? Wait till I tell Mom.''

Just what Molly didn't want—a family celebration for no reason, especially when she didn't know the outcome yet. She injected a note of boredom in her voice.

"Just keep your cool, Mandy. Nothing special happened. I'm just tired of scaring the guests.''

Dead silence at the other end. Maybe she'd gone too far.

"I'm kidding, sis. The hotel's great, and the guests are happy.''

Amanda didn't reply for a moment. ''Not funny, Molly. We love you, and if anyone dares threaten your job…''

"I know, I know. Attorney Amanda Shaw Porter will slap a lawsuit on them. Forget it. Everything's cool.'' She paused to think and then said softly, ''I guess it's just time.''

"Time? Well, hallelujah! If you're sure, then let's talk makeup. First, get a paper and pencil to take notes. I've kept a list of everything I gave you. I knew one day you'd call.''

Five minutes later Molly looked at two pages of handwritten directions and felt dizzy. Her sister had left nothing out. Skin, eyes, colors, techniques. Daytime, evening. She should have known better than to ask an expert. She looked at the receiver in her hand. Amanda was still going strong.

"I've researched your situation with every makeup artist I worked with in New York,''

Amanda said. "So you can feel confident about how you look if you follow directions."

"Couldn't you have asked for *simple* directions?" Molly pleaded.

And then Amanda laughed, and Molly heard unrestrained joy in her sister's voice. For the first time in too long.

"My goodness," said Amanda. "I think I have my little sister back. The original model. I'm crying, Molly. I'm actually crying."

Molly could picture Amanda so clearly, her heart ached to be home.

"So talk to me," said Amanda. "What's happening in Texas?"

Erase that thought. Home was a bunch of too-curious people.

"Nothing specific," replied Molly, as an image of Sam flashed through her mind. "I guess I just needed to get away. Be on my own." Which was also very true.

"Oh."

"Away from the mountains," Molly said quickly, detecting the hurt in her sister's voice. "I needed to see something different. And I needed to work hard."

"Well, sure," came the reply. "I guess we let you off too easy, didn't we."

Molly's hand tightened on the receiver. *Eggshells.* Sam's word echoed in her mind. Leave it to her nosy sister to probe a nerve.

"I made life very difficult for all of you," said

Molly slowly. "And I'm sorry. Recovery can be a long, complicated process and you all helped me through the first part. You and Zach, as well as Mom and Dad. The rest, however, is up to me."

As the words came out of her mouth, Molly could feel the truth of them in her soul. She was responsible for the rest of her life. She, alone. Not her family. Not her friends. And not Sam.

A long, low whistle hit her eardrum across the wires from Vermont. "We'll always be here for you, Molly. We love you."

"Back at you, Mandy. Kiss the folks for me."

Molly replaced the receiver in its cradle, acknowledging the complexities of relationships. The power of relationships. The changes in them. She and Amanda had always been close. Amanda had helped to raise her while their mom and Molly's dad worked to build the business at Diamond Ridge. Despite their age difference, she and Amanda had basically enjoyed a relationship of equals, of mutual respect. Until the accident. Then Molly became the child. But that was changing again because of her effort.

She glanced into the mirror once more. A *woman* looked back. And Molly smiled.

SAM WAS TIRED from lack of sleep, hungry from lack of food and irritable from lack of Molly. Where was she? He glanced at his watch and groaned. Like any normal person, she'd still be dressing for the day.

His eagerness to see her merely reflected his concern after last night's conversation, he told himself. His tough words could have shaken her up after she was alone in her apartment again. Not to mention the kisses. Sweet, tender kisses, the memory of which kept him awake last night.

He looked at the business plan for the new training center, which lay all over his desk. Best-case scenario. Worst-case scenario. A project he believed in. And he couldn't concentrate on it.

If he was totally honest with himself, he'd admit why he felt so edgy. A night of tossing and turning had resulted in a decision to keep his relationship with Molly strictly platonic. Neither of them were ready for intimacy. Both were still finding their own way. But dang! It would be so easy to fall onto the path of least resistance.

Sparks had flown between them last night. A definite awareness, a definite mutual participation in those kisses. He closed his eyes and thought about kissing Molly. So different from kissing Adrienne. Kissing Molly was special. Like holding a jeweled butterfly on his finger. Beautiful, innocent and delicate. He knew nothing about her past love life, but he'd guess from her hesitation that she hadn't been intimate with anyone for a long while.

And he? He certainly wasn't ready for another relationship. Hell, did he even know what a real relationship with a woman was supposed to be like? Obviously not. So it was fortunate that he and Molly both needed to concentrate on the hotel. For both their sakes, he'd eliminate kissing from the approved activity list—kissing and what usually came afterward.

But as a friend, he had some great ideas for her. Places to go, activities to enjoy. Fun stuff. Business stuff. A whole mess of things.

"Good morning, Sam."

Startled by the sound of Molly's voice, he swiveled his chair around, a smile ready on his face. And said not a word. He couldn't.

She leaned casually against the door to his office, her honey-blond hair falling loosely to her shoulders, the blue of her eyes set off by her matching blouse and her lightly colored eyelids. And her face—he had to look twice to realize her scar was still there. If he'd thought Molly was pretty before, she was stunning now. A knockout.

He rose to his feet. "Good morning and wow!"

She grinned, and he could imagine that expression on a younger Molly growing up, the adolescent Molly in high school and the young-adult Molly on her ski team.

"Did your dad have to chase them off with a shotgun?" He winked and enjoyed her laughing response.

"Not quite," she replied. "If they couldn't ski, I didn't want 'em. And then later—" she sobered quickly "—they didn't want me." She straightened up and gave him a gallant smile. "So here I am. Ready to start the day."

"Good. There's a lot to do." He forced himself

to look away. "I'll be with Gladys this morning. Then I'll meet you to put up posters for next week's Fourth of July barbecue and dance. Proceeds go to the volunteer firefighters, so we want a good attendance." He spoke so fast he felt as if he was racing to a fire himself.

"I know all that," said Molly. "I've already co-ordinated the whole thing." She tilted her head and narrowed her eyes. "What's wrong with you, Sam? You're acting funny."

"Nothing. Just a lot of work." He nodded at his desk.

"See you later, then," Molly said, waving her fingers at him and leaving the office.

He watched her go and snatched up some tissues from a box on his desk and wiped his neck. If he worked up a sweat just looking at her this morning, he'd need a cold shower by the afternoon. He took a deep breath. Then another.

Damn! He didn't want to be attracted to her! She didn't even like him very much. Fighting his awareness of Molly presented a challenge he hadn't foreseen. He shook his head and grunted. Just what he needed. Another challenge.

THE HISTORIC DISTRICT in downtown Oak Creek combined the beauty of historical and recently renovated buildings with an upbeat retail and entertainment environment. From the passenger seat in Sam's car, Molly's eyes swept the area, noting the variety

of dining establishments, craft shops, stately govern-
ment edifices, banks and legal firms.

"This is a gem of a town," she said to Sam as
he backed into a parking spot on Main Street.

"It *is* a draw for visitors. We need to capitalize
on that to grow the Bluebonnet and market the busi-
ness-training center," he replied, studying the area
the same way she did. "Between the village and the
attractions beyond, we've got everything. We just
need to be creative in our marketing."

"True enough."

"Funny how I barely noticed all this when I was
a kid spending summers at the hotel," Sam continued. "Back then my perspective was limited to
Gessners' Ice Cream Parlor right down the street."
He pointed to the spot. "Look Molly, it's still there.
The Gessners made the best ice cream and fudge. I
wonder if they still run it."

Molly smiled and reached for her tote, which held
a stack of posters. "I can't blame you for concentrating on ice cream. Summers are darn hot in
Texas!"

A frown suddenly appeared on Sam's forehead.
"Maybe you should wait in the air-con—"

She put a finger over his lips. "I'll be fine, Sam.
I'm not an invalid. Everyone feels the heat, not only
me." She laughed and looked into his dark eyes.
And then stopped laughing, stopped moving. His
eyes were as hot as the Texas sun and much more
dangerous.

"You're driving me crazy," he said in a voice

husky and low, his lips against her fingers, bestowing small kisses.

She gulped. "I'm not feeling too sane myself."

He gently held her wrist while he kissed her palm. A shiver ran through the length of her, followed by a flash of heat. She pulled her hand away from him, her eyes still locked with his.

"We've got work to do," she whispered.

He nodded. "Yeah. Meet me at the car in an hour. Let's go."

Molly grabbed her tote, pushed open the car door and didn't look back. One by one, she visited the proprietors of the shops on "her" side of the street, putting up posters, talking about the upcoming dance and generally filling her mind with people, sights and sounds—anything but Sam.

Finally she pushed open the door of her friend Carla O'Connor's jewelry shop and enjoyed the mellow chime of the bells announcing her arrival. Carla smiled at her from behind the counter where she was waiting on a customer, and then like a scene from a movie, turned her head to look at Molly again. Her gentle smile turned into a wide grin.

"I'll be with you in a few," she said, waving her hand to indicate the rest of the shop. "Make yourself at home."

Molly didn't mind meandering around this oasis of beautiful jewelry and gift items. Earrings, lockets, bracelets. Antique, contemporary, originals. Something for everyone. Maybe she'd buy a present for her sister, who surely deserved one after the hour-long cosmetology lesson that morning. She glanced at her watch. Still had ten minutes before she had to meet Sam.

The bells rang again as Carla's customer left the store. Molly waved a poster in the air, and at Carla's nod, placed it in the window with tape she carried for that purpose.

"You look great!" said Carla, coming out from behind the counter. "Let me see."

Molly stepped toward her. After all, Carla was an artist with a discerning eye.

"Excellent use of color, a perfect match," Carla observed in a clinical tone. "With the attention drawn to your eyes, the scar on your cheek is barely noticeable." She beamed at Molly. "Good job. Couldn't have done better myself."

"Modesty becomes you," teased Molly. "Now let's change the subject. How about taking ten tickets to sell for the event? If we combine advance sales with door sales, we should get the three hundred admissions we want, maybe more. If we add in the silent-auction donations from all the shops, we should reach our overall goal for the fire department."

"Just hand the tickets over," said Carla, a grin on her face, her palm open. "I can sell anything."

The bells rang again. Molly saw Carla turn toward the door, saw her smile fade, her posture straighten. A man and little girl entered.

"Hello, Travis." Carla's voice was low, her tone flat.

"Carla." He nodded.

Molly studied the newcomer, her senses alert. A potentially handsome man, his curtness and severe expression detracted from whatever charm and kindness he might have possessed. Until he glanced at the child. Then, warmth flooded his hazel eyes.

The little girl's eyes matched the man's, but her red hair, although drawn back into a long braid, could have been cut from Carla's thick tresses.

Carla squatted to be eye level with the child. "Hi, Amy darlin'," she said softly, ignoring the man and opening her arms. "I'm so glad you've come to visit me."

The girl glanced up at the man. He nodded, and she ran into Carla's arms.

Astounded at the drama being played out in front of her eyes, Molly's imagination raced to fill in the blanks. She needn't have bothered.

"Amy is my favorite niece," said Carla as she hugged the little girl, who immediately started to giggle. "And this is my brother-in-law, Travis Miller."

Molly turned toward the man and smiled. But his eyes were fixed on Carla. "I'm assuming she's not only your favorite but your *only* niece," he said, a note of bitterness permeating his tone. "But I couldn't swear for sure."

Carla got to her feet, still holding Amy's hand. Molly watched as her friend unfolded to her full height, then tilted her head to look the man in the face. "Whether you believe me or not, Travis, I can't swear, either." She barely blinked. "Free spirits like Meredith was are tough to pin down," she added softly.

His lips hardened to a straight line. "I guess you would know."

Molly gasped at the insult. Carla's eyes widened, then narrowed. "And you can go straight to—"

The mellow tones of the bells interrupted and Sam's voice cut through the tension.

"Are you ready Mol— Hey! Look who's here. Travis Miller! How the heck are you?" Sam shook the guy's hand as though he was a long-lost brother, and the transformation in Travis's demeanor—slow grin, sparkling eyes, eagerness—revealed a different person. Act two of the drama, Molly thought.

"Talk about Jekyll and Hyde," Carla murmured, disgust infusing her voice. "If he weren't such a great dad, I'd—"

"Talk about being saved by the bell," said Molly simultaneously. "Or," she added, nodding at Sam, who although the same height, was broader than his friend, "by a bull in a china shop."

"At least he's a friendly bull," Carla said, glancing meaningfully at Travis.

The "bull" reached for Molly. "Meet my old buddy, Travis Miller. He runs the Rocking H Ranch back a few miles from the Bluebonnet." Sam turned to his friend. "Molly runs the Bluebonnet now. She's the hotel-management expert who will increase cash flow and improve the bottom line. I'm staying behind the scenes trying to develop other business in conjunction with the hotel.''

The rancher's eyebrows touched the ceiling, but he didn't comment. Instead, he said, "I was at your uncle's funeral, Sam. Guess you didn't see me in the crowd. We'll all miss him." He reached for Amy. "And this little gal is my daughter, Amy Elizabeth Miller. Four years old next week—on the Fourth of July."

"Wow," said Sam, hunkering down and giving the child his whole attention. "Everybody celebrates your birthday."

The youngster nodded. "It's loud."

"She means the fireworks the night before," explained Travis. "You remember our tradition around here to celebrate for two nights. Big fireworks on the third and a barbecue and dance on the fourth. We took her to the big show last year."

"And she was scared to death," Carla said wryly, extending a hand to Sam. "Nice to see you again. And by the way, Amy is my niece."

Molly watched Sam look from the woman to the child, a grin crossing his face. "Never would have guessed," he joked. "DNA doesn't lie."

"And that's a pure fact," said Travis Miller in a tone drier than the Texas desert. "Genes run as true with people as with horses." He shook Sam's hand again. "I've got errands to run and not much time. Come on out to the ranch when you can." He looked at Carla. "I'll be back in an hour. Does that suit you?"

"A lifetime would suit me better, but I'll take what I can get."

"You're a stubborn woman." He walked out the door, bells ringing behind him.

Carla wrinkled her nose and scooped Amy up into her arms. "You know what, darlin'?"

The child shook her head.

"Your daddy needs a big ol' tickling so that the only thing he can do is laugh, laugh and laugh some more. Just like this." Carla wiggled her fingers under Amy's arm and on her belly.

Amy began giggling and squirming until Carla put her gently down on the floor. Then she turned to Molly and Sam.

"My sister died in a car accident while with another man. It's a long story and not a pretty one. I'm a dead ringer for her, so Travis takes his anger out on me. And there you have it. Short and simple."

Molly squeezed her friend's hand. "Well, it looks like if anyone can handle him," she said nodding at the door, "it's you."

"Yeah. There's a lot at stake," Carla replied, looking at her niece. "And I *am* too stubborn to give up. Travis is right about that."

"Sounds like someone else I know," Sam offered, reaching for the door handle. "See you, Carla. Good luck. He's really a great guy."

A wistful smile crossed her face. "I know."

EVIDENTLY NEITHER SAM nor Molly wanted to break the silence as they walked to Sam's car. Molly paused while he held the door for her, a courtesy she'd learned to accept after arguing in vain.

"Equality," she'd said, reaching for the handle when they'd left the hotel earlier.

"Indulge me," he'd replied, opening the door, making sure she was safely inside before slamming it.

It wasn't worth the argument, she'd decided, knowing there would be bigger disagreement along the way in her working relationship with Sam. So she allowed him to open the door for her.

Sam started the ignition and the car purred to life. Molly leaned back in her seat, enjoying the air-conditioned comfort of the Beemer. She sighed.

"Was the heat too much for you, after all, Molly? Or was there too much walking?" asked Sam, turning toward her. "Tell me the truth."

"I'm absolutely fine," she replied. "Stop worrying about me. Worry more about your friend back there."

"Who? Trav? He'll handle it."

"Or she will," said Molly. "Carla's no dishrag."

Sam grunted. "I'm sure Travis figured that out. He wouldn't have to be concerned about a dishrag. But I know what I'd do."

"Really?" Molly was curious to discover more about how Sam's mind worked. "And what's that?"

"It's very simple. I'd do whatever was best for Amy. Her childhood counts. Children count. Don't you think so?"

The Harlequin Reader Service® — Here's how it works:

If offer card is missing write to: Harlequin Reader Service, 3010 Walden Ave., P.O. Box 1867, Buffalo NY 14240-1867

BUSINESS REPLY MAIL
FIRST-CLASS MAIL   PERMIT NO. 717-003   BUFFALO, NY

POSTAGE WILL BE PAID BY ADDRESSEE

HARLEQUIN READER SERVICE
3010 WALDEN AVE
PO BOX 1867
BUFFALO NY 14240-9952

NO POSTAGE
NECESSARY
IF MAILED
IN THE
UNITED STATES

Sam could sometimes throw her off base. "Well, sure they count." Molly grinned, thinking about her own niece and nephew. "My sister's kids are very vocal about being counted. Marc and Rachel have opinions about everything."

"It's amazing how many of my old friends from town are married with children now," said Sam. "Besides Travis, I ran into two other guys I used to hang around with during the summers here. They each have one child and a pregnant wife."

"Jealous?" she teased.

An intense expression consumed his facial features for a moment before turning simply thoughtful. "No," he finally said. "But one day…"

"You want children." Molly completed his sentence like a stated fact.

"Well, sure I do. Don't you?"

She forced a smile, trying to ignore the knotting of her stomach. "Maybe one day. But not now."

They'd reached the Bluebonnet, and Sam laughed as he pulled into his reserved spot. "Of course not now. We're not ready yet, Mol."

"That must be it," Molly agreed, getting out of the car quickly, away from the conversation and away from Sam. She needed time alone. "I'm going to have an early night, Sam. See you tomorrow."

"What about dinner?"

"Not hungry, thanks." She headed for her suite, absently rubbing her thigh while blinking back tears. She'd never have children. She'd never be a mother. Her broken pelvis had healed narrower than it was originally, and bearing a child was not possible. Doctors had already suggested she put her mind to adoption when the time came.

She'd been running from this truth, too, and now her heart ached, the pain staggering. Falling in love was not an option for her. Not when normal men wanted full lives with healthy partners and families. Sam was very much a normal man and had unknowingly reinforced that truth. He'd made it clear how much he wanted children.

She let herself into her apartment and immediately ran the water in her tub. How would she deal with her situation? Then she laughed, a hollow sound. There was only one way possible. She'd use the same survival method that had served her earlier.

She'd concentrate on work, managing the Bluebonnet where success was based on effort and business skills. Eventually Sam would find a buyer—she knew she couldn't stop him—and move on, and she'd move on, as well. Her new career had to be everything and everlasting. She could handle that reality, but she wouldn't be a hermit about it. She'd make friends with both men and women along the way.

When it came to sheer hard work and dedication, she'd take home the gold.

A WEEK LATER Molly sat behind her desk, looking at Sam standing in front of her.

"But, Sam," she said patiently, "it's not necessary to be at the high school field to enjoy the fireworks. I'm told they can be seen from almost anywhere in town.'' And besides, she thought, going to the fireworks with Sam would be like going on a date, and she wanted to avoid that.

''It's bigger and better there,'' he argued. ''Tonight's forecast is perfect—clear skies with a zillion stars as background. You'll enjoy it.''

The problem was she'd enjoy it too much. She shook her head. ''My job is at the hotel, Sam. We have guests…''

''…and a night staff to take care of them,'' he finished.

''But one of us should be here,'' she argued, searching her mind in vain for a stronger argument.

''Nonsense.''

She took a breath. ''I'd really rather not go, Sam. Please don't nag.''

Her words hung in the air. ''I wouldn't dream of it,'' said Sam quietly, turning to leave. ''Enjoy your evening.''

She watched him go, eyes fixed on the door he'd closed behind him.

She wanted to erase her last words to him, but remained silent.

Falling in with Sam's plans would be so easy. She could picture them side by side on a blanket or on two lounge chairs, oohing and ahhing at brilliant colors and fantastic shapes as the fireworks exploded in the night sky. She closed her eyes and leaned back in her chair. Not hard to imagine the evening's progress. Their fingertips would touch, they'd hold hands…

She thought of the kisses she and Sam had already

shared, and her heartbeat accelerated. She wanted more! Tears prickled beneath her lids for her own loss, as well as for his, because she knew without a doubt that the attraction was mutual.

She also knew without a doubt that to act on the attraction was to invite heartache. For both of them.

A rap on her door was followed by Sam's voice.

"You're on your own, Molly. I'm leav—"

She opened her eyes and saw that he'd come back into her office.

"Mol?" With that one syllable, his voice changed instantly, becoming gentle and concerned. He stared at her. "What's the matter?"

She swallowed hard, not able to answer for a minute. "I bitched and moaned and was moody for years after the accident. Everyone suffered because I'm not made of martyr material."

He looked confused.

"But for your sake, Sam, I wish I were," she whispered.

"You want to explain that?" he asked. "Do you think I need protection because I want us to see the fireworks together?"

"Yes." She stood up and walked around the desk to him. "Yes," she said again, reaching her hands up to caress his cheeks. "Kiss me, Sam."

She didn't have to ask twice. She felt the sizzle instantly. The kiss deepened, and when she finally pulled away, she and Sam were both breathless.

"So much for platonic," Sam mumbled.

"There's the explanation," Molly gasped at the

same time. "I'm afraid we'll ignite our own fireworks."

A half smile appeared on Sam's face. "You may have a point. But," he said slowly, "would that be so bad?"

"Yes." She brushed her hand down her body as a reminder of her accident.

His smile disappeared. "Ancient history," he said. "You're too sensitive, Molly. I'm your friend. I'd never let a few scars come between us if our relationship grows more, ah...intimate."

"You don't know what you're saying," Molly replied. "You don't know everything about me."

"I know enough," came the instant reply. "Trust me."

She did trust him. But the issue was bigger than Sam could possibly realize. She needed to take a step back. For both their sakes. "Do you think we could just be friends?" she asked in a small voice. "Plain old friends?"

His eyes sparkled with laughter. "You mean with no kisses?"

She nodded.

"I'd actually convinced myself we could, but it's too late, Molly," he replied, humor still apparent on his face. "Platonic passed us by a while ago."

Sam seemed pleased, and suddenly Molly felt alive again, skiing on the edge once more. The risk increased every day. The only difference was the arena.

CHAPTER SEVEN

MOLLY USHERED SAM from her office, determined not to examine their relationship too closely. One day at a time would work for her. Light lovemaking didn't require a confession of her most painful secret, did it? She ignored the idea and thought, instead, about the open acreage surrounding Oak Creek High School where the fireworks would take place. Wearing her sandals was out of the question.

"I need five minutes," she said to Sam. "I'll meet you in the lobby."

"Sure," he replied, looking quizzical. "Anything wrong?"

"Shoes," she replied. "The shoes are wrong."

She walked to her apartment as quickly as she could, conscious of Sam's gaze and more conscious of her limp than usual. She'd change into white slacks to go with her specially built-up sneakers. Not as lightweight as sandals, but she'd be able to keep up with Sam and not stumble on the rough ground.

She paired the slacks with a white sleeveless shell, applied a hot-pink lipstick and returned to the lobby, feeling good about how she looked.

Sam's eyes snared hers. A smile of approval followed, and she was glad she'd bothered with the lipstick.

"Did you think I'd let you fall?" he asked, glancing at her feet.

Not exactly what she was expecting to hear. She rolled her eyes. "What's with you guys? You, my dad, even my brother-in-law, Zach! No, I didn't think you'd let me fall," she mimicked, "but I have to be able to take care of myself. So for Pete's sake, forget the macho!"

Sam grinned. "Your menfolk and I have a lot in common besides owning a hotel."

The truth in his words struck Molly. Sam did indeed share qualities with the men who'd shaped her life.

"But I'm not your dad," Sam continued, "and I won't overprotect you." A solemn promise resonated in his voice as he faced her, one hand on her shoulder, the other lifting her chin. "I saw you in that video. You were the best in the world once, and that same Molly is still inside. Now you'll hone your skills again. This time, the goal is more than skiing. The goal is life. And you, Molly Ann Porter, are going to come out on top."

She could have fallen in love with him right then if she'd allowed herself. His philosophy matched hers exactly, and it had only taken him a month to understand what she needed to accomplish. It had taken her four years.

"Have you ever been serious about sports?" she

asked as they headed for his car. An idea had begun to grow in the back of her mind.

"What a question!" replied a familiar male voice.

Molly turned around to see George and Irene Kincaid approaching. "How nice to see you again! We weren't expecting you until tomorrow." Perfect timing. The Kincaids would dilute the intensity developing between her and Sam. "Do we have a room available for you?"

"We're bunking with Sam for the night," Sam's father explained. "Already stowed our gear."

"We wanted to catch the fireworks," said Irene, looking fondly at her husband. "But George didn't know if he could get away until the last minute."

"Shorthanded at the store," George said with a shrug. He then gave Molly his attention. "Now what were you asking about the starting pitcher of his high school baseball team?"

"Baseball?" Molly glanced at Sam, trying to picture him as a teenage athlete.

"Let me grab these folding chairs and get everyone in the car," Sam grumbled. "Baseball is ancient history."

Molly turned to George with a smile. "That's one of his favorite expressions. But sometimes ancient history comes in handy." Pitching? What good luck. Of all the positions on a baseball team, the pitcher probably had the most skill, the most discipline and the greatest ability to focus—sharpened so that the crowds were mentally silenced when he stood on the mound. Her thoughts raced along, gathering momentum.

"So tell me about your coach," Molly said once she was seated in the front passenger seat, his parents in the rear.

"My coach?" A slow smile started a montage of expressions crossing Sam's face as he probed his memory.

By the time they reached the site for the fireworks, Molly had her answers. Sam did understand what happened behind the scenes; he also understood the characteristics of a good coach. Both would be essential to her. If he wanted to help, she was ready to go back into training. Her palms tingled at the thought. All she needed was a sport.

HE COULD SEE through her as clearly as if she were lighting a beacon to point the way into her mind. She wanted a coach and was interviewing him for the job! And Sam was more than ready to oblige a woman who had the heart and soul of an athlete, but not in the way Molly probably thought. Not as a personal trainer, not as a physical therapist and not as an individual or team coach. Molly needed to unlock some doors, to explore options for an active, fuller life. Sam had every intention of exploring them with her.

He held Molly's hand as they walked from the parked car to the crowded field, about a quarter-mile distance. His parents followed. He let Molly set the pace, able to feel her stride as she walked, her normally uneven gait barely perceptible in the sneakers she wore. No wonder she wanted to change shoes.

"So which bones were broken?" He asked the question as casually as he could, as a reporter might. And probably did at the time.

She didn't hesitate. "Multiple femur fracture on top. A steel rod now goes through the bone and is held there with pins. A lifetime guarantee," she said with a laugh, "unless, of course, a reason develops to take them out."

"Don't borrow trouble," he replied, squeezing her hand.

"I don't intend to." She paused and looked at him. "Want to hear the rest?"

"Sure."

"Multiple tib-fib fractures on the lower leg. You know, the tibia and fibula bones."

He nodded. "Anything *not* broken?"

"Oh, yeah." She grinned. "I had great boots. Perfect ankles."

He glanced down. "I noticed."

She responded with a blush and he couldn't contain his smile. Molly was a sweetheart. A true-blue sweetheart.

"Stop flirting, Sam," she finally said in a fierce whisper.

"Yes, ma'am."

Now she chuckled, and he loved the sound of it. "Am I old enough to be a 'ma'am'? I don't know the rules down here!"

"Those gosh-darn rules again," he teased. "They keep popping up."

"I think this one is quite harmless," she said.

"One of the easy ones." Sam glanced at Molly, finding it difficult to take his eyes from her and almost stumbling on a tuft of grass. He looked around for an area to claim and finally set the chairs down, making sure to open them fully before placing them on solid ground. No holes or rocks beneath them. With Molly and his parents safely ensconced, he prepared to enjoy the fireworks.

His eyes kept straying to Molly's face, however, as she stared at the night sky, her eyes wide, her mouth a circle of wonder with every colorful rocket bursting above. Her hair fell casually behind her, her body resting against the back of the lawn chair. She could have been anyone in the crowd looking forward to the fireworks display.

In the month he'd known her, she'd changed 180 degrees. Was it her new environment? Her new job? Was it just the passage of time? Or was it, at least partly, him?

He had to admit that the last option intrigued him most, especially when Molly's hand kept squeezing his.

"Did you see that, Sam?" she said time and again. "Look at those colors! Look at the shapes! Gorgeous. I'm so glad I decided to come."

"So am I," he said, resisting the temptation to kiss her in front of his parents.

By the time the fireworks were over, he half ex-

pected Molly not to have enough energy left to walk
to the car. But she surprised him.

"Why don't we all play hooky a while longer and
get some ice cream at Gessners' downtown? It's a
holiday weekend. I bet they're still open."

Sam turned to his parents. "Are you game?"

"Sure. Let's go."

The place was as packed as the ice cream. Sam
spotted an empty booth in the far corner and started
for it. "Just follow me," he said to Molly and his
folks.

But he was stopped along the way several times,
recognized by friends from his childhood, by new
friends made when he was handing out posters, and
friends of his uncle. Irene and George were greeting
people, too. He glanced back at Molly, hoping she
wasn't feeling left out and wanting to introduce her
to folks.

He needn't have been concerned. She was still
near the door talking to a customer, then another
one. The woman knew half the people in the shop!
Hadn't she only been in town a couple of months?

He paused to speak with Travis and his sister, Liz,
promising to visit the ranch soon. "Amy's home
with Mom," explained Liz in answer to his inquiry.
"An early night for an excited birthday girl."

"No fireworks this year?" Sam joked.

"There'll be plenty tomorrow when her aunt
shows up," Travis grumbled.

"Oh, hush," scolded Travis's sister. "Carla is a
terrific person."

Molly joined them and Sam made the introductions. "Liz runs the Rocking H riding school," said Sam, nodding at the female version of blond, hazel-eyed Travis.

"Well, we're in Texas," replied Molly. "People are supposed to ride horses."

"Oh, I like her!" Liz laughed. "A walking advertisement."

"But she's absolutely right," said Sam, turning to Molly. "Riding horses is for everyone, even for new Texans like you."

He watched Molly's reaction. Surprise, then caution. But in the end, curiosity won. He watched her lean toward Liz. "Horses," she said. "Just how big are we talking about?"

Everyone laughed. Sam reached around Molly and hugged her. He'd have her on a horse before she knew what hit her. His plan to help broaden Molly's life was on its way to fruition sooner than he'd imagined.

"Before I forget," said Travis, taking two business cards from his shirt pocket. "These are friends of mine with small businesses that are growing. I spent an evening with them a week ago and got my ear talked off about how they both needed better business-applications systems. One's a limited partnership in the oil-and-gas industry, and the other's a mortgage company. They were also squawking about their Web sites." He placed the business cards on the table in front of Sam. "Told them you'd consult and design at a reasonable price. Told them to expect your call.''

Sam reached for the cards and met Travis's gaze. ''They'll get called quickly. And thanks.''

Sam Kincaid, software-design consultant. His networking in Texas had begun.

MOLLY KNEW THAT the proceeds of the Fourth of July festivities were to benefit the town's volunteer fire department. She didn't realize, however, that a good portion of the twenty-five-member department was going to arrive at six in the morning to set up for the event. She stumbled out of bed after receiving a call from the registration desk and headed for a fast shower.

''You should have slept in,'' Sam said when he spotted her in the lobby a few minutes later. ''I purposely didn't ask anyone to call you.''

''The employees take direction from me, Sam,'' she responded. ''And they have instructions to let me know about everything that happens at the Bluebonnet.''

He put his hands on her shoulders. '''Know about' is one thing. Participating is something else. Come with me,'' he said, leading her to the back of the building and outside. ''Take a look. This has been going on every Fourth of July for the last ten years.''

Molly watched the volunteers begin to transform the back lawn and patio into a dining area for several hundred people. Party tents were being erected, long tables and benches were being set out, and more than two hundred pounds of brisket had already started cooking in huge cast-iron smokers.

"It'll all be decorated in red, white and blue somehow," said Sam. "Everyone's donating something, including us."

"I know," said Molly. "The red beans and rice."

"And pitchers of our specialty beers—one per table. And security personnel. This is an important community event." He turned her around. "So how about getting some more rest? I want you energetic for tonight."

"I'll be fine," Molly replied quickly. "I know everyone will be wondering if we can live up to expectations, but I won't let your uncle's memory down. I won't let Oak Creek down." Didn't Sam realize that success on this job was as important to her as it was to him? "You can trust me, Sam. I'll be on top of my game tonight, a good hostess."

She looked up into his face, wanting him to believe her. And he leaned down, his forehead touching hers. "You're very confused, Molly, if you think I give a hoot about how great a hostess you'll be. I only care about you not working yourself to a frazzle."

The warmth in his eyes caused a shiver to ripple through her. His words could have been the words of any good friend, but his tone spoke of more. Memories of his kisses caused another delicious shiver, and she was tempted to taste their reality again. Lord, she was tempted. She had only to raise her chin and their mouths would meet.

But the timing was wrong. She wasn't ready. Before she could enjoy Sam's kisses or anyone else's, she had to become, once again, the best and strongest Molly she could be. She had to reach beyond her new career to the total Molly inside.

"Thanks for caring, Sam," Molly replied, taking a step back. "But you won't achieve your goal that way." She rubbed the tip of her thumb against the other fingers of the same hand, the universal gesture for money. "Only by increasing revenue can you make the Bluebonnet desirable and sell it quickly. Not by worrying about me being tired or not. So the hotel has to shine—every single day and for every single event."

"Then get those department managers helping you more before you lose *your* shine. Molly Porter and the Bluebonnet Hotel are becoming more intertwined every day. So take care of yourself, Molly, for the hotel's sake, sure, but more important, for your own sake."

Could he have read her mind? Could he know she wanted more than a career now? That she wanted a whole life?

MOLLY STOOD in the doorway of the Grand Ballroom that evening, scanning the crowd, the staff and the activities in general. After a nonstop day, she'd taken another shower before getting dressed for the evening and was satisfied she fit in with the event's atmosphere. She'd chosen a sleeveless navy-and-white polka-dot dress with a sweeping skirt and V-neckline. Lightweight and cool. She exchanged the matching sash for a red one and was happy with the patriotic result. It had been a longer day than she wanted to admit, and wouldn't admit if Sam asked, so she reluctantly left her sandals in the closet and chose supportive shoes.

The ballroom was pleasantly crowded, with most people dancing to the country-and-western band. Other guests were visiting the dessert tables in the Houston Room or were submitting written bids for the donated goods displayed in the Austin Room. Molly took a deep breath and exhaled with relief. The evening was going beautifully.

She glanced toward the band and saw young Judy take the microphone. Then Molly corrected herself. Their lovely, funny, everyday Judy Schneider wasn't taking the stage. Instead, she'd assumed the sophisticated, confident Judith Sands persona. And darn, if it wasn't Patsy Cline singing "Crazy" at them a minute later. Some of the guests stopped dancing just to listen, and Molly marveled at the talent born to and developed by some special people. Judith slid into another number, and once again, the guests began moving to the music.

Molly watched them and remembered when she danced the night away a lifetime ago. She absorbed the music now, too—country-and-western—strange to her rock-and-roll ears. But the beat was strong and she swayed in time.

"I believe it's our turn."

Molly swung around quickly and saw Sam approaching, holding out his hand.

Lost in the music at the moment, Molly stared at Sam and didn't move. "I don't think so," she finally said. "I don't dance." She glanced around for inspiration. "Why don't you ask Carla? Or Liz? They're both here."

"This is a simple Texas two-step, Molly. You can do it," Sam replied patiently, ignoring her references to the other women.

Was he trying to embarrass her? Or was he just being insensitive?

"Maybe I wasn't clear, so I'm giving you the benefit of the doubt, Sam. For the record, I don't dance. And I certainly don't know the Texas two-step or any other dance. That's the bottom line. But thanks for asking."

She returned to scanning the ballroom, relaxed once more.

"If you can walk, you can do the two-step."

She glared at Sam. "Sometimes walking's a challenge. Now will you leave me alone?"

But he remained there, his brow wrinkled as though he was in deep thought. "Hmm." He shook his head. "Leave you alone? I don't think so." He stepped next to her, took her hand and placed his other hand around her waist.

He moved so smoothly she was in his arms before she could protest further without causing a scene. "I'll get you for this," she whispered with a vengeance, praying she wouldn't fall on her face. How could he?

"Now calm down, Molly-girl. We're going to stand right here away from the crowd just listening to the music, listening for the beat. Hear it?"

She heard his heart—or was it her own?—beating double time. The music was secondary to being held in a man's arms once again. So good. So normal. The way she remembered, but better. It was Sam who held her now. She took a deep breath and felt herself begin to relax, to sway with him.

"When I tell you, take three small steps backward starting on your right foot, then pause," he whispered.

But she didn't need his words. She heard the music and felt his body get ready. And she moved with him.

"One more step and pause," he added.

She did it.

"That's the whole thing," he said as he led her into the six-beat grouping again. "Four straight steps out of six beats of music. Can't get more simple than that."

He was right. And if her foot dragged a smidgen, so what? Seemed like a shuffle step in this dance was okay, too. Molly peeped up at Sam. "Let's keep going. This works for me."

He laughed heartily, and Molly felt her cheeks catch fire. "Shh!"

"What were you afraid of, Mol? Did you think

I'd let you fall?'' He shook his head. ''Not a chance.''

His question was getting to be a habit. But then he led her into the actual ballroom, and Molly realized that now she was one of the crowd, enjoying herself like everyone else on the dance floor. A good feeling, yet odd for someone who always yearned to stand out. To stand above. To be the best in the world.

But her world had shrunk in the past four years. Now, however, Molly felt it begin to grow again. Tempting her with infinite possibilities.

The music changed to a slow waltz, and Sam's arm tightened gently around her. She couldn't resist laying her head on his shoulder, relishing the strength of his broad chest, powerful arms and the total masculine entity that was Sam. She stroked his back where her hand rested, feeling the hard muscle beneath and enjoying it.

She felt a butterfly kiss on her temple, and tears threatened to fall. She felt so normal! Totally feminine and desirable. Just like other women. Just like she used to feel before the accident changed everything.

But now she knew differently. Now she understood that she had the power to change her life yet again.

THE MUSIC ENDED, but Sam didn't release her until they were approached by Judy Schneider's parents. And even then, Molly felt one of his hands lightly on her waist.

"A wonderful party, Molly," Judy's mother said.

"Thanks," Molly replied. "We're hoping it's a big success for the firefighters." She turned toward Sam and introduced him as the hotel's owner.

"We're delighted that your daughter is working here," Sam said to Judy's parents. "She's great in both jobs."

Molly glanced at Judy, still on the stage. "With Judith Sands in the spotlight, we can't go wrong this evening. She's a wonderful singer."

"That's what they tell us," said Judy's dad, but he didn't sound too happy.

"She had me riveted the first time I heard her," said Sam.

"I'd rather she be riveted right here in Oak Creek, or at least at the university in Austin," grumbled Mr. Schneider. "Eighteen years old and all my girl ever talks about is New York. Sometimes I wish she couldn't sing a note."

"Shh, Matthew," Judy's mom cajoled. "She'll come around. Don't worry."

Is that what they really thought? Molly studied each parent and plunged in. "She won't, you know."

Three pairs of eyes turned to her.

"She won't come around," Molly repeated.

The dad's eyes hardened, but his tone was gentle. "If you know something about my little girl, ma'am, I would sure appreciate hearing about it."

"I know nothing that she hasn't shared with you, Mr. Schneider. But look at her." Molly turned toward the stage. "Don't you see it? The passion. The want. The dream. She's not going to give it up."

"That's my great fear." Judy's dad ran his fingers through his hair. "Do you know how many fine voices there are in this country, how many young'uns run to New York or Hollywood aiming for a star? And then falling hard on their tails?"

Molly felt Sam's mouth on the back of her neck. "Stay out of it," he whispered. "She's their daughter."

But Molly had been where Judy was now. She shook her head and reached for Judy's father's hand. "They don't do it thinking there's a guarantee, Mr. Schneider. It's the dream. That's what keeps them going. And Judy's got everything. The talent, the tenacity, the yearning."

"And a full scholarship to the music program at the University of Texas! A spit down the road. Now what's so bad about that?" The man's frustration vibrated in the air.

"Oh." Molly's surprise limited her response. Judy had never shared that tidbit with her. "Guess you've got me there, sir. Has she been accepted to a New York school, as well?"

Now Judy's mom spoke up. "She never applied. We forced the issue at UT. My daughter thinks she'll waltz into a New York audition and 'knock 'em dead'. Those are her words."

"More likely she'll knock herself out," said Molly. "Success on a professional level takes time to achieve. I'll talk to her. Tell her about how I did two years of college before making the team and practicing full-time.''

''What team, Molly?'' asked Mrs. Schneider. ''What are you talking about?''

Startled at the ease with which she revealed her past, Molly was silent for a moment, confused. She glanced at Sam, knowing he was the only person other than herself who was aware of her background.

A gentle smiled played on his face. ''You have nothing to hide, Mol. You've accomplished what only a few in the world can equal.''

She refocused on Judy's parents, who were still waiting. ''I was a member of the U.S. Olympic ski team but never got to participate in the Games. Instead, I clashed with a snow fence and wound up limping.'' She motioned them to silence when they would have spoken, then leaned toward them. ''But I'd do it all again in a heartbeat.''

She could have heard the proverbial pin drop in the silence that followed. ''And that's the whole point,'' she continued. ''If Judy's dream is as strong as mine was, she won't give it up. So find a safer way to give her a chance.''

''Skiing?'' Mr. Schneider turned to his wife. ''And I thought singing caused problems!''

''We'll figure something out,'' replied Judy's mom, hugging Molly. ''Thanks for sharing that. We've been drifting, just hoping she'd change her mind. Now I see we need to take some action.''

''Good luck.''

Sam reached for her when the Schneiders walked away. "My turn to give advice."

"Oh?"

"Oh, yes. I advise you, Ms. Porter, to dance with me again."

"And I advise myself to accept."

"Good decision."

Stepping into his arms felt as natural as skiing down a mountain. Familiarity with a thrill.

HE'D BEEN RIGHT yesterday. Holding Molly in his arms was not a platonic event. Not when his heart kicked up a notch every time he inhaled her perfume. Not when she cuddled her head on his shoulder. Not when he felt her legs press against his while they danced. In a minute he'd need a cold shower.

He scanned the room looking for a distraction and found it. "Take a look over there, Mol," he whispered, nodding at a dancing couple—a red-haired woman with a fair-haired rancher.

"Whoa!" said Molly. "What do you know! A ceasefire."

"But for how long?" Sam pulled Molly closer to him again. "Whatever's eating Travis will have to be resolved before he lets it go."

"Carla's up for it," Molly replied.

Sam glanced down at the woman in his arms, suddenly not caring about the other couple. Molly's eyes were closed, her long lashes fanning her smooth cheek, her delicate profile almost cameo perfect.

He laughed inwardly. Perhaps she looked delicate on the outside, but Molly was about as delicate as a linebacker on the inside. A strong-minded woman. But he wasn't complaining. He was goal-oriented himself and liked that characteristic about her. It was one of the traits he'd admired about Adrienne.

The name from the past provided the cold shower he'd been contemplating. How could he have forgotten the price of ambition among some women? He looked at Molly again. Nah, she'd never sacrifice family for career, would she? No. She said she liked children.

And what did it matter? He and Molly had been thrown together for professional reasons and were dedicated to achieving them. So what if he admired her courage? So what if she felt perfect in his arms? Adrienne had moved fluidly with him, too.

None of it meant anything. Certainly not love. Not with Adrienne and not with Molly. He and Molly would each go their own way when the hotel was finally sold. He'd probably network himself back to California, and Molly...well any hotel would be lucky to get her.

In the meantime, however, he'd inhale her sweet fragrance and keep on dancing.

CHAPTER EIGHT

SAM REPLACED the telephone receiver, a smile tugging at his lips. The bank had blessed his business plan.

A month had elapsed since the Fourth of July activities at the hotel. A month of intense business effort that seemed to have paid off. In addition to his consults and follow-up design work for Travis's two friends, he'd made countless phone calls and company visits and had spent hours completing and presenting his business plan to potential backers. The Oak Creek Technology Center was a reality, at least on paper.

Suddenly a broken sigh escaped him and his hands trembled as the significance of the accomplishment sank in. Fear of failure had driven him like hot flames licking at his boot heels. He'd never failed at anything before his dot-com ventures, and if he had to work his tail off to earn another chance, he would. In fact, he just did. And he had plenty more work ahead of him.

So, his worst fears hadn't been realized. He was not a twenty-nine-year-old has-been with no future. The demise of his dot-coms hadn't ruined him forever. He'd work for another chance to prove himself on his own terms, and dang if he wouldn't succeed this time around.

He leaned back in his office chair, one hand massaging the nape of his neck. He'd been conservative with this plan, not assuming grandiose success. He'd fully explained the risks and advantages to every potential investor, especially to his old friends in California. He'd followed up with small software companies in Austin, coordinating a consortium of them as part of the investment group. He'd paused only to eat and sleep, often crawling blindly into bed in the wee hours of the night.

No one had forced him to add on to the traditional Bluebonnet business. He could simply have taken over the hotel after his uncle's death, managed it the way John had, and with some extra effort, gone on paying the new mortgage. But he'd shied away from doing that. He hadn't worked for it. Hadn't built the hotel. Had never thought in terms of hotel management and didn't want anything thrust at him as a gift. Especially something as mature and valuable as the Bluebonnet.

But now he owned her! Molly provided excellent leadership, but ultimately, the Bluebonnet was Sam's responsibility. He hoped his new ideas would coexist nicely with the hotel and bring in new revenue. He owed that much to his uncle—Uncle John, who'd believed in Sam to the tune of three million dollars.

He rose from the chair and started pacing. He

hadn't deserved to inherit the Bluebonnet. That was the crux of it. Deep inside, he'd known it. Molly had known it immediately. And that bothered him. For some reason he cared about her opinion. But why?

Images of Molly spun through his mind, her moods, her beauty, her achievements. She had the same effect on him as a ninety-mile-an-hour base-ball striking him in the gut. Knowing Molly was a powerful experience, intense and exciting.

He'd hardly seen her all month, not since they'd danced the two-step. He missed her! Due to his trav-eling, their nightly dinners had diminished into brief meetings. But each time he returned, he looked for-ward to reconnecting with her. In the future, he would spend more time right here, overseeing con-struction, having dinners with Molly and providing her with greater support.

He'd have to reconnect with the department su-pervisors, as well. His morning meetings had proved productive, and his knowledge of behind-the-scenes hotel secrets had grown enormously.

He walked next door, eager to brief Molly on the progress he'd made with the tech center. Her office was empty. He glanced at his watch. Almost five. Maybe they'd dine together that night.

He approached the registration desk and spoke with Judy.

"Molly took the day off, Sam. Didn't she tell you?"

A day off? He couldn't remember her taking a

day off. A horrible admission, when she had certainly earned as much time off for herself as she wanted. "Guess we missed each other. If anyone deserves to relax for a while, it's Molly."

"I don't think she's relaxing in Houston."

"Houston? That's almost a three-hour drive. Some day off."

Judy shrugged. "I got the feeling she was going there for business, not pleasure, but she didn't tell me any details."

Business? His mind raced. The only piece of business she could have in Houston was a new job. With a variety of first-class hotels, Houston could draw her like a magnet. What else could possibly tempt her to the fourth-largest city in America? Damn!

"Will you let me know when she returns, Judy?"

"It's almost five, Sam. I might not be here, but I'll leave a message for the night shift."

"Thanks."

Sam spent the next few hours patrolling the hotel like a hound searching for a scent. Then, at eight o'clock he spotted her at the main entrance, a plastic shopping bag in her hand.

Shopping? Was that it? The world-famous Galleria would be tempting, but Molly only had one bag to show for her efforts.

"Hey," he said. "Let me help."

"Hey, yourself," she said, looking up at him with a quick smile.

She seemed exhausted and a bit pale to his concerned eye.

"I've brought these for you. And for the staff," she said, offering him the bag. "I want opinions. Ever eat *kolaches?*"

He nodded.

"These are from Olde Towne Kolaches. I stopped off for a cup of coffee and tried them. Now I'm thinking of adding them to the breakfast buffet. Go ahead—taste one."

He just stared at her. "Are you telling me you went all the way to Houston to buy *kolaches?*"

"Let's call it a happy coincidence and leave it at that." She yawned behind her hand. "I really need to turn in now. Good night. And let me know what you think of the pastries."

Sam watched her walk toward her suite. Was it his imagination or was her limp more pronounced than usual? He checked her footwear. Flat sandals. He breathed a sigh of relief. No mystery. So that left his original idea intact.

Molly had to be searching for another job.

The thought twisted his insides. Made him ache. The Bluebonnet without Molly didn't sit well. In less than three months, she'd made an enormous impression—all good! The staff loved her, the guests appreciated her, and the whole town had complimented them on the holiday festivities. It was Molly who managed to retain the Bluebonnet's positive image in the eyes of the community. Sam knew it, and he'd immediately given the credit to Molly whenever anyone thanked them.

He walked toward the pub, intending to get himself a hamburger, then decided to call Molly's apartment. He'd distribute the *kolaches* to the staff, get their opinions and take two burgers to go.

"Sam, I'm really tired," Molly replied to his suggestion.

"Have you had dinner?"

"I don't care about food right now."

"You need to eat, Mol. How about taking one of your hot baths," he cajoled, "and I'll bring the nourishment you need afterward. Right to your door. You can't turn down a deal like that."

She didn't reply immediately.

"I'll take that as a yes," Sam said. "How much time do you need?"

"You don't give up, do you?"

"No. I guess I don't." Sam mulled the words over, then nodded to himself. He'd spoken the truth.

"Then give me forty minutes. I still have to do my exercises."

"I thought you were tired."

"I never skip my workout," she said, "no matter what. Guess I'm still in training."

"Then I'll see you in forty," he said, hanging up the phone. It was time to implement some of the ideas he'd had a month ago before he got so busy. She may have thought she needed a coach, but what she really needed was a handler. Sam was happy to oblige. Surely Molly deserved time to play! And so did he.

SHE COULD EASILY have fallen asleep in the bath and probably would have if she hadn't expected Sam.

Dangerous to doze off in a tub of water, anyway, she thought as she toweled off and slipped on a short-sleeve cotton-knit sleep-T that ended below her calves. Modest. Comfortable. She nodded in the mirror as she brushed her hair. No makeup tonight. She was tired. Sam would just have to bear looking at the real Molly, at least for a while longer.

She heard the knock as she walked barefoot into the living room, liking the shoeless state best of all her choices. Seemed she'd adapted well to warm-weather living.

She opened the door, but before she could say hello to Sam, the delicious aroma of the grilled burgers hit her with full-force. Her stomach rumbled like a volcano ready to erupt. She met Sam's amused gaze and burst out laughing with him.

"Come on in. I guess you're just what I need right now, after all."

Sam rolled his eyes. "I'm crushed. You love me only for my culinary treats."

Molly continued to smile as she led him to her kitchen area. "I thought that was the way to a man's heart, not a woman's."

The amusement left Sam's face as he laid the dinner on the coffee table and turned to look at her. From head to toe, without pausing at her scar. "It's going to be the way to *your* heart if you don't start eating more. Come on," he urged. "Dig in. Then we'll talk."

She didn't hesitate, surprised at how hungry she

was. It had been a long day. The food was delicious, and when she finally came up for air, she found Sam watching her.

"Hire an assistant manager," he said. "ASAP."

"An assistant! Sam! We're trying to save money. I don't need an assistant." Her appetite vanished. What was he trying to tell her? His expression revealed nothing, which was unusual. Sam didn't have secrets and didn't play games with her regarding the Bluebonnet.

"What's wrong, Sam?"

He snapped to attention, then reached for her hands. "Are you happy here, Molly?"

What in the world was he getting at? "Happy? What do you mean? I have a contract, don't I?"

"Forget the contract. Just answer the question. Are you happy?"

She could reply to that one honestly. "I have absolutely no regrets about taking this job. It's challenged me from the start. Skiing will always be my first love, but if I can't race down a snow-covered mountain, then for me, this career is as good as it gets."

"But are you happy here at the Bluebonnet, Mol? With me?"

The intensity of his voice vibrated in the air, and when she looked into his dark eyes, now filled with concern, she knew her answer was important to him. He cared about her feelings. His hands still engulfed her smaller ones, his fingers gently squeezing hers, and suddenly she wasn't sure they were talking about a hotel. "I'm happy," she whispered.

He raised her hands to his mouth and brushed soft kisses against her fingers. "I'm glad," he replied.

Her breath caught as his lips traveled to her palms; her heartbeat quickened and her mind became mush. Did he realize what he was doing? He couldn't know that she sometimes fantasized about making love with him. She dreamed until the reel broke, which took about thirty seconds. But they were hot seconds. Worth the pain of every reality check.

"Mol?"

"Mmm?"

"We start construction on the new facility very soon. It'll be a done deal within a month."

His words brought Molly crashing back to her kitchen table. She disengaged her hands from Sam's, slowly absorbing his meaning, and became focused once again on business. Sam's eyes shone with pleasure at his news.

"The tech center is a go," he restated. "And I wanted you to be the first to know about it.

"And that's why you insisted on dinner," said Molly matter-of-factly, pasting a smile on her face. "Now I understand."

Sam's brows furrowed. "No," he said. "I insisted on eating with you after I saw you. Exhausted and...no sparkle. And to me, you always sparkle, Mol." His voice trailed away, the concern back in it.

She blinked at his words. At his sincerity. His vision of her…he'd never know how much it meant. Yes, Sam's opinion mattered, but his choice of ''sparkle'' caused her heart to squeeze. ''Sparkle'' reflected a person of action, exactly the way she'd always seen herself. Now she knew he viewed her the same way, despite his first impression when he'd arrived for his uncle's funeral.

Sam's hands clasped hers again. ''Which brings us back to—'' he seemed to pick his words carefully ''—your need for help running and growing this hotel. I'm not enough, especially now with the construction under way and the hotel's need for new clients. So we'll advertise for your assistant. I don't want you keeling over on me.''

He was being generous to her, so why did she feel so threatened? Most hotels had assistant managers. It wasn't a sign of failure if she hired one, but…but she'd thought she'd be working with Sam. And she wanted Sam!

Lord, she was taking his defection personally. She should have expected him to be successful with the new enterprise. He went after what he wanted. Well, she understood that. But she'd thought it would take longer. Or maybe she thought it wouldn't happen at all, and Sam would direct all his energies into the hotel.

She was an idiot! Everyone pursued their own dreams.

''Congratulations, Sam,'' Molly said. ''I know

you've worked darn hard putting this together. You can count on my cooperation in every way.''

"So you are happy here?'' He leaned forward, eyes shining.

"Yes, yes, of course.''

"And you're not looking for a new job in Houston?''

Surprise made her mute for an instant. Then she burst out laughing. "So that's what this little repast is all about! Wining and dining me to discover if I'm looking for another job.'' She laughed until tears ran down her face. "You've made my day! If I ever decide to leave you, Sam, you'll be the first to know. I haven't felt this wanted in years.''

He leaned toward her, still holding her hands. "Then people are fools. You're wonderful.''

She saw the kiss coming an instant before his lips touched hers. Gently, reverently. A prayer. Her eyes closed, her senses alert to his featherlike touch. He brushed a path to the hollow of her neck, and she shivered. A delicious sensation.

"Mmm,'' she murmured.

"Mol?'' Sam's voice sounded funny.

She opened her eyes. Sam looked funny. "I...I think our dinner is getting cold,'' she said.

"Right,'' Sam replied, blindly reaching for his burger, his eyes never leaving her face.

"Sam?'' asked Molly. She needed to concentrate, to bring their conversation back to business. "You need to do something about our Web site. It's awful.''

She saw his eyes refocus, saw understanding register in his expression. And then she reached for his hand and pressed it firmly. "You know what they say about mixing business with pleasure?"

He hesitated for a fraction of a second. "Sure," he said. "It doesn't work."

"I rest my case." She'd keep her fantasies to herself. The disappointment of an eventual breakup would be too much for her. And that was what would happen. She and Sam were at loose ends. Especially Sam. Wasn't there a recent girlfriend in his life that didn't work out? "But," she added with a smile, "I need all the friends I can get. Remember, I'm the new girl in town."

"Hard to believe. You know more people than I do." He took a bite of his burger. "So tell me more about the Web site. I'm ashamed to admit I haven't studied it."

She gave him credit for bouncing back. "You've been so busy I hated to bug you, but I think a better Web site could be key to improving the reservation rate in the off-season."

"I'll make it a priority," he replied, "as long as you find an assistant…"

She nodded.

"…and save tomorrow night to have some fun. I'm taking you out."

Fifteen minutes later she walked Sam to the door and wished him good-night. He hesitated on the threshold, his hand on the doorknob.

"Sleep late tomorrow, Molly. I want you rested

for the evening.'' He leaned toward her. ''We're going to have a great time.'' He kissed her lightly on
the mouth. ''Night, Mol.''

''Night, Sam.'' Molly locked up after him, almost
in a daze, stroking her fingers against her lips. She
padded to the bathroom, brushed her teeth and
climbed into bed, wanting a minute to figure out
why she'd just contradicted herself, agreeing to mix
business with pleasure. But her eyes closed and she
fell asleep immediately.

SAM COULDN'T SLEEP. A strange phenomenon for
him especially when he'd enjoyed his evening so
much. In fact, he'd enjoyed it too much! Kissing
Molly could become a habit, despite his reservations. He couldn't resist when the delight in her
laughter combined with the joy on her face, produc-
ing the most beautiful picture he'd ever seen. He
wished he'd had a camera to capture her expression.
But he didn't. So he captured her lips with his own,
instead.

And now sleep eluded him.

Her ingenuous remark about not being wanted in
years bothered him. Of course, she had to be referring to skiing. But he'd teach her that there were
other options in life. She'd already discovered another career, but she hadn't discovered how to have
fun. And that was where he came in.

Since the night of the fireworks, he'd wanted to
provide Molly with a new playground to replace
those Vermont mountains she loved so much, but

his work had gotten in the way. And he still had major work ahead. But he also had a million ideas for Molly—places, activities—and she'd love them all. Tomorrow night would be a beginning. By the time he finished his campaign, she'd be sparkling all the time. Just the way he liked to see her.

He threw on a shirt and shorts, went back to his office and booted up his computer. No use wasting time. Might as well go online and examine the Bluebonnet's Web site. Molly would appreciate his fast response.

At nine the next morning, he walked into her office, a report in hand. Either she was wearing cosmetics or she blushed when she saw him. He couldn't tell. But she looked lovely.

She had the phone against her ear. He sat in the guest chair and stretched his legs in front of him just as Gladys Pierce came to the door.

"I'm down two full-time staffers. We need to advertise," she announced.

"Tell Bonnie to run an ad," he replied, referring to their Human Resources manager. "Didn't we decide that you all could make more decisions?"

"Bonnie's on vacation. I don't know what to put in the ad copy and I don't know the number to call, and I've gotta run and do some hands-on bedmaking. Could you ask Molly to take care of it? Thanks, Sam." And she was gone.

Sam crossed to Molly's desk and went through her Rolodex until he found the card for the *Hill*

Country Gazette, their regional newspaper. He took it to his office, made the call and returned to Molly.

"They're still coming to you for everything, aren't they."

"I like to know my staff," she replied, a wary expression on her face.

"Good," he said. "I'd like you to know a new member of your staff—an assistant manager! Now, where's the best place to find one?"

For a moment he thought she wouldn't go along with him. He waved his report slowly in front of her. "Web site," he whispered. "Want to do some creative thinking?"

Her eyes lit up and she reached for the envelope, but he held it just out of her grasp. "After we discuss your assistant."

Surprise. Outrage. Laughter. Molly.

"You're a tease and a pest!" she sputtered.

"Yup, the world's biggest pest and proud of it." He waited while she moaned, groaned and protested. Then he continued his pressure. "You've got to be in charge of the big picture, Mol, while the assistant is focused on the day-to-day operations."

She didn't say anything, but her forehead creased in concentration, and Sam was encouraged.

Then inspiration hit with the force of a locomotive. "How many run Diamond Ridge in Vermont?" he asked.

Her eyes snapped open wide.

"Come on, Molly," he coaxed. "I know there's your mom and dad and...what's his name? Your brother-in-law? Zach! That's it. So that's three major players. And what about your sister?''

"Sometimes," Molly replied. "When she's not buried in her law practice or supervising the kids' homework."

"Okay, tell me something," Sam said quietly. "Why do you have to run a one-woman show?"

He could have lost himself in her shining blue eyes, which just opened wider, if that was possible.

"What do you want me to say?" Blinking furiously, she rose from her chair. "A one-woman show is what I do. What I've always done."

She walked toward him and waved her arm at the window. "Just look out there and pretend for a minute. Pretend you see a mountain, instead of tiny hills, a snow-covered mountain so high you can't see the summit. Don't you understand? It was just me and the mountain out there. Do you think skiing is really a team sport when you're alone at 2500 feet going like the wind, cutting those turns, finding the edge, always aiming for a new personal best?"

Magnificent in her passion, with her blazing eyes, swirling hair and proud carriage—as sexy a woman as he'd ever seen—Molly held him mesmerized. He pulsed all over, his arms aching to hold her, his mouth desperate to kiss her. He breathed deeply. In and out.

"This hotel is a team effort," he finally replied, forcing himself back to the topic at hand. "And you can't play every position. But you are the captain. Now learn to delegate."

She stepped toward him, her eyes locking with his. "But I thought I'd have you," she whispered.

Now he couldn't breathe at all. And didn't care. He moved closer, reaching for her, his fingers trembling as he caressed her cheek. And then she was in his arms. His mouth covered hers, so sweet, so soft. He felt her response and suddenly was kissing her with an intensity that bordered on the savage—his idea of a supportive friendship left in the dust, his comparisons with Adrienne shot clear to hell, along with Molly's fear of mixing business with pleasure.

HE DIDN'T TELL HER their destination that evening and had the satisfaction of hearing Molly squeal, "An amusement park!" when he pulled into Six Flags outside of San Antonio.

"Let's go," said Molly, unsnapping her seat belt. "I haven't been on rides in…can't remember when. And I've never been to Six Flags. It seems huge."

If Sam had wondered about Molly's reaction to such a large venue, he worried no longer. He was sure now that her enthusiasm would overcome any physical discomfort. And he intended them to be on the rides more often than walking.

"Game for heights?" he asked, eyeing the Ferris wheel.

"Are you kidding?" Molly replied. "The higher the better."

She told the truth. Most gals would be squealing and snuggling into their dates as the giant wheel turned, especially if their car paused at the top. Not

Molly. Sam watched her close her eyes, smiling face to the breeze, hands braced on the safety bar and clearly loving every moment in the air, especially at the highest point.

When she finally opened her eyes eighty feet off the ground, Sam took her hand and squeezed it. "Look out there, sweetie." He waved his arm in space. "The evening's just beginning. We've got a whole playground waiting for us."

"And I guess I'm ready to play." She looked at him and reached over to cup his cheek. "Coming here was a great idea, Sam. Thanks."

His satisfaction couldn't be beat. Making Molly happy was a pleasure.

They disembarked from the Ferris wheel and Sam watched Molly look around. "Your choice, Mol."

He might have known her gaze would rest on a monster roller coaster.

"I choose that," she said, pointing to a huge maze of twisted steel loops and corkscrew turns built for a seventy mile-an-hour thrill.

"Why am I not surprised?" he asked, taking her arm and walking with her to the roller coaster. He sat down next to her in the lead car.

"Maybe one in the middle would be less forceful," he suggested.

"Maybe."

"But you want this one."

"Yup. Being first is always better." She turned to him, suddenly concerned. "But if you want to take another car, it's okay. I'll be fine up here alone. Don't worry.''

Not a chance. He grinned. ''And let you have all the fun? No way.''

But Sam knew it was more than fun for Molly. It was almost ecstasy. When he could fight the wind that tried to blow his eyes closed, he watched Molly's face. Her happiness on the Ferris wheel was only a prelude to the joy he saw now. She reveled in the speed. Her body moved with the coaster, balancing against its force, and when that force lifted them away from the seat, she returned almost exactly to the same position. Neither the speed nor the centrifugal force could eliminate Molly's natural grace and balance.

When the ride ended, Molly turned to him, her eyes shining with excitement. ''Let's do it again.''

Lord, she was beautiful. And so alive! His body tightened, wishing her words referred to another kind of activity.

''Sure.''

Three hours and countless rides later, Sam held Molly's hand as they walked back to the car.

''Those hot dogs were great. Aren't you glad we waited to eat until after the rides?'' she asked.

''Smart move for people addicted to roller coasters,'' said Sam as he patted his stomach. ''I like my food to stay down.''

Molly's fingers tightened around his. ''I had a wonderful time tonight, Sam. Thanks so much for thinking of it.''

"My pleasure. And now I've got another idea."
He opened the passenger door and tucked Molly
inside.

She looked up at him. "If it's as good as this one,
let's hear it."

"How'd you like to go skiing?"

CHAPTER NINE

MOLLY CLUTCHED the edge of her seat. Her stomach knotted and her skin felt clammy. Skiing? Was Sam crazy?

"You'll love it, Mol. We can rent a boat and skis at one of the lakes, take a picnic lunch. And you'll be skiing again."

Waterskiing. He was talking about waterskiing. She took a deep breath, then another, and forced herself to relax as she watched Sam walk around the car and climb behind the wheel.

"I don't think so." She tried to make her tone as light as possible. "You'll have to come up with something else."

He reached for her hand, brought it to his mouth and kissed her fingers. "Hey," he said, "would I suggest anything that would hurt you? Waterskiing is easy. And you can ski on one foot. It's fun. I've done it loads of times."

"Your heart's in the right place, but no thanks," Molly replied. "I don't do water sports."

"Why not?" He paused, his brow furrowed, before his eyes widened in an expression of horror.

"Don't you know how to swim?" His rising voice reflected his incredulity.

"Of course I know how to swim," she replied, removing her hand from his.

"So what's the problem?"

She heard his honest confusion and couldn't blame him for it. For all he'd done for her, he deserved a truthful response. She took a deep breath.

"Sam," she began, "have you ever seen me wearing a pair of shorts?"

"Huh?"

She shook her head and sighed. The guy was oblivious. "So you're not a leg man?"

He grinned. "Legs are nice, Molly, but they're not the total package." He reached for her again. "See. I like your hands. I like kissing them. Like this." He demonstrated.

She leaned back in her seat, relaxed again. He was making her revelation easier for her. "The scar on my thigh is a foot long, Sam. It's too ugly for anyone to see, including you. So I don't wear shorts or bathing suits."

Molly waited for him to respond, but he didn't, except to squeeze her hand. Then she watched as Sam scanned the side of the road. "What are you doing?" she asked.

"Shush."

She remained quiet as he pulled into a fast-food parking lot and shut off the ignition. He wasn't smiling. In fact, his expression was as serious as she'd ever seen. He reached across her and unlocked her seat belt.

"Turn my way, Molly. I want you to see my face while you hear my words."

"You're scaring me, Sam," she whispered. "What's going on?"

"Just this." He leaned forward and brushed his mouth on hers, then moved back again before taking her hands in his. "Now you listen to me, Ms. Molly Ann Porter. And listen hard."

She couldn't move away if she wanted to. And she didn't want to.

"There is nothing, not one thing about you that is ugly. Do you hear me? Not this," he said, raising his hand to touch her cheek, "or any other reminders of your skiing career. You're a beautiful woman, Molly. In every way. And too smart to let a scar keep you from doing what you want."

He kissed her again. "And besides," he whispered, "you have the cutest tush. The skirts you wear don't hide everything! And then there are those jeans. But, hey, I'd love to see you in a pair of shorts."

She giggled. Then felt tears well and run down her face. Then felt Sam's mouth on hers again, this time kissing her with an intensity she'd known only in her fantasies. She leaned toward him and his arms came around her, crushing her to his chest, and she stayed there, not wanting to move away, maybe not ever again.

He may have turned her safe world upside down, but he'd offered her glimpses of a better one.

"Tell you what," she whispered.

"What?"

"I'll cut down a pair of jeans and we'll go skiing some day."

"Atta girl," he murmured.

THREE MORNINGS LATER Molly headed to her office prepared for a meeting with Bonnie Carter, whose job it was to coordinate personnel. It was mid-August, and new staff had to be hired to replace the college students who were returning to school. With their targeted marketing campaign, the reservation rate had held steady, and Molly hoped it would improve during the upcoming fall-festival season. Oktoberfest weekends plus a special fly-fishing day, a music fest in nearby Gruene—it seemed every weekend had some kind of theme.

As she stepped over the threshold to her office, she saw a package on her desk the size of a shoe box. It was wrapped in red shiny paper with a pretty white bow on top. She put her purse down and reached for the small envelope with her name on it, tucked under the ribbon.

Why would anyone leave her a gift? It wasn't her birthday. She hadn't done anyone a favor significant enough to necessitate a thank-you. She opened the envelope and read the card: "Hope they fit. If not, we can take them back for an adjustment."

It was signed with a capital S. Had to be Sam. She shook her head. What was he up to?

She slowly removed the red paper to reveal an actual shoe box. Her size was printed on the outside. She lifted the lid and stared at a pair of pretty sandals, the type she liked so much. But she saw at a glance that this pair was a little different. She picked up the left shoe. The sole had been built up just about an inch.

She sat in her chair and slipped off the unmodified sandals she was wearing, then put on the new ones and stood up. She rocked back and forth, heel to toe. So far, so good. She put one foot in front of the other and walked the length of her office. The limp was as slight as when she wore her closed shoes.

She blinked back tears, then shut her eyes and pictured Sam. Her lips trembled and she pressed them together. How many guys would have thought of doing such a thing on their own? How many girl-friends would have? Maybe not even her own sister.

"So do they fit?"

She whirled around and saw Sam standing in the doorway, a big grin on his face.

"Perfectly," she said in a husky voice. "I'm overwhelmed. It was so thoughtful…and…thank you."

"As long as you like them, and they fit. We can fix the height if it's not right."

"They feel fine," she said, walking the length of her office again. "I guess I never seemed to have time for shopping, but sandals were definitely on my mind.''

Sam walked closer to her. ''You never *made* time for shopping. But that's going to change as soon as the new assistant comes on staff.'' He paused and looked her in the eye. ''You have started the search, haven't you?''

''Today, Sam, today. I'm meeting with Bonnie today,'' she replied quickly.

''Good.''

Darn! Now she'd really have to hire someone or Sam would be nagging her forever. It seemed *she* cared about the bottom line more than he did. Didn't he realize they could save thousands by doing without an assistant? She studied his expression. Stubborn as a Texas fence post. If she didn't go along, he'd speak to Bonnie himself about advertising for the position.

He met her gaze and held it. Suddenly the office became as quiet as a library after closing time.

''You have a good day, Mol,'' he finally said.

''You, too.''

He nodded but just stood there. ''The architect is meeting me in a little while with the blueprints for the conference center.''

She groaned silently. ''You've done a lot in a short time,'' she said.

''As soon as all the i's are dotted and t's crossed with investors, I want to be ready to roll. The sooner we're up and running, the sooner the debt on the Bluebonnet becomes more reasonable. The profitability projection becomes real. And that's the goal.''

"But what if you're wrong?" Molly heard the cry in her own voice. "What if your idea flops? We'll lose everything! The hotel will be bankrupt, and God knows what will happen to her then.''

His lips thinned, his dark eyes glowed like burning coals. "Failure is not an option here. Not on my radar screen.'' A flash of hurt crossed his face. "Are you predicting I'll fail?" he asked quietly.

"Of course not!" Molly replied, shaken that she'd unwittingly planted such an idea. Shaken that he'd believe that of her. "But I lose either way,'' she said, sadness permeating her voice, "because even when you succeed, you'll sell her.''

Sam started to speak, but Molly held up her hand. "I know, I know,'' she said. "Your heart's not in the hotel business.''

"And you couldn't care less about information technology,'' he retorted.

What could she say? He was right.

"My heart may not be in the hotel business in general, but it is with the Bluebonnet,'' he continued softly. "Just as yours is.''

"Yes,'' she said, looking into his caring face. "But it's slated to be a short-term romance.''

He shrugged, his expression becoming a bit cynical. "That's the way it goes sometimes, Molly. A nice honeymoon, but no golden anniversary. Jobs, people, ideas. Often, it's for the best.''

"I wouldn't know," she replied. "I tend to stick when my heart's involved."

"Yeah," he said, "you do. You love hard. You give your all to everything, and then have to pick up the pieces when it comes crashing down."

She tensed, her body frozen. Then she grabbed him by the upper arms. "So what? I'd do it all over again. I loved my sport. Everything about it. If I hadn't tried, I'd never have known how good I was. I would have missed so much, so many challenges, so many people, so many experiences and places. My God," she cried, "*I was so lucky!*"

Her heart pounded, her hands throbbed from squeezing him and she let go. She looked at Sam's face and saw her own feeling of wonderment reflected there. She felt a smile start to grow. She wanted to dance, wanted to fly. She felt as light as a gently swirling snowflake.

"And you know what else?" she asked, not expecting a reply.

"Yes," he said. "You are an amazing woman."

She stopped midsentence. "Amazing? No." She paused. "I was going to say 'happy.' It's as though I've loved and lost, but the experience was worth everything. And I'm still a happy person. I'm still me. And I think that's quite enough."

"Then I hope your good feelings last a lifetime. Only the best for you, Molly." He leaned toward her and kissed her gently on the forehead.

His lips were warm, but Molly felt a chill travel

through her body. Sam's voice, his touch, his words—all were appropriate, but suddenly felt like goodbye.

SAM LEFT HER OFFICE, his mind reeling from what he'd seen. The Molly he'd just left was the Molly in the skiing video. Alive, intense, powerful and confident. That was the real Molly. And now she was on her way to becoming that woman once again. Dang, she was something!

He let himself out the back entrance of the hotel and paused, as usual, to enjoy the colorful masses of flowers. Then he scanned the acreage where the new building would go. Constructing a technology center was a sound plan. He'd decrease the debt on the hotel. Pay back his uncle in a way. But his heart didn't pound the way it did when he was developing software solutions or creating his Internet companies.

He walked the land to the actual site of his new venture. Stood on the walking path, visualizing the completed structure and knew he was going backward. He was looking at creating something that was tried and true. Not cutting edge. He'd be setting up a facility to teach what was already known. Which was fine—for someone else.

His heart was in Silicon Valley. He wanted to be where technological developments were made and integrated into everyday life. Where software-design teams came up with new applications for business, for medical research, for entertainment, for any possible need. He wanted to be where his creative energies would be challenged.

He turned around and looked back at the Bluebonnet. Stately. Mellow. Welcoming. She was a beauty all right.

Just like the woman who managed her.

Why the hell had he kissed Molly politely on the forehead when he really wanted to wrap her in his arms and kiss her till she couldn't think straight? Because he was an idiot. Or because he was a coward. Maybe both.

When she'd turned to him with her thousand-megawatt smile, her blue eyes glowing, her excitement was almost palpable. Her body moved as fluidly as a dancer's. She was easily the sexiest, most mesmerizing woman he'd ever seen. But in that moment he barely recognized her as Molly. His Molly. And then came the peck on the forehead.

The hell with it. He could rectify that mistake. Molly would still be in her office. He strode toward the entrance and almost crashed into Judy Schneider, who seemed to come from nowhere, racing toward the door.

"Sam! You're just the person I need. You and Molly." She grabbed his hand. "I'm so upset. Come with me. You won't believe this."

She was worked up about something and it wasn't all good. Her excitement was laced with dismay. He followed her—not that she gave him much choice—right into Molly's meeting with Bonnie.

"Sorry, ladies," he apologized immediately.

"Our songbird seems to need an ear right now." He met Molly's questioning eyes, then shrugged and shook his head.

Molly turned to Judy. "Bonnie and I just have a few more things to go over. What's going on?"

"It's my mother."

"Is something wrong?" asked Molly, concern etching a line on her forehead. The forehead Sam had kissed so recently.

"Yes, something is wrong!" said Judy, eyes wide, almost wild. "My mother is crazy. She says she's going to New York with me. And that we'll share a cute apartment together. Can you imagine?" She looked totally outraged. "She'll ruin my life!"

Sam glanced at Molly, whose hand was covering her mouth as she coughed. Or pretended to cough. Sam fought his own grin.

"Hey, it could work," he said. "Supper on the table every night, a supply of clean clothes…"

Judy glared at him. "Not funny."

"So what's the alternative?" Molly prompted.

"How about you talking to her? She likes you."

"Oh, no. I've already done my bit." Molly glanced at Sam, who nodded approvingly.

The youngster collapsed into a chair. "Shoot! It's embarrassing to wind up going to college twenty miles away at UT."

"Hey, my alma mater's a great school," said Sam. "And they have a great music department."

"Yeah, but I want to go to New York!"

"And you will," said Molly. "But not this year."

She approached Judy and sat in a chair facing her. "Your dream and your voice won't disappear by going to school. A professional music program can only help you. In fact, it might make you stronger for when you do hit the Big Apple."

"Mmm. Maybe."

"My sister went to school in New York, but she stayed in the dorms, not her own apartment. Not until law school when she was older."

"Shoot!" said Judy again. "It's my own fault. I should have applied to Juilliard. If I had gotten in, then my going to New York would be a done deal."

"Plan now for next year, Judy." Molly paused. "When you want something—no, not want. When you *love* something so much you can't breathe without it, you figure out how to get it."

Molly's eyes had darkened with strong emotion as she spoke, and Sam knew she believed every word.

"But now it's over for you, Mol," he said, "and you're still breathing."

"That's right." She stood up and walked to within a inch of him, chin raised in challenge.

"And earlier this morning, you told me you were lucky," Sam continued, inhaling her light scent and almost losing himself in the depth of her blue eyes.

"I meant it."

"Good." He nodded at Judy who hadn't said a word. "She's just starting out. Any words of wisdom for her?"

"I can think of a few." Molly gave her full attention to Judy. "You're familiar with my background, aren't you? The skiing? The Olympics?"

Judy nodded.

Molly clasped the girl's hands. "When you have a dream that takes hold, when you eat, sleep and drink that dream twenty-four hours a day, seven days a week, there's only one thing to do." She squeezed Judy's fingers. "You go for it with everything you've got."

"Yes!" Judy jumped up from her chair, eyes glowing. "That's just the way I feel, too. I will get to Broadway some day, soon. Thank you, Molly. You're the greatest. You too, Sam." She moved toward the exit. "I'm going to go talk to my mom. Bye." And she walked out, singing.

"Bye," said Sam with a grin as he opened the door and watched her step toward her future. Then, still holding the door open, he turned to Bonnie. "Would you mind?"

"No problem." Bonnie followed Judy out of the office.

Now Sam closed the door. Approaching Molly without hesitation, he placed his fingertips underneath her pugnacious chin and kissed her the way he should have kissed her earlier that morning.

Molly responded to Sam's kiss with an urgency that surprised her. Her heart raced as she wound her arms around his neck, her mouth on his, eager to taste the sweetness that was Sam. What an improvement over the early-morning brush-off! Which obviously had not been a brush-off. She moaned with joy as his lips continued to claim hers, thankful for being wrong about their first encounter that day.

She pressed herself to him, inhaling his unique blend of spice and man. His lips became gentle, and she felt a parade of soft kisses travel from the corner of her mouth down her neck and across her shoulders. She shivered as his tongue seared the return path to her mouth, his lips capturing hers once again.

There was no one like Sam! At least not for her. The thought startled her, and Molly almost lost her balance.

"Easy, baby," he whispered.

She felt Sam's hold on her tighten immediately and reveled in the safety of his arms.

"I'm fine," she whispered. "You've got me."

She looked into his dark eyes and saw the concern, the admiration, the…love shining there and knew her heart was his for the asking.

She loved him.

TEN MINUTES LATER Sam had gone to speak with the architect, Judy had reappeared at the front desk for her final week at the hotel, and Molly sat in her office with Bonnie Carter, trying to continue their conversation about staffing. Her mind had to focus on business; she'd wait until later to daydream about Sam.

"In the past, we didn't replace summer help," Bonnie said. "The reservation rate dropped after school started up again, so we didn't need as full a staff. Except for weekends with all the festivals."

"So midweek is dead?" asked Molly.

"Not exactly dead, but not really alive, either."

"I've already started an independent advertising campaign in addition to the co-op one we share with the whole community—Texas travel magazines, Internet Web-site expansion, and I've even invited some big travel agents for a visit."

Molly leaned forward in her chair. "I'm looking to increase business wherever we can. We'll target midweek autumn stays first. So replace the college kids with folks who want jobs. The managers will train them. Follow up with housekeeping first. Gladys lost a couple of people already, but we put in an ad."

"And what about the assistant-manager position?" asked Bonnie. "Sam seemed pretty insistent about that one."

Sure he did. He wanted her to have more free time. But his words ran through her mind. Did she have to run a one-woman show?

"The salary's high on that position," Molly finally said. "Create the ad, show me the wording, but hold off on placing it until I tell you."

"You're the boss," said Bonnie. "But I don't want to be around when Sam finds out."

"He won't blame you," Molly said quickly. "You report to me. In fact, I'll tell him myself so there's no misunderstanding."

Bonnie smiled. "I'd appreciate that, Molly. I know you're the manager, but Sam's the owner and John's nephew, so it can get a little confusing."

Molly made a mental note to "unconfuse" the staff. She'd make herself more visible, be out and about more, instead of spending so much time in her office.

Bonnie left just as the phone rang. Molly picked it up. "Hello."

"Molly? Liz Miller here. You remember, Travis's sister?"

"Of course I remember. How nice to hear from you."

"I'm calling to invite you to our ranch this Sunday afternoon. Real Texas barbecue, real Texas horses and real Texas margaritas."

"Sounds like fun. How gentle are the horses, though?"

Liz's laughter was contagious and Molly found herself smiling.

"Sam's being invited too. So you can travel together or not. Your choice."

"We'll be together," Molly replied. "If we can get away. Oh, dear. Maybe only one of us will be able to go. I'm not sure now, but I'll let you know."

"No problem. We're having a group of friends and I think you'll have a good time."

"Thanks, Liz. I really appreciate being included." Molly hung up the phone, noting that she *did* appreciate the invitation. Who would have thought a couple of years ago that she'd appreciate anything ever again? She'd thought her life was over and had actually wanted it to be over.

And now, another world had opened for her. She had a future.

"Incredible," she murmured. A great job in a beautiful place, new friends, a community, even horses. But most important of all—Sam. A smile grew on her face as she thought of him. His eyes dark with heat when he looked at her, his sense of humor, his intelligence, his warmth, his...deep desire for children.

Suddenly her stomach cramped, her vision of happiness dimmed, and she figuratively hit the ground with a great thump. How could she have forgotten that part about him? She distinctly remembered their conversation about kids when she and Sam distributed July Fourth fliers and Travis Miller and his daughter came into Carla's shop. Sam had been very clear about wanting children in his future.

She rubbed her stomach, tried to relax and decided she didn't have to do or say anything now. If their relationship continued to grow, she'd find the right time to confess her reproductive problem. She'd lived by the rules of good sportsmanship all her life and wouldn't change now, whatever the outcome might be.

JEANS AND A V-NECK BLOUSE tied around the waist qualified as barbecue casual, Molly decided, glancing in her bedroom mirror. She picked up her tote, in which she'd placed a pair of sneakers and socks—just in case she actually got on a horse.

A knock sounded. "Ready, Mol?"

"Coming." She opened the door to find Sam with a wooden keg of their home-brewed beer hoisted on his broad shoulder. The man had triceps and biceps to spare. Molly gulped.

"I'm almost ready." She threw her sunglasses into the tote and retrieved a tray of sliced fresh fruit from her refrigerator. She eyed the display, pleased that it looked great, especially with the chocolate-dipped strawberries in the center.

"Hmm," said Sam, catching a glimpse of the tray. "Almost as pretty as you."

Molly felt heat rise to her cheeks and wished she wasn't one of those people who blushed easily. "Let's go," she said, closing the door behind them.

"Pretty, feisty and looking really good in those jeans."

"You're impossible," said Molly, blushing even more. "I've worn jeans before."

"And I've noticed every time," replied Sam, opening the back door of his car and depositing the keg. He placed the fruit tray next to it and escorted Molly to the front passenger door. "Climb in and buckle up."

Five minutes later Molly craned her neck left and right in order to absorb the beauty of the passing scenery. Hills, lakes, trees—the countryside enticed her to relax. Much gentler than the Green Mountains of Vermont where ski slopes of more than two thousand feet were common.

"It's lovely here," said Molly. "I'm glad Liz invited me."

"We were lucky the Eberhardt wedding took place at the hotel last night, instead of today," said Sam, "or neither of us could have gone. Good thing we're hiring an assistant for you."

"Yes." Molly looked straight ahead. "But it may take a while to find the right person." She glanced sideways at him, her conscience tugged. "Especially if the ad hasn't gone in yet," she added in a small voice.

Total silence met her remark. In the well-built automobile, there wasn't even the hum of tires on pavement to provide a background of white noise. Maybe she shouldn't have said anything while he was driving, Molly thought. Sam kept his eyes on the road, his lips tight, their color gone.

At last he spoke. "Why hasn't it gone in?"

He was angry. His clipped words proved it. But her reasoning was for his own good. "I want to save the money. It's a hefty salary, which could be put toward the mortgage."

"Not at your expense." His tone was low and emphatic. "Now, either you do it or I will."

Her best defense was an offense. "Do you always bully your employees?"

"Bully my employees?" he almost exploded. "Woman, you're the only 'employee' that's ever caused my blood pressure to skyrocket!"

Interesting.

"My employees *loved* working with me," Sam continued. "And notice I said *with*, not *for*. We were a team, but I was the leader. And I made the final decisions, so the debacles were on me. I'm not looking for scapegoats here.''

No, he wouldn't. Molly patted his arm. ''I know, Sam.'' She felt his anger drain away, felt his muscles relax under her fingers.

''Thank you, Molly. But that doesn't resolve our issue. That salary you're so concerned about is part of the cost of doing business. So what's your pleasure? Do you find someone or do I?''

She sighed deeply. ''Okay, okay. I'll tell Bonnie this week.''

He glanced at her, suspicion in his eyes. ''Promise?''

''Promise? Don't you trust me?''

He snorted. ''To teach me alpine skiing? Yes. To hire yourself some help? No.''

His expression, his tone—she laughed until her sides hurt. ''You are so funny, Sam!'' And then she heard his baritone chuckle join hers, and she wanted to hug him. Oh, man! He was special. He had to be. She wouldn't have given her heart to anyone who wasn't.

Sam turned onto the Rocking H road, and Molly looked about her with interest. Fence posts with barbed wire strung between them lined the road. Trees adorned the land either singly or in copses, with scrub grass here and there. Sam stopped the car and got out to open the entrance gate, drove through, then stopped again to get out and close the gate.

''Travis runs a relatively small operation, maybe three thousand acres,'' said Sam as he continued driving. "So forget what you've seen on the tube, where the King Ranch with over eight hundred thousand acres was used as a model."

"Eight hundred thousand? I can't even imagine such a size."

"Think Rhode Island."

A ranch as big as a state. "That's a lot of cows," she said.

"Yeah. Travis raises cattle, too, but he also breeds quarter horses. And Liz runs a riding school."

Molly remembered Liz mentioning the school. "It's a whole other world to me. I know about skiing and hotels, not ranching and horses."

Sam chuckled. "I have a feeling you'll be a quick study."

"Look." Molly pointed through the windshield. "Travis does have a corral—just like on television. And what are those big tanks way out there?"

"Water," replied Sam. He parked at the side of a large, white, two-story farmhouse with a wide wraparound porch, from where a half-dozen people waved at them. "Let's go."

Within five minutes, Molly was surrounded by Liz and Travis Miller and friends, who greeted her like long-lost family. She glanced at Sam and he winked at her, then turned his attention to Mrs. Miller, Travis's mom.

Liz took Molly's arm. "C'mon. We're all going for a trail ride, but I wanted to get you on a horse beforehand. Buttercup will be perfect for you."

Molly's palms tingled, and she halted her stride. She absolutely could not afford to break her leg again. "What's the chance of falling off her?"

Liz stopped, also, surprise on her face. "Almost none," she replied. "But, Molly, I'm not going to force you—"

"Do it."

Molly whirled at the tone in Sam's voice. "What?"

Sam turned to Liz. "Saddle the horse for her. She's already gone seventy miles an hour on the damn roller coasters for two hours nonstop, so she can certainly ride one of your sweet mares."

"Uh, hel-lo, I'm right here," said Molly, looking at Sam. "And I'll make the decision."

"When you fall off a horse, you're supposed to get right back on," said Sam. "And that goes for any sport." His eyes bored into hers, a message in them. "C'mon, champ," he continued. "You'll always be a competitor. Get on the horse. Next time it could be alpine skis and you'll want to be ready."

A picture of Vermont's mountains flashed through her mind and her legs turned to jelly. And in that instant, in that exact instant, she knew. She knew what she had to do...one day. Even if she ventured no further than the bunny hill.

She nodded at Sam. "You're one hell of a coach." Then she turned to Liz. "Lead the way."

CHAPTER TEN

MOLLY LEANED DOWN and patted Buttercup's neck. "You're a real sweetheart," she murmured. The horse's ears twitched and Molly laughed, satisfied that she and Buttercup were establishing a rapport. She'd had no trouble mounting, vaulting on her right leg on the horse's right side, the untraditional one. Buttercup was so well trained, she tolerated a rider's mount from either side. After ten minutes in the corral at a walk, Molly was now part of the group riding out.

Ahead of her, rode Travis, at one with his stallion. Little Amy rode next to him, sitting proudly on her pony, looking as though nothing ever fazed her, which Molly knew to be untrue. She'd sensed that tension between Amy's dad and her aunt Carla confused the child. She'd heard Travis's sigh of exasperation when Carla had shown up. And she'd seen conflicting expressions on Travis's face when Amy ran into her aunt's arms.

Molly sighed, sympathizing with her new friends. Relatives and relationships could sure be less than perfect, even on a beautiful day with gorgeous blue skies and a delightful breeze.

"Having fun?" asked Sam, riding next to her.

She flashed him a grin. "Everyone's equal on top of a horse, aren't they."

"What about the fun part?" he asked, pushing up the brim of his hat and looking at her.

"For sure," she replied in a low voice, her body automatically adjusting to the rhythm of the horse. She held the reins loosely, totally relaxed now, wondering why she'd ever had one droplet of concern. "I wouldn't mind visiting Buttercup on a regular basis," she said, "and, of course, a little more speed wouldn't hurt."

Sam chuckled and turned around. "You've hooked another one, Liz," he called. "Molly might be haunting you in her spare time."

"No problem. And I'm not surprised. She's got a natural seat."

Molly didn't bother saying a word. She was getting used to Sam and his friends talking about her as though she wasn't there.

"We're crossing an arroyo now," Travis said. "We're lucky to have these streams on our land. Fresh water for livestock all year round."

"It wasn't luck, Trav," Liz said. "Granddad was no dummy. He was thinking about survival and growth even then."

Molly smiled. "Sounds like a businessman with a dream. Families and their dreams, whether they're ranches, hotels or ski resorts, seem to be the same everywhere, don't they?" She looked at Sam. "And you know what else? I think you and your dreams fit in here, as well as anyone. You don't need Silicon Valley to be happy. You think you do, but you don't.''

"Hear! Hear!" Travis exclaimed. "Listen to the woman, Sam.''

"Thank you, Travis,'' said Molly, encouraged to continue her argument, despite Sam's stunned expression. "You once told me you'd bring high tech here to you, and now you're actually doing it.'' She paused. "Could it be your heart was talking?''

"Nah,'' Sam replied quickly. "Just my mouth. I'll make sure the tech center is in good hands when I leave.''

She shrugged, but bit her lip. He didn't realize the opportunities he had here. Well, there was still plenty of time before the project was done, and perhaps she'd planted a seed. She patted Buttercup's neck. "So how do I make this little girl go faster?''

"Your love of horses took all of twenty minutes to nurture,'' said Sam dryly, looking at his watch.

Travis turned in his saddle. "We'll pick up the pace now,'' he called to the group, then turned to Molly. "Buttercup will follow the lead horses. Kick her gently in the flanks if you want more speed. Tighten your knees to slow down.''

But she didn't want to slow down. Riding the mare at a trot was an adventure in balance and coordination—her outstanding traits. Galloping would come next. She could visualize it. Just as she used to visualize every twist and turn of the mountain before she took off on a run.

Travis slowed them down a mile later, and Molly leaned over the horse again, stroking her, talking to her. "I love you, Buttercup."

Laughter surprised her. Molly looked at her friends and brought herself back to reality. She'd been in her own world, back in the zone she hadn't experienced in years.

"Thanks, Sam," she said.

He tipped his hat. "Annie Oakley lives again."

"Not quite," she said, laughing, "but this sport feels real good."

"Maybe to you," chimed in Carla, "but I prefer a nice soft cushion to hard leather when I sit down."

"For God's sake, Carla," Travis snapped. "If you can't learn to ride from Liz, then you're hopeless. Maybe I should take you out myself. We can't have my favorite sister-in-law falling from a horse, can we?"

Carla's eyes blazed. Molly thought their heat would turn Travis into a human torch.

"I wouldn't give you the satisfaction, you blind, stubborn...horse's hind end. Oh, I give up." Carla turned her horse toward home, kicked hard and took off like a shot.

"Oh, hell," growled Travis, riding after her. "Why do I always do that? Liz, take care of Amy," he shouted over his shoulder.

But Sam was already next to Amy, talking quietly. Molly couldn't hear his words, but the little girl kept looking at him and nodding. Then she offered a smile of pure joy, and Molly's heart lurched.

Sam was a natural with kids, she thought, admiration and guilt mingling inside her. He'd make a great dad. She brushed aside the thought and concentrated on the return ride to the house.

A peaceful barbecue and a cold beer sounded awfully good to her.

SAM LEANED BACK against the corral fence, elbows on the railing, and watched dusk turn to evening. The sounds and smells were familiar. He breathed deeply and almost tasted the flavor of ranching—horse, hay, leather, earth. And man. Hardworking man.

"So, was Molly right about you?"

Travis's question startled Sam out of his reverie, and he frowned at his friend, who was walking toward him, draining the liquid from his plastic cup. "What do you mean?"

"Do you really need to go back to California?"

Sam grunted. "Only if I want to spend my life where the action is."

"What about the training center you're opening? Isn't that all about the latest software?"

"It's about providing a facility where customers, such as finance or insurance companies, can send employees and clients to learn software, standard packages or customized. In the long run, it's cheaper for them and more efficient. Most companies don't want permanent overhead for training."

Travis nodded. "I'm following you. It makes sense, Sam."

"As a business, yeah. But personally I'll get bored in no time. It touches only on my managerial and sales skills, not my design skills, and that's the most creative part. I design programs that haven't been invented yet. I'm a renaissance man, Travis. I like to get involved with everything."

"How's the work for my friends going?" asked Travis.

"Actually," replied Sam, "it's going very well. I'm working on their Web sites and they both want to go forward with their business applications. I *will* be doing the design."

Travis clapped him on the back and grinned. "That's great! You might get more referrals. This might grow. Maybe you'll be known as a Web-site designer."

Sam shuddered. "No, thanks, buddy. Web-site design grows stale pretty quickly if that's all you do."

Travis shrugged. "But it doesn't change the point I'm making. You'd be mighty welcome back here, Sam. Just wanted you to know. Can't imagine the town without a Kincaid in it."

Sam sighed heavily. "You're grieving for my uncle John, is all. Just like me."

"Could be. Could be I'm looking back on a lot of things lately."

"Yeah. I hear you." Sam let silence take over. A companionable silence between friends. Then he said, "It's like that sometimes, looking back. Wondering about doing things differently."

"But if I'd done things differently, I wouldn't have Amy," Travis said in a heartbeat. "And that's the thing that gets me. Every time."

Sam heard the love in Travis's voice as clearly as the ringing of church bells on Sunday morning, but he couldn't resist teasing him. "And you wouldn't have Carla."

Travis glared at him, then sighed. "Right."

Sam laughed and punched him lightly on the shoulder. "Molly and Carla hit it off right away, and now it's as though they've known each other for years."

"Women!" Travis snorted.

Sam chuckled. "Well, pal, in this case you might want to reconsider. I trust Molly's instincts. She's a natural. Look at her with that horse today! First time, and they're a duo already. She's good with people, too."

But his friend's expression made Sam pause. "And your point is…?" Travis asked, suspiciously.

Sam put up his hands. "Hey, you did me a favor. I'm trying to return it. But I'll shut my yap now."

Travis's shoulders slumped, his eyes closed. "Sorry, Sam. I guess the woman's like a cactus under my skin."

Aren't they all. "Could be you're only seeing Amy's mom when you look at Carla. You don't really see Carla."

Travis straightened up and glared. "I see Carla O'Connor in my friggin' dreams! I can't sleep. I snap at everybody. Especially at her." He gazed over Sam's shoulder, his expression thoughtful, sad. "I know I'm not being fair—and then I snap some more. There's just something about that woman…"

"…that's getting to you," Sam said. "And I know you'll figure it out mighty fast, because she's coming our way."

Sam watched Travis eye his pretty sister-in-law as she approached in another colorful outfit, purple this time. The woman had legs that didn't quit, and Travis's face reflected his hunger…and his caution.

"Hi, Sam," greeted Carla with a smile. "Dessert's being served." She glanced at her brother-in-law. "Amy's falling asleep sitting up, and she'll probably want us both to tuck her in."

"I'm coming," said Travis, moving toward the woman, barely waiting for her to complete her message. "Why don't you stay and keep Sam company?"

"Because," Carla enunciated, "my niece wants me." She turned around and strode toward the house without waiting for Travis's reply.

Sam chuckled as he watched Travis catch up to her. What a pair! And then he thought about Molly and quickened his own step toward the big front porch.

He spotted her, rocking gently in a comfortable-looking, cushioned chair. Her head rested on the back, her arms dangled over the side, one hand gently ruffling the neck of the Millers' Labrador retriever. He'd never seen her as relaxed or as still in the three months he'd known her. A new facet of Molly. At least to him.

He caught her eye as he approached. And then she smiled at him. Slow, warm and sultry.

He forgot to breathe.

"Ready for dessert?" she whispered.

Was he ever. He leaned down and kissed her. And felt her eager response. "That's better than cake and ice cream put together," he whispered, then saw the happiness shining in her eyes. Happiness, tenderness...and love.

"Mol," he whispered, his spirit full of wonder, of discovery, "we have to talk."

"Yes," she agreed softly, pulling him down beside her. "I agree."

But two hours later Sam let himself into his suite after gently kissing Molly good-night at the door. There would be no talking that evening. Molly had fallen asleep on the way home and was probably on her way to dreamland again by now. She worked hard, played hard and must have a clear conscience. Who else fell asleep as easily?

Sam chuckled as he got ready for bed. Molly was a sweetheart, and as she said between yawns, "I'm not going anywhere. We can talk tomorrow."

He was looking forward to it.

SHE WAS DREADING IT. Two hours after crawling into bed, Molly was wide awake. Her fingers traced the railroad-track scars on her leg, still easily felt after four long years. They'd always be with her.

They'd always be visible, a reminder of a day she'd like to forget. A reminder of other damage invisible to the eye, but with permanent consequences affecting the rest of her life.

Somehow she'd have to tell Sam. Their relationship was shifting. The warmth in his voice and his eyes, his loving expression when he'd said, "We have to talk," were both thrilling and scary. And full of promise.

Molly got out of bed and wore out a path across the bedroom floor—short step, long step—before jumping onto her exercycle. She had an overabundance of energy, both mental and physical, and her uneven gait provided no satisfaction. Her legs pumped the pedals. Her mind explored the problem.

She'd lose Sam. No question about it. And the kicker was she couldn't blame him. He wanted children. Was very clear about it. Of course, he didn't know he stabbed her heart every time he mentioned it, so she couldn't blame him for that, either.

Her balance sheet was lopsided if she added up wins to losses, so she usually didn't weigh them anymore. Instead, she tried to focus on her second career and her new life. But the past seemed to have a way of catching up. One mistake at seventy miles an hour—one stupid mistake—had affected everything. Her lifelong dream of an Olympic victory followed by a career in sports, the romantic dreams of love and marriage, the vague notion of a "happily ever after," all the hopes in a young girl's heart killed in one wild moment.

Molly looked down at her feet, at her scarred thigh, at her hands gripping the bars of the bike. She touched her cheek, running her fingers along the remains of the imperfect surgery.

Her ambition had cost her. Had cost her plenty. She smashed her fist against the handlebar. But dammit! If she had the chance, she'd do it all again.

She'd lived her life taking risks. Now she'd take another one, because taking risks was part of who she was. Just as playing fair was.

She loved Sam. She had to tell him the truth because she loved him. Because he deserved to know. Because she couldn't live with herself if she didn't.

She had to tell him even if she lost him.

Her legs felt like rubber when she walked to her bed, and she let herself plop down on the sheet.

If she lost Sam, the scars on her heart would dwarf the ones on her leg. And the never-ending darkness would come again. It might overwhelm her next time. What a horrible thought. But life didn't include a guarantee of happiness.

She felt tears gather and blinked them away. No crying allowed! She had to be strong, no matter what happened next.

THE NEXT DAY dragged by. And sped by. Simultaneously. By dinnertime Molly thought she was living a double life. She and Sam had not had more than a moment alone together from the time he'd said, "Good morning, sweetheart," and kissed her in her office before running out to meet the architect again, to half an hour ago when Sam said he'd meet her in five minutes for dinner and still hadn't shown up.

As she'd completed one task after another during the day, her impending confession hovered like a shadow in the back of her mind. And now, as she straightened up her desk, she was torn between relief and anxiety at the delay of their talk.

"Hey, Mol," said Sam, suddenly appearing in her doorway. "I'm starved. Are you ready?"

She looked up at the sound of his voice and wanted to run her palm over the dark stubble on his face. Her arm rose, almost by itself, and his eyes warmed as though anticipating her touch. He was sweet and sexy. A wonderful combination in a man. And this man wanted her, cared about her, acted in every way as though he loved her. All she could ever hope for was wrapped up in the six-foot package standing directly in front of her.

Her fingers brushed over his mouth, and then she was in his arms, his lips on hers.

"The hell with dinner," Sam groaned a minute later. "I want you."

She hugged him hard, inhaling his familiar spicy fragrance, conscious of his hard muscle beneath her hands, the broadness of his back, how her head felt against his chest, how she fit against him so perfectly. How she wanted to be able to embrace him exactly the same way fifty years hence.

She slowly released her hold and glanced up. "I

know,'' she whispered. ''But let's go for a walk first, and then we'll see.''

His eyes narrowed, but Molly shooed him ahead of her and locked the office door. The time had come. She wasn't backing out.

Almost blindly she led him to the back entrance, oblivious to the activity around them. For once, oblivious to the riot of color on the patio and in the gardens. Out the door and down the walkway to the meandering path around the property. Then she felt Sam's arm come around her waist and pull her gently back to a slow pace.

''Whoa, girl. Are you so anxious to see the plans for the training center? We can review them any time you want. Just because the Historical Society has no objections doesn't mean I won't let you have a crack at it.''

If only it was that simple! Molly shook her head, understanding Sam's question. They were headed for the acreage where the new building would be constructed.

''I'm not concerned about the center, Sam. I trust you. I know you want the best for the Bluebonnet.''

''So what's the matter?''

She tried to smile. ''I hope nothing. I hope nothing's the matter that can't be worked out.'' She pointed to a bench in the shade of a large live oak. ''Have a seat. I need to tell you something and then I'm going to leave you alone.''

''I don't like mysteries,'' he grumbled. ''Just spill it, Molly. You're scaring me.''

"I'm sorry, Sam. I'm sorry. Just sit down. Okay? This is hard for me to talk about." She heard the desperation in her own voice and knew Sam heard it, as well, because he sat quickly, his eyes glued to her face.

She stood in front of him, memorizing the lock of hair that chronically flopped onto his forehead, the dark-brown eyes, now filled with concern, the strong chin and the full mouth that had the power to turn her to mush. Lord, she loved him.

"Sam," she began, "I love being with you. We might have had a rough beginning, but I want you to know that I think you're wonderful. Special."

She saw his eyes light up and quickly added, "But I don't think you're superhuman. You're a healthy, normal man and you want what every man wants. And I can't give that to you."

Her heart thumped against her ribs as she finally formed the words that would give him the freedom to walk away with a clear conscience. But looking him in the eye was too hard. She couldn't do it. Instead, she focused over his shoulder and saw nothing.

"I can't have children," she said, her voice steadier than she'd anticipated. "The accident caused damage on the inside, too. I can't carry a pregnancy to term." She inhaled. Exhaled. "I know how important children are to you, so before we get more involved, I wanted you to know."

She pivoted away from him, satisfied she'd done the right thing, but needing to leave quickly. "You don't have to say anything," she added. "Now or later. I'll understand."

The hotel seemed to shimmer in the distance as Molly walked toward it, jaw clenched, hands fisted at her sides. Her part was over. She'd done what she had to do, and the next step was up to Sam. Her legs moved one in front of the other until she was safely in her suite.

She collapsed onto the couch, totally wiped out. For the second time in her life, she could lose everything she wanted. It seemed she had a penchant for high-stakes risk.

An hour later she was in the Jacuzzi when the phone rang. She picked up the portable receiver. "Hello."

"It's Sam," he announced without preamble. "I'm coming over."

Her heart galloped at the sound of his voice. "No, you're not, Sam. I'm in the tub, finally unwinding from the day. Can we postpone until tomorrow?" If he was going to add stress to her life, she could wait.

"You left me poleaxed on that bench, Molly. I needed time to take it in. And now I want more information."

She closed her eyes tight, gathering her control. "I'm sorry, Sam, but there's no silver lining. I broke my pelvis in the accident. And now it's too narrow for a full-term pregnancy. If I became pregnant, I'd miscarry. That's the whole story." She took a breath. "I'll say good-night now and leave you to your thoughts. See you tomorrow."

She put the phone down gently and let the tears flow. What had she expected? That he'd come over with a diamond ring and say he loved her so much that her problem didn't matter? *Get real, girl. That kind of ending happens only in dreams.*

She should never have gotten involved with him. She'd known from the beginning to concentrate only on her career. Marriage and a family were out of the question for someone like her. She winced at her own words. *Someone like her.*

Maybe she'd cancel the plastic surgery she had scheduled for the end of the week in Houston. Her fingertips traced the scar on her face. Did it really matter anymore if she had it done? The cosmetics she used to hide her scar were good enough for a woman alone. And she would be alone from now on. She'd been fooling herself thinking her relationship with Sam could grow into something permanent.

She slammed her palm against the bath water, taking satisfaction in the splash. Dammit! Was Sam the only reason she'd scheduled the surgery? No, he wasn't. Although he may have been the catalyst, he wasn't the real reason she'd finally decided to go ahead with her plan. In fact, Sam never mentioned her facial scar. It was Molly herself who wanted to get rid of it. Finally.

After having had a hell of a good time in her new job, in a new place, meeting new people and making new friends, she knew how important her career had become. And good first impressions counted in business. She'd be moving on in a while; she had to be ready. She couldn't count on meeting up with another John Kincaid, so she'd go through with the surgery. For her career's sake.

In the meantime she would continue to enjoy life at the Bluebonnet, no matter what happened between her and Sam.

WHEN SHE WENT to her office the next morning, Sam was waiting for her. He lounged in her doorway, arms crossed and shoulder resting against the frame, looking so good her heart tripped.

"Hi," she said in a quiet voice, avoiding his gaze and hoping her hands wouldn't shake as she took out her key ring to open the door.

"Good morning," he replied, not moving out of her way. "Aren't you going to look at me?"

Molly took a deep breath. Might as well get it over with. She raised her eyes and in Sam's recognized compassion, warmth and concern.

He was a kind human being. One of the many reasons she loved him. She turned away. Stop it! Stop thinking. Distracted by her mental efforts, she allowed Sam to take her keys. He opened the door, then closed it behind them.

"Please leave it open," Molly said at once. "I feel a bit claustrophobic." She'd never been bothered by closed spaces in her life, but suddenly she needed air.

"Are you afraid to be alone with me, Mol?" Sam asked incredulously.

She'd love to be alone with him for the rest of her life!

"Afraid? No." Incredibly she felt herself smile as she altered her position to look at him. Study him. Full in the face.

Sam's eyes heated, his hand rose, fingers brushed her cheek. "God, Molly. I see you and I..." His words trailed off.

"It's all right," she whispered. "I understand."

He shook his head. "No, you don't," he said. "And there's no way you could." Pain-filled eyes stared at Molly for a moment, and she inhaled sharply. If she'd thought Sam would or could walk away easily, she'd been wrong. Very wrong. He was suffering, too. Then he blinked and said, "I need a little time, Molly. Just a little time."

Impulsively she squeezed his hand. At the very least, Sam was her friend, and he needed her to be a friend, no matter the stakes. Maybe even because of them.

"I release you, Sam, of any guilt you may be harboring. I know you want a full future. And I don't blame you. I'm sorry. I just...I just didn't know how quickly we'd grow to lo— care so much about each other." She tried to smile. She really did. "Especially after our disastrous beginning."

The corner of his mouth quirked up. "We were like oil and water."

"Oh, not exactly," she replied, remembering those first days. "I think we were more like the fireworks we saw back then."

"My problem is," said Sam slowly, "I like the fireworks we make together."

She moved away from him. He spoke in the present tense, and she couldn't carry on the conversation or pretext of conversation. She felt, rather than saw, Sam leave the office.

"I know you need time," she whispered to the empty room. "Just...don't take too long."

In the meantime, however, she'd move ahead with her own plans. She'd survived life after disaster once; she'd survive life after Sam, too. Her only wish was that she didn't have to.

SAM STRODE to his suite, put on a pair of running shoes and jogged out back to the walking path behind the hotel. He didn't want to think; he didn't want to feel. He just wanted to run.

He should have known better.

Pictures of Molly superimposed themselves on the fainter images of Adrienne in his mind. Was he always destined to get involved with women who had problems having children? Whether due to attitude or physical condition, the result was the same. But the women sure weren't!

He'd completed one turn around the track and glanced up at the Bluebonnet. Molly! Never a boring moment with her. She could fill him with delight and drive him crazy both within the same five minutes. When they were together, he laughed, he gasped, he cheered. He had fun!

He had admired Adrienne. Her drive, her intelligence, her striking good looks. And what else? He frowned as he thought back. Maybe the mutual excitement of their professional climbs influenced their feelings. The smell of success, the lure of power.

The empty apartment after he'd disappointed her. When he didn't live up to expectations.

Rivulets of sweat ran down his face as he rounded the track for the second time. The morning heated up quickly in late August. Too bad they had no pool at the hotel. Something to talk to Molly about. Molly! He'd bet swimming would be great exercise for her.

He eyed the hotel again as he started his third lap. In the meantime he'd follow up on the waterskiing idea. She'd love it.

Whoa! Better rethink those plans. Not fair to get too involved if he wasn't serious. He could walk away from her now.

Sure he could. He was surviving without Adrienne and he'd been together with her longer than he had with Molly.

But he'd never had as much fun with Adrienne. They'd never taken time for fireworks or horseback riding. Or the Texas two-step. They'd never taken time to fall in love.

He stopped dead in the middle of the path. Was that what was happening between him and Molly? Dang! He'd seen her eyes light up when he approached. He'd seen the love for him shining there. And he'd felt his heart pick up speed when he saw her. Even when he thought about her. Feelings were growing. Love was growing.

But would he do something about it? Could he sacrifice having children? Would he come to resent her, or would loving Molly be enough for the rest of his life?

CHAPTER ELEVEN

"MOLLY'S GONE till Monday, Sam. Are you going to be available all weekend?"

It was midmorning on Friday and Sam looked up from the piece of paper in his hand to see Bonnie Carter standing in his office doorway. "Do I have any choice?" he grumbled, then quickly apologized. "Sorry, Bonnie, but I just don't get it," he said, shaking his head. "She leaves me her phone number but doesn't tell me where she's going."

"If it makes you feel better, she didn't tell me anything, either. I've got the same piece of paper you do."

Sam heard himself sigh. It had been a long couple of days since he and Molly had spoken, both going about their business with a tacit agreement to focus all conversation on the hotel and expansion plans. They had no agreement at all, however, on where to focus their eyes. And their glances had spoken volumes, which had nothing to do with hotel business.

Sam blinked and reset his mind on his work. Ground breaking for the technology center was scheduled to begin a week from Tuesday, right after Labor Day—no complications from the Historical

Society—and Sam couldn't have asked for a smoother time of it.

He returned his attention to Bonnie. "My folks are coming in tonight for the weekend, so I'll have some backup. Don't worry about the staff. Enjoy your time off."

"Time off?" said Bonnie with a grin as she dropped a stack of paper on his desk. "I have two young kids. I don't get time off!"

"And you sound really miserable about it," Sam joked. He glanced at the stack of paper. "Résumés?"

The woman nodded. "For Molly's assistant." She winked at him. "Just in case you have time on your hands, you can read these. I've culled the ones I thought were the best and clipped them on top."

"Has Molly seen them yet?"

"Amazingly, she made time to scan them. In fact," continued Bonnie slowly, "there's nothing she hasn't done this week. I've never seen her quite as frenzied. She's been like a whirlwind the last few days."

Sam closed his eyes and winced. He knew exactly why Molly was going for the gold in her job. So she wouldn't think about him. Them. Her personal life. Her coping mechanisms were back in full force.

"She hates being bored," he explained, hoping Bonnie would accept the explanation.

"Bored?" the HR manager repeated incredulously. "In case you haven't noticed, Sam, nobody is bored around here. I think she just wanted to accomplish a lot because she was taking a long weekend off.''

"A well-deserved weekend," said Sam meaningfully.

"No argument from me." Bonnie turned to leave.

"One more thing," Sam called.

The woman paused.

"The résumés are priority. I'll be back to you within an hour, so block some time for phone screening. Molly needs backup immediately.''

"I agree, and I'm glad you're pushing this, Sam. I love working with her, but the woman doesn't know when to quit. The transition from your uncle to Molly has gone more smoothly than anyone anticipated, and we all need her. I don't want her to burn out.''

Sam nodded. "I hear you."

"And, Sam," Bonnie went on, "in case you don't realize it, your presence has been a huge positive factor, as well. Everyone understands that Molly knows the actual hotel business and that you're consulting with her on everything. But they love having a Kincaid at the helm. The old-timers around here are more than content.''

A surprising sense of satisfaction filled him as a picture of Gladys Pierce and the others formed in his mind. They were tough old pros, and he wasn't surprised that they continued to maintain their standards as they performed their jobs. He hadn't realized, however, that he was part of the reason none of those key employees had sought employment elsewhere.

"Thanks for sharing, Bonnie. I appreciate it."

She waved and Sam immersed himself in the résumés. Nothing was more important at the moment. He wanted Molly healthy and happy, not burned out. He still wanted to take her waterskiing. He wanted to dance with her again.

His heart lifted as he thought about his plans, and he almost rushed into the next office to invite her. Until he realized she wasn't there. Disappointment stabbed him. Life without Molly was dull. Flat. Their relationship was stuck at a crossroads—because of him. But he could change that.

At the moment, however, he would focus on making her life easier. He turned back to the résumés and put everything else out of his mind.

SAM'S CELL PHONE rang just before noon while he was in discussion with his general contractor at the site of the new tech center.

He picked it up. "This is Sam."

"Could you come to the front desk please, Mr. Kincaid?" said the voice on the other end. "Some folks are here to see you or, rather, to see Molly."

Molly? "Be right there," he replied before concluding his conversation with the construction boss. "Save every tree possible. We want to retain the same atmosphere the hotel and gardens have."

"I know. We're putting ribbons on the ones we have to cut, so you'll be able to see for yourself.

But remember, we're also creating a driveway from the county road directly to the building, as well as a parking area. So that will require more trees down.''

"No choice there,'' Sam said. "Just be gentle.'' He shook the man's hand and walked toward the Bluebonnet.

Who could be asking for Molly? He walked through the back entrance, down the corridor toward the check-in area. An attractive couple stood there, glancing at their surroundings, then at each other. The woman was blond, slender, wearing a light-blue blouse and white slacks. The man was tall, broad and dark-haired, gray only at the temples. But it was the woman who snagged Sam's attention. She looked familiar.

Sam approached the couple. "Hello,'' he said. "I'm Sam Kincaid and I was told you're looking for Molly.''

"We are,'' said the man.

"So, you're Sam,'' said the blonde at the same time, bestowing a thousand-watt smile on Sam. "I've been wanting to meet you.''

Sam recognized the smile instantly. Identical to Molly's. He shook the woman's hand. "You must be Molly's sister.''

"She is,'' the man confirmed, before the woman could respond. "I'm Zach Porter and this is my wife, Amanda. We're Molly's family. No one around here seems to know where she is. I'm trusting that you do?''

Sam couldn't miss the challenge in Zach's voice. No man alive would have. He met Zach's hard gaze. "Did you tell her to expect you today?"

He saw Zach's lips tighten and knew the answer before Amanda chimed in.

"He's got us there, sweetheart." She looked at Sam. "We had a pair of open-ended airline tickets and we wanted to surprise her. The summer sped by and it was now or never for us. The foliage season starts in a week and we'll have to be back in Vermont. But I did leave a message on her phone last night."

Sam shook his head. "She probably never got it. She left yesterday evening."

"Left?" asked Zach. "What do you mean, left?" He looked at his wife. "Did Molly say anything to you about a trip? Where did she go?"

The woman's face stilled, her smile gone. "No, definitely not." She turned toward Sam. "Where's my sister, Mr. Kincaid?"

How did he get to be the bad guy here? He'd strangle Molly after he found her.

"She's in Houston. Why don't we all go into my office where there's some privacy?" Sam suggested. "I'll have your bags brought to your room."

"Forget the bags," said Zach. "I'm not checking in until I know exactly where Molly is."

Sam called to the desk clerk. "Please hold the Porters' bags behind the counter for the moment. Thanks." He led Amanda and Zach to his office and pulled out the piece of paper Molly had left him.

"She's in Houston, but I don't know why or where. All I've got is a phone number for emergencies." He looked from Molly's sister to her brother-in-law. He doubted either of them were drawing breaths. "I guess we'll call this an emergency."

He dialed the number. And listened. And felt the blood drain from his face.

"Methodist Hospital?" he whispered.

"Give me that phone," Zach roared.

"Forget it!" Sam said, quickly recovering from the unexpected information. He swiveled his chair around to face the wall, effectively putting the phone out of the other man's reach.

"Molly Porter," he said. "She's a patient there." He drummed his fingers on the arm of his chair. "Surgery?" he repeated when the hospital rep returned to the phone. "Outpatient unit? Give me directions to the medical center from Interstate 10." He swiveled back around and glared at Zach as he reached for a pad and pencil and wrote down the directions.

"Can you connect me to the outpatient unit right now? Thanks." He looked at the white-faced Amanda and the now quiet Zach. "I'll drive us immediately. She won't be alone."

They nodded, and now he rolled the pencil in his fingers while waiting for the outpatient department to pick up the phone. "I want to leave a message for Molly Porter, who's having surgery right now. Please tell her not to leave the unit. Understand? She is not to leave the hospital until her family gets there. Thank you.''

He hung up and shared a brief commiserating glance with the other two before releasing his frustration. ''You realize my orders don't mean a damn thing. Molly does whatever the hell she wants, doesn't she?''

Their silence was answer enough.

''But she's not unreasonable,'' said Amanda quietly. Then added, ''Just why are you so angry, Mr. Kincaid?''

Now Sam's silence rang throughout the room.

MOLLY BLINKED HER EYES and stretched in the hospital bed. She recognized the nurse who was walking toward her as the same one who helped prepare her for surgery a few hours ago.

''You're a little swollen, as expected,'' the woman said, eyeing Molly's face. ''But how are you feeling?'' She took Molly's wrist and looked at her watch.

''I'm okay. A little sleepy, but not sick. And I want to leave as soon as you'll let me.'' Molly pushed at her blanket the moment the nurse completed her task.

''Not quite yet,'' said the nurse.

''But I feel great,'' protested Molly, sitting up in the bed. ''The 'twilight' anesthesia is fabulous. I'm not groggy at all now.'' She paused and put her hand to face.

''Here's a mirror.'' The nurse handed her one.

"But you can't see much. Remember, scar-revision surgery leaves you swollen and bruised in the beginning, and yours was a particularly long scar. The steristrips and paper tapes are protecting your stitches."

"Hmm." Molly examined herself in the glass. "I'd better stay hidden in my office for a while or I'll scare the guests away."

The joke fell flat. Tears filled her eyes and she lay back on her pillows. What had she done? She'd vowed no more surgeries and here she was alone in a strange hospital, in a strange city, having another surgery that as far as her health was concerned, was totally optional.

And then she reminded herself why she'd done it. She wanted to look better. She wanted every advantage possible in order to make it in life on her own. The swelling and discoloration would disappear in time and she'd look damn good. Not perfect. Scars never disappeared completely, but the improvement would be remarkable. She wiped away her tears and sat up again.

"I'm ready to leave," she announced to the nurse and to the room in general.

"Then we're just in time."

She jumped at the sound of the familiar voice and turned toward the door. "Sam!" she exclaimed, her heart racing, her mouth smiling. "What are you... Amanda! And Zach! Omigod! What's going on?"

Molly held out her arms, tears threatening again, reveling in her sister's hug, in Zach's careful embrace. She glanced at Sam, who'd stood aside during the reunion, and then couldn't look away.

"I'm throwing the question back at you, Molly," said Sam, meeting her gaze. "Why don't *you* tell *us* what's going on—if you can?"

She raised her hand to her cheek. "I think what's going on is pretty obvious."

"And I think you've been pretty selfish!"

"What?" she gasped, astounded at his interpretation.

"Sure," said Sam. "You, Molly Porter, still believe in a one-woman show. And to hell with everyone else. You disappear without telling anyone where you're going and cause folks to worry. Folks who care about you. Folks who love you."

Outraged, Molly watched Sam work himself up before she replied. "I don't answer to you!" She brushed her fingers against her cheek. "And just for the record, I didn't do this for you, either!"

"You didn't have to do it for me," he replied, moving closer to her. "I think you're beautiful just the way you are! Or were. There's not a thing wrong with your outside."

But the inside? How dare he open that other wound? "You…you…how could you…?"

Suddenly Sam looked shattered. "I'm sorry. I didn't mean that like it sounded… Oh, hell." He turned to Zach and tossed him a set of car keys. "Take the Beemer. It's a better ride and she'll be more comfortable lying in the back seat. I'll drive her Honda."

Exhausted, Molly fell back against the pillows. But she wasn't quite finished. "I'm not returning to the Bluebonnet till Sunday. I've reserved a room at the Marriott right across the street from the hospital and I intend to use it."

"Smart idea," said Amanda. "We'll all stay and take care of you. I'll find the nurse and check you out of here."

"I'll get her," said Sam, "and then I'll leave you folks to enjoy your visit. I've got a hotel to run in Oak Creek." He walked out the door of the recovery unit, leaving a wall of silence behind.

Amanda spoke first. Gently. "That man is crazy in love with you and you hurt him, Molly."

The accusation was too much. Tears ran down Molly's face; she shook her head back and forth on the pillow. "I hurt him?" she sobbed. "How can you hurt someone who loves you but doesn't want to?"

At her sister's confusion, she added, "He has feelings all right, but not enough. He wants children and I can't give him any." She reached for the ice pack on the adjacent table. "I'm supposed to keep the incision cool. Hot tears do not help." She took a couple of deep breaths and felt calmer. "Everything will be fine," she said. "I'll survive."

The door opened, and Sam walked in with a package and some papers in his hand. He went to the bed and motioned Amanda and Zach to him.

"Here are samples of the antibiotics she needs to

take. Every four hours.'' He looked at Molly. ''Understand?''

''I understand English,'' Molly replied.

Sam glared. ''Leave the steristrips on. The stitches will eventually dissolve. You need to book a follow-up appointment in ten days.'' He thrust the medications and gauzes at Amanda and leaned over Molly. ''And I will take you to that appointment. Do you understand that? You're not driving a six-hour round-trip by yourself.''

''I'm perfectly capable—''

''Sam's making sense, Molly.'' Zach, the man she'd adored since she was born, was a traitor.

''But—''

''No buts,'' said Sam quietly, still leaning over her and touching his mouth to hers as gently as if she were a baby. So sweet. Oh, she'd missed this connection with him during the past week. She pressed her mouth to his, heard his faint groan and felt her entire body relax.

He was not immune to her.

But a minute later he was gone. With her car keys, with warnings about following doctor's orders and with a fond goodbye to her sister and Zach.

''There goes Sam Kincaid,'' Molly said to her family as the door swung shut behind Sam, ''the man who's trying to figure out whether or not he can live without me.''

''Even smart men are stupid when they're in love,'' said Zach.

Was that true? Molly turned to Amanda for her

opinion. But Amanda's eyes were fixed on her husband, along with a smile that could heat up a room on a cold Vermont night.

"Maybe *especially* the smart ones," she said.

Molly grinned. Sam was usually a very smart man.

THERE WERE PEOPLE everywhere, but the hotel seemed empty without Molly. On Saturday morning Sam called Housekeeping. "Gladys, could you arrange for Molly's suite to be cleaned today? I'll take care of the charge as a special request. Thanks. And, by the way, she'll be working a reduced schedule next week... No, she fine. Just some minor surgery... Yeah, pass the word and I'll e-mail everyone. Thanks again."

He checked Molly's schedule to see if he could pinch-hit for any appointments that week, but she'd evidently cleared her calendar.

On Saturday afternoon he called her in Houston, but Molly was sleeping. He spoke with Zach, instead.

"The anesthesia's totally worn off and she's feeling bruised," Zach said. "Amanda and I will stay with her until Wednesday, rather than leave on Monday, but we can't postpone any longer because of the Labor Day holiday coming up. We've been talking about taking Molly home with us for a while."

"No!" Sam said immediately. "I promise she'll be fine here. And she has a doctor's appointment a week from Tuesday."

"Right," said Zach. "I forgot."

Sam sighed with relief, uneasy at the thought of Molly disappearing into the bowels of her family so many miles away. Maybe disappearing forever. She might decide not to return to Texas, even though her contract still had two months to go. He shuddered at the thought of legally forcing Molly to honor the contract. Force was not acceptable, unless he had no choice. The idea worried him until he remembered her response when he kissed her. Nah, he wouldn't have to manipulate her to stay.

"Her timing on this elective surgery could have been better," said Zach. "She's leaving you short-handed before a holiday weekend."

"No problem," said Sam quickly. "My folks will be here and some of the summer help will still be here." The memory of Judy Schneider flashed through his mind.

"Hmm," murmured Zach, "but it's not like her to be so thoughtless. I wonder why she wasn't concerned about the Bluebonnet."

Sam's heart sank. Zach was both astute and absolutely right. Unless she felt severely pressured, Molly would never have done anything to hurt the hotel's operations, including putting herself out of commission.

Sam hung up the phone, knowing that any pressure Molly felt was due to him.

"Were you talking to Molly? How is she?"

Sam raised his head at the sound of his mother's concerned voice. "She sleeping, has some discomfort, but she's fine. That was Zach Porter, her brother-in-law.''

''Funny, they have the same last name.''

''Molly and Zach are also cousins. Molly's dad is Zach's uncle, I think. And Amanda had a different father. Molly explained it to me once.''

His mom sat down across from him, brown eyes twinkling, expression eager. ''Molly is such a lovely girl, isn't she?''

''She sure is.''

''So you think so, too? That's wonderful. She's friendly and smart and pretty…and…whenever Dad and I have come out here, we've both noticed how you look at her.''

He closed his eyes. Just what he needed. An interfering mother. ''Yeah?''

''Yes, Sam. You look at her all the time.''

A chance to tease his mom. ''Well, we work together a lot.''

Irene shook her head and leaned forward. ''No, no. You look at her in a certain way. A special way.''

''I do?'' His mother, the diplomat. ''Mom,'' he whispered, his voice full of drama, ''do you know something I don't?''

She caught on. ''Oh, go away with you. I just want you to be happy and Molly's so…so… perfect.''

Almost perfect. ''She is the kind of girl that many men could fall in love with,'' he replied slowly, waiting to hear what his mom would say, his need to tease evaporating.

"That's right," said Irene, standing up now. "Many men could definitely be attracted to her, so don't wait too long." She leaned closer. "And, Sam, I've seen the way she looks at *you*. I'm not blind."

"And what do you see?" He held his breath, not knowing why.

His mom grinned. "She thinks you're pretty special, too. Definitely special. That girl has good taste." She reached up and kissed his cheek. "Dad and I love you, Sam. Your happiness is everything to us."

He wrapped Irene in a gentle hug and kissed the top of her head. "I know, Mom, I know."

He stared at the doorway long after his mother left the office. She thought Molly was perfect. "But you'll never have a grandchild, Mom," he whispered. "You'll never be blessed with what you long for."

SUNDAY AFTERNOON Molly glanced at the assembled mass—Amanda, Zach, Irene, George and Sam—keeping her company while she reclined on the couch in her suite at the Bluebonnet. The only reason she was on the couch was because everyone forced her to be.

"I feel like a princess on display," said Molly, "a princess with an aching face!"

"You're a beautiful princess." Irene glanced at Amanda as though for support.

"She sure is," replied Amanda.

Molly groaned. "I wish the kids were here. They'd distract everyone from me."

"Distract? You mean they'd drive us all crazy!" said Amanda. "But it's funny how I miss them even after only a few days."

Molly looked at Sam. "Rachel and Marc are the best children in the world. Funny, adventurous, and they ski like poetry in motion."

"Just like their aunt," said Zach.

She glared at him. "Just like their father."

"Coward," he replied. "The hills are waiting."

His eyes felt like a spotlight searching her face. She'd kill him. "Break your own leg," she said.

"Wait a minute. Just a minute," interrupted Sam, looking from Molly to Zach. "Am I missing something here?"

"Not a thing," Molly replied. "He gets a kick out of torturing me."

"I do not." Zach looked from her to Sam and held Sam's gaze. "She thinks if it's not for a gold medal, it's not worth doing. Can't understand that people take pure pleasure in the sport."

"Of course I understand!" Molly retorted. "In fact, Sam's going to take me skiing, aren't you?" She waved her arm at him for emphasis, hoping he remembered.

Zach pivoted toward Sam, a grin covering his face. "You are? That's great. Where? Colorado?"

"Not quite," he replied. "We're going waterskiing. Whenever Molly's ready."

"Waterskiing?" Molly saw Zach's forehead crease in thought. "I suppose it's a start," he finally said, "but it sure doesn't compare to a five-thousand-foot run or even a five-hundred footer."

Molly watched Zach approach. She wished she was standing eye to eye with him.

"Picabo Street, one of the best in the world, got back up after a severe break and skied an Olympic run. You can ski the bunny hill," he said.

"That's enough, Zach. Leave her alone." Amanda's voice.

Molly looked at her sister, saw her biting her bottom lip, saw the uncertainty on her face and knew that she herself had made the right choice. Coming to Texas was her salvation. Being with her family caused rifts and anxiety.

"Molly's not a coward." Sam stepped next to her and reached for her hand. "This gal has ridden seventy-mile-an-hour roller coasters and five-mile-an-hour horses. She's organized last minute feasts, handled an eighteen-year-old wannabe superstar with anxious parents and won over an entire staff of employees who think they run the hotel. My uncle, a man who spent his life building the Bluebonnet, had complete confidence in her. Molly's made friends all over town. And she's only been here four months. I'd say she's pretty amazing. Wouldn't you?"

Molly felt the impact of his hot glance before he glared at Zach. She watched the two men's silent battle.

"Absolutely," Zach finally replied. "She's truly amazing. And I think I can return to Vermont with a peaceful mind."

"I'm just glad Pops isn't here," said Amanda.

"You mean, there's another one like him back at the Diamond?" asked Sam, nodding at Zach.

Suddenly tears filled Molly's eyes as she thought of her loving dad. "Not exactly," she replied, her voice trembling. "Daddy thinks his girls are perfect. He thinks that neither of us can do any wrong, while Zach calls it as he sees it."

"Fathers," explained Amanda, "are not the same as husbands or brothers."

"That's because husbands expect more," Zach said.

"Well, this husband," drawled George Kincaid, breaking into the conversation, "thinks his wife is absolutely perfect! So there goes your theory right up in smoke." He put his arm around Irene and kissed her on the cheek.

To Molly's delight, everyone burst out in applause, and she relaxed against the cushions.

She wasn't perfect, and she didn't have to prove anything to Zach. Or to Sam. The only one she had to satisfy was herself. George and Irene were as wonderful together as her own mom and dad. And if husbands expected perfection, well, she didn't need a husband.

CHAPTER TWELVE

SAM WATCHED MOLLY hide her third yawn behind her hand as she lay on the couch. He nodded at her relatives. "Come on. I'll give you a tour of the hotel while our patient snoozes. With your focus on Molly, you haven't seen any of it yet."

"Good idea," Molly agreed. "Make sure you show Amanda the gardens." She looked at her brother-in-law. "And, Zach, if you're really nice to Sam, maybe he'll cast his eagle eye over the Diamond Ridge Web site and fix it up. He's really good at that stuff." Another yawn cut her off, and her eyes closed, then opened. "Good Lord, it's only the afternoon and I'm tired."

"You've had surgery, girl," said Sam as he walked toward her. He bent down and kissed her briefly on the lips. "Even an outpatient procedure takes a toll. Get some sleep. Mom and Dad will mind the store while I roam the halls with Amanda and Zach."

He made his way to the door and opened it. "The tour is beginning. Let's go."

He didn't know what to expect from Zach as they strolled through the Bluebonnet. Perhaps a few questions about the hotel's history, perhaps some observations on the decor or even some curiosity about the guests. What he got was an interrogation rivaling that of the Spanish Inquisition. But it wasn't hard to see Zach's increasing enthusiasm.

"You've got a sweet operation here, Sam. Great facility, great property. The Bluebonnet is physically different from the Diamond, yet the atmosphere is similar. Maybe it's the guests. They're smiling, happy, busy. Just like ours are."

"All Molly's doing," Sam replied easily. "So you can take credit, I guess. She grew up at Diamond Ridge."

"But it's your business," said Zach. "Your show."

Sam shook his head. "I may own it," he said, "but it's Molly's show until I sell it."

Zach stared at him in disbelief. "Sell it? You're not thinking clearly. People would kill for this operation. I don't get it."

The genuine amazement on Zach's face started Sam laughing. "You and Molly sure are related. Hotels must be in your blood."

"Maybe," Zach replied. "My uncle and I built the Diamond from nothing. Year after year we improved it."

"I can understand that," said Sam. "My aunt and uncle did the same here. But I don't feel the way they did. Sure, I have a soft spot in my heart for the Bluebonnet because of happy memories, but running it doesn't excite me. And before devoting a lifetime of work to something, I think a person should be exited. Don't you?''

Not expecting or receiving an answer, he led Zach and Amanda to his office and logged onto the Internet. ''What's your Web-site address?''

Moments later strains of ''Winter Wonderland'' filled the room as Sam studied the Diamond Ridge home page. ''Pretty,'' he said, nodding at a picture of the ski resort covered in snow, ''but consider getting rid of the music. Most site users are annoyed by music that automatically downloads.'' Then he explored the site. And didn't say anything else.

''So,'' Zach said a few minutes later. ''What do you think?''

Sam rotated his chair so he could see Zach's expression. ''The truth?''

Zach nodded.

''The site's not compelling enough and you're losing potential customers.''

Zach's eyes widened, then blazed. ''I'm paying a monthly fee to a designer to maintain our site. We need a strong presence on the Web.''

Sam pressed a few keys and the Bluebonnet's home page came alive. ''Sit down,'' he invited as he rose from the chair. ''I've recently reworked our site. Browse. You'll see the difference.''

Sam waited while Zach explored. Amanda stood behind her husband, looking over his shoulder.

''Jeez,'' she said. ''We have lots of pictures, but Sam has a lot of interaction with the visitors. He's got a contest for winning a weekend here in the fall and he's posting weekly activities."

"We needed to increase business," Sam said, "and the Web site is a relatively inexpensive way to do it. We're also linked to many related sites from the local Chamber of Commerce to national hotel associations, travel agencies and the state tourism department. I want visitors to return to the site, so I try to tempt them with new happenings. At some point I'm betting they'll book a stay with us. It does seem to be working. Business is actually picking up."

"Why do you care, if you're going to sell?" asked Zach. He still looked disturbed by the idea.

"I'm not a hotelier," said Sam, "but I am a businessman."

"And a Web-site designer," said Amanda.

Sam smiled. "Software engineer and business manager. This is just a sideline."

"So you play with computers while Molly runs the hotel," Zach said thoughtfully. "Well, how about taking on a new customer?"

"No problem and no charge," Sam replied. "Not to Molly's family."

Amanda looked at her husband with a grin. "This one's a keeper."

Zach leaned back in the chair until his gray eyes held Sam's. "That remains to be seen."

Sam understood the message. *Don't hurt Molly.* He didn't need the warning. The thought of ever hurting her made his stomach roil. And yet he couldn't swear he wouldn't. He clenched his jaw, impatient with himself. Why couldn't he just relax and follow his heart?

TWO WEEKS LATER Sam picked up the ringing phone in his office. He'd just come in from admiring the foundation of the new Oak Creek Technology Center, and his mind was racing ahead to all the appointments he'd made over the next several weeks. Most were revisits with potential computer-training clients.

"Sam Kincaid speaking," he said into the phone.

"Hello, Sam. This is Bob Allen. I got your name from Jeff Rosen. I believe you're doing some software design for him."

Sam smiled. Jeff was one of Travis's friends. "Sure, and I'm still at it. How can I help you?"

"I own a small chain of bookstores, fifteen of them, spread between Texas and Oklahoma. I need an inventory-control program that does what *I* want it to do."

Sam listened as Bob explained his ideas.

"I can do the work," Sam responded, "but isn't this town loaded with tech folks? There must be dozens of established design firms you could call."

"I did make some calls. Frankly, the big guys don't have time for little fish like me," said Bob good-naturedly. "I'd have to wait quite a while to get results. So when Jeff heard about my experience, he suggested I call you."

Interesting, Sam thought as he hung up the phone

a minute later. The big firms were getting major projects, leaving a niche in the marketplace for smaller ones. Suddenly his breath caught. Realization dawned. Whether he'd planned to or not, he had become part of the local business community—the technology branch.

The total amount of work he'd taken on separate from the hotel was enormous. Not only was he establishing the Oak Creek Tech Center by handling the major sales effort, planning the facility and recruiting backers, he was now also a software designer for clients in a variety of industries. Seemed he was filling a niche in the area, maybe more than one. A long, low whistle escaped his lips. In essence he was being himself, with fingers in a lot of pies.

The door flew open and Sam was jolted from his thoughts. Molly stood on the threshold, excitement radiating from every inch of her, but especially from her knockout smile.

"We've done it, Sam!" She rushed in and shoved something at him. "Look at this spreadsheet. Look at those numbers. We are booked and overbooked for every weekend through Thanksgiving. If my figures are correct, the Bluebonnet's business is going to improve by approximately twenty-five percent."

Her smile captivated him.

"I think we've equaled any growth spurt Zach and my dad ever managed. I'm going to call them."

He didn't care about comparisons. "You're beautiful."

A flush spread over her face, and she laughed.

"Sure, I am. It's the profits that are beautiful. You'll be able to sell the hotel sooner than you thought." Her words slowed and a crease appeared in her forehead. "And I don't know why I'm so happy about it."

"That's easy. It's because you like success. Because you're a pro and you've proved it."

The corners of her mouth turned up again. "Yes. I guess I did. A great accomplishment for my résumé when the time comes."

Her résumé! His heart twisted. When he sold the hotel, she'd be looking for a job. He watched her head for the door and didn't want her to go. "Mol...let's celebrate your success." Sam stood up and walked toward her. "How about our waterskiing date?"

She stared at him until he thought she wasn't going to answer. Then she whispered. "Date? I don't think so. Not a good idea." She waved and left the room.

MOLLY LECTURED HERSELF as she returned to her office. It wasn't Sam's fault her heart was breaking. He'd never promised anything. Never said he loved her. Never misled her. In fact, he seemed to be very conscious of *not* misleading her.

But if *her* heart was broken, *his* must be splintered. The situation was almost funny. He sought her out constantly. They dined together almost every night. He'd taken her to the doctor's office in Houston and asked the surgeon a million questions.

But most important, his eyes devoured her whenever he thought she wasn't looking. And on the occasions when he kissed her good-night, she thought they'd both melt. Sam usually took a step back, breathing hard, dark eyes tortured. Trying to be honorable.

She almost felt sorry for him. Almost. But not enough to help him out, not enough to invite him inside. That privilege would come later when Sam finally woke up. *If* he woke up.

Molly sighed. Sam loved her. He showed it in every way. Too bad his heart and his brain weren't in sync yet. She tossed her papers onto the desk and stretched. She needed a break. Maybe she'd visit the Miller ranch later and take a riding lesson from Liz. Or maybe she, Carla and Liz could go to a movie that evening. She reached for the phone just as a quick knock at her door announced a visitor.

She looked up, then grinned. "Well, thinking of the devil." Molly walked around her desk to greet Carla with a hug. "My hand was on the receiver to call you. How about a girls' night out tonight?"

The svelte redhead paused, then stepped aside and placed her hand on the back of the visitor's chair before answering. "Actually," she said, her voice slow and husky, "I'm here to talk about a wedding."

"A wedding?" Molly repeated, motioning Carla to sit down and wondering if one of Carla's friends wanted to use the hotel for the occasion. "Sounds like fun. Whose? And when?"

"Well…a lot has happened in the past month between Travis and me." Carla's glance swept the floor, the ceiling, the windows before finally settling on Molly.

"Whom did you say?" Molly stared into Carla's green eyes, the normal emerald lights now a dark-forest shade. The knuckles of her hand were white as she clutched the edge of Molly's desk. Then she seemed to get a grip on herself, leaned back and flexed her fingers.

"Here's a confession you'll find hard to believe." Carla looked away for a moment, then met Molly's glance again. "I've loved Travis for years. My sister knew that, of course, and then did what she always did— Oh, sometimes men are so dumb!" She stared at her hands, her voice dropping as she mused.

"I'm sorry, Carla—" Molly began.

But the other woman interrupted. "Well, my sister's not important now," she said. "Not anymore. Travis and I… God, Molly, I've loved him for so long! He…he's been confused, distrustful. So in recent times, I've focused only on my sweet little niece. Amy's my only family and I'll do whatever I have to do to be part of her life."

"But you *are* part of her life," said Molly. "You don't have to marry Travis in order to see Amy."

A luminous smile inched across Carla's face. "But, Molly, I *want* to marry him. He's allowed me to push my way into Amy's life without even having a court order. My visits are at Travis's will. I moved to Texas on the chance that he'd be decent about it, and in the end, he has been—most of the time. Sure, he's made me sweat at times, but in his heart he knows I love Amy. And that I'm not my sister.''

"He's made you sweat," Molly echoed, "and yet you love him."

"I do," Carla reaffirmed quietly. "He's a wonderful father, Molly. And the qualities I admired years ago are still there—tarnished by experience, of course, but still there waiting to be polished again."

Molly studied her friend. She'd seen Carla in many roles, in many moods—conducting business, playing and laughing with Amy, volunteering for community events, dancing with Travis—but she'd never seen high-energy Carla so subdued and serious. "And he's asked you to marry him?"

"Yes. Oh, yes."

"So he's not confused anymore? Not distrustful?" Molly probed.

"I didn't say that! He so desperately wants a relationship he can count on." Carla got up, strolled to the window and gazed out at the gardens. "I've thought about it until my head hurts. I've always loved him and I know he's not indifferent to me! And the bare facts are that if I don't make a move, one day Travis will marry again, and my presence in Amy's life might become incidental or inconvenient." She turned from the window. "I won't let that happen, Molly. And it's not just for my sake, but for Amy's. Isn't she entitled to know her mom's only sister? Her mom's only living relative?"

Molly heard the passion in Carla's voice, but said nothing. Her friend wasn't finished yet.

"Not every courtship follows the same rules. I may have had to light his fire, but I think he may come to love me."

Molly laughed. "One look at you would light any man's fire!"

"Pooh. Everyone's taste is not the same," replied Carla. "But Travis—his taste suits me just fine."

"So," said Molly, trying to be diplomatic, even though her thoughts were spinning, "would you like to tell me how this all came about? The proposal, I mean."

"You know," replied Carla, wrinkling her forehead, "I'm not quite sure. But two nights ago when I was at the ranch, Travis said something... something like, 'Amy needs a mother and you might as well marry me.' I must have agreed."

Carla seemed both confused and amazed as she recalled the evening, and Molly started to chuckle as she pictured the scene. "You know what I think?" she said. "I think Travis might have surprised himself, as well as you, but now he's got you right where he wants you! Don't you see it? Amy may have started out as the catalyst, but she wound up as the bait—God only knows how a man's mind works—but in the end, Travis made sure you'd marry him. Oh, Carla! Who trapped whom? You'll have a great future, my friend, and I'll be happy to help with the wedding!"

Molly couldn't stop laughing at the redhead's expression. She pointed at her. "He caught you, Carla. Not you, him. Maybe not fair and square, but he did it."

She didn't hear Sam approach until his voice rang out. "Is this a private party or can anyone join?"

Molly motioned him in.

Carla still stared at Molly. "You mean that man had me worried about Amy for nothing? I'll murder him!"

"No, you won't," said Molly firmly. "You'll love him. And he'll love you." She turned to Sam, who looked totally puzzled. "Carla and Travis are getting married."

A wide grin split Sam's face. "Heck, it was only a matter of time. Anyone could see that."

Molly stared at Sam, amazed at his insight.

"He just wants a mother for Amy," Carla explained.

"Shoot, girl!" said Sam. "He's got Liz right at the house to act as a mother and his own mom, as well. A built-in grandma if that's all he wanted. Nah, he wants you!"

"But what if there were no Amy?" Carla's question sliced the air, her unexpected anxiety surfacing. "Would he...would he..."

"The man's head over heels in love with you," Sam retorted. "He can't even speak coherently when you're around. He loves you with or without a child. It doesn't matter to him. And that's the way it should be between a man and a woman."

Molly's breath caught in her throat as his words

registered. Did he realize what he was saying? She looked at him and caught a surprised expression, before a tiny smile appeared. And then a grin.

She forced herself to concentrate on Carla again, watched her friend blush, a soft radiance in her expression. She couldn't resist continuing Sam's thought and revealing the heart of the matter. "Amy was just a convenience, Carla. You both used her as an excuse to be part of each other's lives."

She had some satisfaction when Carla hung her head.

"Well, maybe I did, but it was unconscious!"

"And what would you have done about Amy if you had no feelings for Travis at all?" asked Molly.

"I would have fought for court-ordered visitation rights."

"Atta girl." Molly looked at Sam. "Call Travis and congratulate him. Then let's all go out to celebrate and plan a wedding."

"All right," Sam replied softly, but he didn't move, just kept his eyes on Molly.

"What's the matter?" asked Molly. "Are you okay?"

"I think I'm going to be very okay. I just need a little time to get my house in order."

SHORT STEP. LONG STEP. Short step. Long step. Sam gently clasped Molly's arm and paced himself as he escorted her down the aisle at Carla and Travis's wedding. It was a beautiful Sunday in mid-October. A month had flown by since the announcement of the marriage, and now an intimate number of guests were seated in the autumn sunshine on the back lawn of the Bluebonnet, watching the best man and the maid of honor pave the way for the bride and groom.

Sam glanced at Molly and almost lost his breath. Her blue eyes sparkled, her smile dazzled, and her skin looked so smooth he had to check twice to detect her scar. As usual, he felt energy and warmth radiate from her. She made him laugh. She made him think. She argued with him and drove him crazy.

And he loved her.

His breath whooshed from his lungs. A weight lifted from his shoulders. The feeling had been growing for months and suddenly he had the urge to shout it to the world. Real love felt fantastic, not like the habit he'd fallen into with Adrienne. He wanted to spend his life with Molly! They might develop some routines, but he'd never be bored.

He looked at Travis waiting for his bride and pictured himself waiting for Molly before clergy. Oh, yes! Wonderful thought.

He and Molly had reached the flower-strewn gazebo where the ceremony would be held. He leaned over and kissed her lightly on the cheek. Then on the mouth. Her eyes widened. The kisses had been unplanned, not part of the rehearsal.

"Will you be okay?" he whispered, about to leave her. He had to stand on the other side of the aisle and couldn't support her if her leg ached during the next half hour.

"Just fine," she replied, giving him a warm glance before nodding at the empty front-row seats. "Don't worry. There's a Plan B."

He squeezed her hand and took his place, but his mind never left her. He was going to pop the question, but not tonight in the midst of their friends' wedding. He'd take no chance of Molly thinking he'd been carried away by the beauty of the occasion. He wanted their moment to be special. Maybe on top of a Ferris wheel or during a roller-coaster ride. Of course, she hadn't gone out with him on a real date since her surgery. What if she said no? What if she didn't love him? What if he'd waited too long?

His hands started to sweat, and his mouth became dry. He inhaled deeply and tried to calm down. He wouldn't think that way; he hadn't waited too long. No, that smile she gave him—it was special.

He glanced at the woman he loved and wanted to kidnap her right then and there. Love is everything, he thought. If he told Molly how much he loved her, all would be well.

He heard a titter run through the crowd and looked back up the pathway to where Amy tossed rose petals in front of her as she walked toward her dad. The child was the image of her aunt. Travis's family circle would be complete, hopefully this time with a happier ending.

In the meantime, Sam and Molly would create

their own world. Maybe they'd adopt. Maybe they
wouldn't. It didn't matter to him anymore. As long
as he had Molly.

The music changed and once again he looked toward the back of the aisle. And there stood Carla,
in a simple white gown and light veil. Smart lady.
With her height and coloring, she didn't need anything more. Sam grinned as he studied the figure
next to her. Carla had no family, so Sam's dad was
giving Carla away. In fact, George had felt honored
to be asked. In a town like Oak Creek, the community pulled together.

SAM HADN'T LEFT HER alone all evening, and now
he wanted to dance again. Something had happened
to him in the past few hours. Molly didn't know
exactly what it was, but she liked it.

She moved into his arms as though she'd spent
her lifetime there.

"Ah, Molly, Molly," he murmured against her
neck as she followed his lead. He held her firmly
around the waist and she felt both secure and comfortable.

"You're beautiful, Mol," he said.

"Thank you. And have you had one too many?"

"No way." His voice was indignant. "I've had
one vodka-and-tonic and one beer. You've been by
my side almost every minute, so you know it's the
truth." He leaned in and whispered, "Do you think
I have to be intoxicated to tell you you're beautiful?"

"Well, so are you." She dimpled.

"Maybe you've had one too many," he teased. "Men are not beautiful."

"So you're handsome."

"You think?"

She grinned. "Definitely. Tall, dark and handsome. And very attentive."

"My pleasure. I love having you in my arms like this. I love dancing with you."

Love. Why was he using that word without really meaning it? Suddenly Molly didn't feel like bantering anymore, but Sam was still talking.

"I need to see you tomorrow night. It's important."

Molly heard no laughter in his voice. Seems he wasn't kidding around anymore, either. "Sure," she said. "What's going on? And if it's so important, what's wrong with tonight?"

"Tomorrow's better," Sam replied. "Just block out the time. I know how in demand you are around here, so we'll need to go out. Just you and I. Away from the hotel. To someplace special. Very, very special."

He didn't sound tipsy anymore; he sounded intense. And he looked intense, with his eyes blazing into hers. Molly couldn't look away. She followed his lead on the dance floor as if in a dream. There was a promise in his eyes. A promise she wanted him to keep.

She smiled slowly at him and immediately felt his arms tighten around her. He may have had some plans for tomorrow evening, but she was thinking about tonight.

She'd been patient while he digested the news about her reproductive disabilities. She'd had to be realistic and give him the time he needed. Sure, deep in her heart she'd hoped Sam would have pooh-poohed her problem and said children didn't matter to him as long as he had her, but she was practical enough to know that kids did matter. So she'd gambled. What was she losing except time? What was she chancing except…a broken heart?

The familiar fragrance of his cologne made her tingle. Maybe, just maybe, her gamble had paid off. She closed her eyes and leaned against Sam's broad chest, absorbing his strength. She was exactly where she wanted to be.

The music changed and Molly heard Judy Schneider's beautiful voice singing a special love song for the bride and groom. Molly glanced at the young singer and sighed contentedly. Judy's easy commute provided her with a chance to work weekend gigs at the Bluebonnet or at the many clubs Austin boasted. Her life seemed to be working out just fine. Then Molly glanced at Carla and Travis. Despite a topsy-turvy start, their lives together should work out fine, too.

So that left her. And Sam.

She reached up and stroked the shell of his ear and heard him inhale. "If you lean a little closer," she whispered, "I'll puff gently on it."

Now she heard him groan.

"If I lean a little closer, I won't be responsible for my actions," Sam growled before his lips found hers.

Her arms wound around his neck as she melted into his kiss. His tongue traced her lips and she shivered; then he covered her mouth hungrily and she burned. Cold and hot. Hot and cold. Crazy! He invaded her mouth and she met his thrusts eagerly, blindly. "Do you want to get out of here?" she whispered when she could catch her breath.

"More than you know," Sam replied.

She took his hand. "Let's go."

He didn't budge, just nodded at the crowd. "Just inhale and exhale," he whispered, "like I'm doing. And we'll get through the moment." Then Sam winked. "Damned glad these tuxedo pants are roomy."

Molly's eyes jumped to the spot, and Sam hustled her into another dance. "They're not *that* roomy." He laughed. "Keep looking there and I *will* have to excuse myself."

Molly felt the heat travel to her ears. But she was having fun. And had more to look forward to—with Sam. Alone with Sam...

Alone and intimate. And naked. And he'd never seen her in a pair of shorts.

"How about taking a midnight swim later?" Molly whispered.

Perhaps her scars would be easier to accept under the cover of darkness. A step-by-step approach.

"One small problem," said Sam as he kissed her

temple and continued to dance her slowly around the floor. "We have no pool."

Right. What was she thinking? Historic restrictions. "How about the lake? We could go to the lake."

"Sweetheart, the only water I anticipate is a cold shower before the evening's over. And if I keep kissing you like this—" he demonstrated "—we might wind up taking one together."

"Together?" Her voice squeaked and a wave of panic traveled through her. "But you've never seen my leg." She blurted the words, unable to follow through on her graduated approach.

"Molly!" He paused in midstep, staring at her, his eyes reflecting his hurt. "Please give me some credit. Do you think I care about old scars when I've got you alive and well and in one piece?" He pulled her close. "The topic's closed. Now be quiet and dance with me."

But she couldn't move. She just held Sam and felt tears run down her cheeks. She buried her face in his chest.

"Ah, Molly," he whispered, "don't cry. You're the most wonderful and beautiful woman in the world. And I love all of those things about you."

She snuggled closer, enjoying his words and the kisses he bestowed on her forehead and cheek.

"The accident's history," he continued in a quiet but firm voice, "so put it behind you. And look ahead to the future."

She peeped up at him from under her lashes.

"That's what I thought I was doing ever since I got to Texas," she said, a bubble of laughter coming through with her words. "But it's great to hear we're on the same wavelength."

"You're an idiot, Mol," Sam said. "And so am I. A while ago, I was scared to death you'd run back north with Amanda and Zach."

"You were?" She'd had no idea.

"Sure," he admitted. "Zach suggested it and I said no."

"And he listened?"

"I didn't give him much choice." Sam took a breath. "I was buying time, Molly. Now tell me, was I wrong?"

Wrong? Molly looked into the eyes of the man she loved, eyes that warmed, then heated, as he stared back at her. She shook her head. "No," she said softly. "You were very right."

He captured her mouth again, gently this time. "Thank you," he whispered between kisses.

"Hey, none of that stuff when I've come to claim my dance with the maid of honor."

Molly pivoted at the sound of Travis's voice, then grinned.

"He's right," said Carla, standing beside her groom. "This is our party. We're the ones who are allowed to kiss all the time."

Sam folded his arms and mockingly complained to Molly. "No fair. They just want to have all the fun."

"Come on, Molly," said Travis, reaching for her. "Let's dance."

Molly watched Sam immediately put his hand on Travis's arm and stop the other man from leaving with her. "You be careful out there, my friend. Molly's special."

Travis nodded, his smile lingering. "She's sure been a special friend to us. And to you, too! Don't look so concerned, buddy. I know how to hold a lady. I won't drop her."

Molly caught Carla's glance and threw up her hands. "The music's changing while they're discussing my fate. Come on, girlfriend, let's show them how it's done!"

Rock. Fast rock. And Molly felt the beat as much as anyone there. She stood facing Carla. "I don't know how this is going to end. I may wind up face-down on the floor, but I want to dance."

"Go for it, girl. The worst that can happen is that we'll all think you're drunk!"

Molly giggled, planted her feet and started her hip action. She could do that much. She looked around. The floor was crowded and she was just one more guest having a good time.

Arm action next. All right! Out in front, then over her head. Lord, she hadn't danced to rock and roll in more than four years. And it felt so darn good. So normal.

She glanced at Carla and saw her friend's gaze shift to somewhere behind her shoulder. "What?" she shouted over the loud music.

"Sam." Carla shouted back.

Molly chuckled, then shrugged. This dancing wasn't about Sam. It was about her. Suddenly she stopped thinking. She stopped focusing. Great ice skaters were trained to "skate dumb." She now let her body "dance dumb." No thinking allowed.

Instead of using heavy foot action, she leaned and shimmied from the waist. Carla danced around her, while Molly changed position by quarter-turns. And every time she turned, Sam was there. Dancing by himself.

She finally waved him in. "Come on," she invited. "You, too," she called to Travis who was politely hovering and dancing behind Carla. The groom lost no time joining them.

Molly looked around the room, then imagined the rest of the hotel. The Bluebonnet was in full operation—private parties, tourists, business guests—the works. Just like a hotel should be. She was not too modest to recognize that much of the credit was due to her.

An hour later she was still feeling the euphoria as Sam walked her to her suite. "I don't think I could have danced all night," she said very matter-of-factly, "but I had a great time. A wonderful time!"

"I know," said Sam dryly. "In fact, we all know."

Molly giggled.

They reached her door and Sam pulled her close. "I had a wonderful time, too." He leaned down and kissed her, slowly, thoroughly.

She shivered, desire for him coursing through her. She tightened her hold on him, wanting to stay forever in his arms. And when he kissed her again, crushing her to him, she knew she'd found her future. Wherever it might be.

"Molly, Molly, lovely Molly," Sam murmured.

She looked into his dark eyes, full of desire, hot for her. "Want to come in?" she whispered.

CHAPTER THIRTEEN

THE AIR STILLED; waves of silence pulsed against Molly's ears, drowning out any other sound.

"Hell, yes! I want to come in," Sam said in a strained voice. "I want to touch every inch of you. I want to learn every inch of you. But not tonight. I want no misunderstandings the morning after."

Molly startled. Wasn't that usually the woman's concern?

He must have seen her confusion. "Too much wedding," said Sam, waving his arm in the direction where the party had taken place. "Save tomorrow night for me."

The longing she saw in his face left no doubt of his veracity. "How about a cup of tea?" she offered, reluctant to end their evening.

"Do you want to kill me?" Sam's whisper was determined. His hands clenched into fists at his sides, and Molly suddenly understood that in front of her stood an honorable man. A throwback to an earlier time? An old-fashioned Texas cowboy? She thought of Sam's dad, and her hypothesis made sense. A touch of gallantry was inherent in George.

And the honorable man now facing her needed her cooperation.

She placed her fingers gently over his mouth. "Let's just say good-night, and we'll make tomorrow evening ours." Then she crossed the threshold into her suite.

"Wait," said Sam. He stepped forward, kissed her once more—fast and hard—then turned and walked down the hall.

Molly closed the door behind her and leaned against it for support. Sam had a way of keeping her off balance. She finally turned the key, locking herself in, and changed into her comfortable cotton nightshirt. She meandered through the small apartment, unable to sleep despite the late hour until she spotted her old video on the night table. Without hesitating, she inserted it into the VCR and stretched out on the living-room couch. Then she pressed the "start" button on the remote.

There was the snow, the American and Olympic flags. The sign displaying Lake Placid's name. The voice-over announcing the date and the practice run. There was her old friend, Julie Martin. A great run. Julie had never thought she was as good as she really was. And when she'd taken the bronze that year, she'd credited Molly for her increased confidence. Molly had scanned the papers many weeks later, but had never gotten in touch with the other girl.

Out of the start house came the next skier, her long blond hair whipping behind her. On the couch, Molly watched, dry-eyed. Her heart beat steadily and for the first time, the woman on the screen seemed like someone else. For the first time, Molly watched the disaster unfold with a critical eye as though she was watching a stranger. She stopped the action, started it, adjusted the film to slow motion.

"The speed, the ice and the edges," she murmured. "I guess it wasn't my day." She clicked the video off and stood up smiling. "But who cares now?" She spread her arms and twirled around. "I'm alive! And I'm in love! And I have a new career! And a great life!"

Molly paused in her glee. "What do you know?" she said out loud. "I've got it all."

WHEN SHE AWOKE from a dreamless sleep the next morning, Molly was still smiling. She stretched lazily. A wonderful day beckoned, with the promise of an unforgettable evening to top it off. She rolled to her side and glanced at the clock radio on the end table. Her lethargy vanished. It was after ten and she was late.

She scrambled out of bed, hopped into a quick shower and put on one of her usual long-skirt-and-blouse ensembles. She gathered her hair into a ponytail at the nape of her neck and didn't bother with makeup. The hell with the surgical scar; it was much fainter than the original one, anyway.

She snatched her purse from the living room, slipped on her sensible, sturdy shoes and let herself out the door. The newlyweds had the luxury of sleeping the day away, but Molly was a working girl with a hotel to run.

She mentally ticked off the tasks waiting for her as she made her way across the front lobby toward the administrative office wing. Some guests were in the process of checking out. Molly made her way toward them, shook hands and chatted about their stay at the Bluebonnet. She listened to their comments, happy to hear their praises, but noting any items that needed improvement.

"Safe trip home," she called as the couples made their way to the door. "And come back and see us again."

"We will, Molly. We had a great time here."

"I'm so glad," replied Molly as she waved them goodbye.

She was about to resume her trek, but paused again, content to observe new guests checking in. Good. Just the way it should be. A revolving door that maintained high occupancy rates.

The clerk behind the front desk motioned her over.

"Morning," said Molly walking toward the desk.

"Good morning. Sam's cell phone is off. Do you know where he is?"

Molly shook her head. "But it was a late night. Maybe he's still sleeping."

"Sam never had trouble with late nights before," said a sultry voice next to Molly, "and I doubt he's changed."

Molly spun around. A young Elizabeth Taylor

look-alike stood before her, stunning with violet eyes and thick, wavy hair as dark as ebony. Her complexion was porcelain pale and smooth. She didn't need cosmetics, but she'd used them to glorious effect. As for the rest of her, the woman bloomed with pregnancy. Glowed with it. In short, Molly had never seen a more beautiful woman.

"Welcome to the Bluebonnet," said Molly warmly, after catching her breath. "Do you know Sam?"

The woman's demure smile told its own story without words, but she replied, "We're old friends."

Molly nodded. "I'll try to track him down. Is he expecting you?"

"Actually," said the woman, "I'm about the last person he expects to see. I knew Sam in California and I'm surprising him."

Molly smiled. "That should be fun, but I'm afraid I didn't get your name."

"Adrienne Burke," said the brunette. "But just tell him a friend is here."

Click. Click. Click. The name sounded familiar. "No problem," said Molly. "Would you like to sit down and wait or are you checking in?"

"Oh, I'll definitely be checking in—a suite, perhaps, on the ground floor would be best."

With raised brows, Molly looked over at the desk clerk, who was busy punching computer keys. The clerk nodded and asked, "How long will you be staying, Ms. Burke?"

Adrienne paused, then patted her stomach. "I'm not quite sure. But the sooner I'm gone, the better."

The clerk looked at Molly.

"An indefinite stay," Molly said before meeting Adrienne's eyes. "We'll do everything to make your stay comfortable, but we have only one suite on this floor. We may have to move you if it's been reserved before you leave."

"I doubt Sam would do that," Adrienne replied easily. "But don't worry about rearranging someone else's room. Your job won't be in jeopardy."

After her initial surprise, Molly almost laughed at the remark, but turned away before Adrienne could see her grin. Sam and Adrienne may have been old friends, but it was obvious they hadn't spoken in quite a while.

"Sam's a very fair person." Molly glanced over her shoulder and kept a straight face.

"Excuse me," said the clerk. "How many will be checking into the suite?"

"Oh, I'm alone," Adrienne replied.

The clerk smiled and continued to punch keys.

"You know," Molly said, "I think you've got a great idea. A last vacation before the baby takes up all your time. Wonder why more people don't do it."

"No," replied Adrienne. "It's more like my last stop to freedom."

That was an odd way to put it. Molly studied the woman for a moment. "I'll track Sam down while you get settled in."

"Good," Adrienne replied. "But remember, I'd like to surprise him. No names, please. I'd appreciate that."

Molly nodded. It was no business of hers if an old friend wanted to surprise Sam. Even if the woman was stunning. And pregnant.

After checking Sam's office to no avail, Molly started toward the construction site. Despite the nature of her errand, she paused briefly on the patio to note the seasonal garden array she so enjoyed. Marigolds aplenty—she knew their names now—and red zinnias. White-and-purple petunias, and snapdragons in yellow, pink and orange. All were part of the fall display. Autumn flowers in Texas had to be cultivated, while in New England, Mother Nature worked alone to produce the magnificent foliage.

Molly struck out on the path and made a beeline for the half-finished building through the trees, and sure enough, Sam was standing in front. His arms were crossed on his chest and he was looking up at the structure.

"Hi," she called.

He turned at the sound of her voice, his eyes sparkling their welcome, along with his smile. Molly reached him and received a kiss as naturally as if they'd greeted each other that way every morning.

He put his arm around her. "Look at the progress we've made." He nodded at the two-story building, now almost completely framed out in wood, with drywall covering the interior walls. "We're right on schedule, maybe a bit ahead. And when the brick work goes up, it'll be a match for the hotel in soft yellow.''

"That's great, Sam.''

"There's a demand for training here, Molly. Folks are calling *me* at this point, checking on when we're opening. And that's in addition to my design clients. In fact,'' he said, "just this morning I spoke with a buddy on the West Coast who wants me to work with him long-distance.''

"Oh?''

"Yeah. We're talking virtual-reality applications, Mol. Not everyday Web sites.''

"Like geek stuff?''

Sam started laughing, and laughed long and hearty until Molly saw tears run from his eyes.

"Yes, Molly,'' he finally said, giving her another hug. "Geek stuff. I haven't been called a geek in years, but I suppose I am one at heart.''

"Speaking of the West Coast,'' Molly said, "that's why I'm here. You've got an old friend from California waiting for you in the lobby.'' She tilted her head in the direction of the hotel.

"Who?'' Sam asked as he turned and headed for the Bluebonnet.

"Sorry, I can't tell. I'm sworn to secrecy,'' Molly replied, keeping in step with him.

Sam chuckled. "Well, the suspense will be over in a minute. Who knows? Maybe another job opportunity has come along.''

"Ahh…I don't think so,'' Molly said.

Sam shrugged and led the way through the patio

and into the hotel. Molly followed slowly, wanting to allow some privacy for the reunion. But Adrienne was no longer at the registration desk. Molly spotted her sitting in a club chair, browsing through a magazine on the other side of the room, and tapped Sam on the shoulder. "Over there," she said nodding toward the woman.

Sam started in that direction, then stopped when the brunette lifted her head and saw him. "Adrienne?"

Adrienne Burke rose from her seat, her fashionable navy-blue outfit leaving no doubt about her advanced pregnancy. She smiled and said, "Hello, Sam," in the sexiest voice Molly had ever heard.

SAM STARED at his former girlfriend. Speech deserted him. Coherent thought deserted him. He stood as though he were made of stone.

"You've turned pale, Sammy. Have I shocked you that much?" Adrienne walked toward him and before he could answer, kissed him lightly on the mouth. "And here I thought you'd be so happy to see me, especially in this condition."

"Happy? I'm stunned. I thought...you said..."

Adrienne closed her eyes and sighed. "Obviously I changed my mind. I guess between your talk of 'miracles' and the fact that when it came right down to the wire, I just couldn't go through with the abortion. So I just...kept growing."

She sounded good. Sounded confident. But now Sam noticed the fatigue around her eyes, and despite his shock, started feeling concerned. "Sit down again, Adrienne. Please."

She complied.

"But why didn't you call me?" he asked. "Let me know? Didn't you think I'd be interested? It's my child, after all."

"I was far away, Sam. I've been working in Paris, France, not Paris, Texas, and plan to return. So nothing's really changed."

Suddenly Adrienne stood up again and whirled on him, her expression desperate. "Do you hear me, Sam? Nothing's changed. A baby was never part of my plans. You're the one who wanted it, not me. And I promise you that when I walk out of the hospital, I'll be a free woman again. With your cooperation or not."

Sam swallowed his shock. Or tried to. "You can't mean that, Adrienne," he said quietly, grasping for calm. "You're the mother. You're not thinking clearly. Your hormones are talking, that's all."

Adrienne eyeballed him with a boardroom look. "My hormones are just fine. Be reasonable, Sam. You know that I never wanted to be a mother. Auntie Adrienne will be happy to send presents for birthdays and Christmas."

Sam couldn't speak. He could barely believe Adrienne's words, but she looked totally serious. She poked him in the chest with her index finger.

"I'm serious, Sam," she said. "Either you claim this child as the father with your name on the birth certificate, or we sign adoption papers. By my calculations, you've got about a week to make up your mind.''

She meant it. Her entire being seemed to reverberate with her own personal truth. He didn't understand how she could feel that way, but there was no question that she did.

''You might change your mind after the baby's born,'' he said gently. ''And you know I'll share all expenses and caretaking.''

Adrienne sat back down, heavily this time, as though she'd used up her energy trying to convince him of her sincerity. She looked up. ''I know you think I'm being hardhearted, but I'm not. I'm being strong-minded and smart—for everyone concerned. I know myself and what I want out of life. And a baby isn't part of it. I'm trying to be as candid as possible so we can plan properly.''

Sam needed a minute. He turned away from his ex-girlfriend with the notion of finding Molly, but she was gone, and the clerk at the registration desk was busy.

He glanced back at Adrienne. ''The baby's mine,'' he said softly. ''It can't be anyone else's.''

''Good,'' Adrienne replied, ''I'm glad. You'll be a good father.''

She meant it, and Sam appreciated her confidence in him, but right then, he needed to speak with Molly. He looked at the desk clerk again, this time catching her eye.

''Molly?'' he called, a question in his voice.

''Sorry. She didn't say where she was going.''

Sam turned his attention back to Adrienne, his heart in his toes. How much had Molly heard? If he lost her...

"So that's the way the wind blows," said Adrienne.

Sam looked grim. "Right now I'm afraid it might be more like a storm brewing. God, I hope not." He held out a hand to the woman who carried his child. "Let's get you settled in."

And then he'd find Molly. And pray she'd listen to him.

MOLLY SLAMMED her car into reverse and peeled out of the hotel parking lot. She'd stopped at her office only to grab her purse before making her getaway. She'd always needed to be in the mountains when she was working out problems as a youngster, but there were no mountains here. No ski runs. No wind in her face. Just tears threatening to fall.

Almost by itself, her car turned toward the Miller ranch. Liz would provide her with a mount. But Liz wasn't home. Mrs. Miller, however, waved her toward the barn. "Help yourself, Molly. You've been back enough times to know what you're doing. And after the great wedding last night, you can have any horse in the place. My son and his bride sure got married in style." Her eyes twinkled as she looked at Molly. "But what a courtship!"

Molly forced a smile. "Thanks. I appreciate it. I just needed to get away for a while."

"Sometimes we all need to do that."

Molly walked to the barn and cast a critical eye over her choices. She stroked her old friend, Buttercup, but chose the gelding that Sam always rode. "C'mon, Bravo," she said. "We are going for a ride!"

He butted her shoulder in appreciation and whinnied. "Oh, yeah," she whispered, patting his neck before saddling him up.

Ten minutes later she finally felt the wind in her face as the big horse maintained a slow gallop down the familiar trail. She'd wrapped her long skirt around her legs as best she could and didn't worry about it. Slowly she emptied her mind of everything but the moment.

There was no Sam. There was no Adrienne. There was no baby. There was only the autumn sunshine, the dappled shade, the rocking of the horse and the quiet all around her. Peace. Peace in her heart and mind. An elusive goal, but she was determined to find it.

The rhythm of the horse was comforting, and she felt her body relax. Soon her mind followed suit, then began to wander.

She'd been through upheaval before. "Ha!" she exclaimed. An understatement. But she'd survived. Oh, yes, she'd survived then, and she'd survive now. Somehow. A fresh start was what she needed, and she'd find one. What was the old saying? "What doesn't kill you makes you stronger," she whispered.

But a sob escaped before she could control it. She didn't want to be tested any more.

Molly slowed Bravo to a walk, took a deep breath and then another. "Good boy," she murmured, patting the horse's neck. A perfect partner, responsive to her wants, comforting to be with. Molly was in no hurry to return to the barn or to the hotel.

She'd make no moves to renew her contract, of course. Her assistant had been hired and would be starting shortly. Sam... Another sob escaped, and she pressed her lips together hard. Sam would go on with his life. He and Adrienne and their child. The hotel would survive.

The horse snickered and Molly realized they had come to an arroyo with clear running water tempting whomever passed by. "Okay, boy," she whispered as she dismounted. "Let's have a drink."

She knelt at the edge of the stream, letting her hands cool in the wetness, before forming a cup to capture some liquid. After satisfying her thirst, she glanced at her reflection before splashing water on her face and neck. She had never looked more disheveled in her life. Her hair was a tangled, flyaway mess. She wore no makeup, not even lipstick, and her clothes were wrinkled from sitting on them.

She started to laugh at herself, but her mirth dissolved into tears almost instantly. With one arm through the horse's reins, she stretched out on the ground next to the stream and sobbed. She cried for the life she had once had, then lost. And she cried for the happiness she had almost found. She cried because the road ahead would be lonelier now than ever before—because she had loved. And lost.

SAM'S MIND was on Molly the entire time he spent with Adrienne. Asking about her medical reports, chatting about the delivery date and possible doctors took a while. Always organized, Adrienne had brought copies of every medical record. But all the time Sam was with Adrienne, he wanted to find Molly, talk to her, explain to her and just be with her.

God, he loved her. That evening was to have been one long romance, one big happily-ever-after event. He'd had it all planned. A declaration of love, followed by a marriage proposal. And now, he didn't have the first idea of where to look for her.

He checked her office; he checked her suite. She often enjoyed meandering through the gardens, so he checked those, also. No luck anywhere. Then he checked the parking lot.

"Damn!" Her spot was empty, but he trotted through the entire lot double-checking. Where would she go? He was frustrated by his own question. She could have gone anywhere.

Sam raced back into the hotel, ready to quiz every employee in the place. Gladys knew nothing. Madeline knew nothing. The front-desk clerks knew nothing. Bonnie knew nothing. But they all knew to call his cell phone if Molly showed up or telephoned.

He strode to her office again. Think. Think! Who

would she call? Who were her friends? Her best
friend just got married last night, so Carla was out
of the picture. He glanced at his watch. Almost two
o'clock. Could the honeymooners still be sleeping?
He shrugged. Neither of them would be aware of
anyone but each other. As it should be.

But how about Liz? Travis's sister had made a
beautiful bridesmaid last night, and she was one of
Molly's close friends.

He picked up the receiver, punched in the number
at the Miller ranch and had to settle for leaving a
message on their machine. He held the phone and
flipped through Molly's Rolodex searching for anything personal. Ace Linen Service, Chamber of
Commerce, Economic Development Board...the list
went on. He slammed the phone down.

If they'd been in ski country before Molly's accident, he'd look on a mountainside. He could picture her taking to the slopes if she wanted to get
away from everyone. But they were in Texas hill
country where Molly's sense of adventure and controlled risk-taking came from roller coasters
or...horses.

Sam raced to his Beemer. The Miller women
could have been anywhere on the property when
he'd called. The ranch was worth a shot.

AN HOUR LATER Sam was mounted on Travis's stallion. He bit his bottom lip knowing that Molly had
chosen to ride his usual mount, Bravo, instead of the
sweet, reliable Buttercup. Leave it to Molly to make

her statement clear without using any words. She needed action and she needed solitude. And didn't hesitate to find both.

He nudged the horse along the familiar path, fairly confident that Molly, who was still a novice, wouldn't decide to blaze her own trail. Molly's car had announced her presence on the ranch, and Travis's mom had confirmed Molly's request for a mount. But Mrs. Miller had been indoors when Molly had taken off and hadn't noticed which horse she'd chosen.

The trees thinned out away from the homestead, but Sam saw nothing resembling a human being. There weren't many places for a person to hide in the mostly wide-open spaces, but why should Molly be hiding? She'd had almost two hours' start on him and could be miles away.

"Find Bravo." Sam leaned over the big horse and talked softly in his ear. "We'll find Molly if you find Bravo," he encouraged, then was startled when the horse whinnied in response. He patted the animal's neck. "Good boy."

After ten minutes of riding, of periodically standing up in his stirrups to survey the horizon, Sam finally saw Molly's mount in the distance. Bravo, without a rider.

He cantered toward the other horse, his gaze constantly scanning the ground between himself and Bravo. Finally he spotted a patch of blue among the scrub grass at the edge of the arroyo. Molly's skirt! Fighting panic, Sam jumped from his horse and kneeled next to the woman who fed his dreams. She sighed deeply at that moment, yawned and turned toward him. And it was then he realized she was only sound asleep and not physically hurt. His relief left him shaking. Until he examined her face.

Tears had left their imprint on her cheeks; they still gathered on her lashes. She sighed again, or maybe it was a groan, and Sam saw another drop find its way down her pale skin.

His own heart twisted; he swore he could feel her pain. Then he leaned over and kissed her gently on the mouth.

"Molly..." he whispered.

CHAPTER FOURTEEN

"MOLLY. MOLLY."

She heard his voice. She inhaled his fragrance. She felt his lips touch hers...and felt herself smile. Turning, searching, reaching. It was a wonderful dream and she wanted to cling to it.

"Molly, are you all right?"

It really was Sam's voice. Sam's arms scooping her up. Suddenly reality hit her, and Molly scrambled to her feet, out of Sam's grasp, almost tripping in her need to escape. She turned away from him, rubbed her face with the back of her hands and tried to finger-comb her tousled mane into some semblance of order. Then she gave up. Took a breath and faced him.

"What are you doing here? How did you find me?" She wished her voice held more authority, more disdain, but he'd caught her off guard.

His eyes sought hers, but she avoided their search. He reached out. She stumbled back. "Mol?"

Did his voice break?

"Please. Don't walk away." His arm remained extended. "I love you, Molly. I love you very much. When I couldn't find you anywhere in the hotel, I went a little nuts. Until finally I thought of the horses.''

She studied his face. He spoke the truth, but... ''Love?'' she whispered. ''Do you know that this is the first time you've mentioned it?''

He took a step toward her. ''It certainly won't be the last. I love you, Molly, and I'll say it every day until all my days are gone.''

Tears welled up in her eyes, but she shook her head and gestured for him to stop where he stood. ''Your timing on the dance floor is a hell of a lot better than your timing for declarations of love.'' She took a deep breath. ''It's too late, Sam,'' she whispered. ''Much too late.''

''Too late? Of course it's not,'' he replied. ''It's never too late for love.''

Suddenly the irony of the situation, the irony of her life, hit her like the pound of a hammer. Molly spun away from Sam for a moment, digesting it, and when she turned back around, the confident Molly, the Molly who controlled the mountain and a hotel, had replaced the unsure Molly.

''Don't talk so foolishly. Of course it's too late. It's too late for many things, so many things.'' Her heart twisted and she blinked back tears. ''For me. For you.''

''You're wrong, Molly! I love you.''

''You love me?'' she cried. ''You can't! Not when there's a woman back at the Bluebonnet. A gorgeous woman, in fact, pregnant with your child, just waiting for you to be a family?''

But Sam was shaking his head. "You don't understand," he said. "She's not waiting for me at all. Not in a romantic way. Nor do I want her in any way—except to give birth to a healthy child."

Molly stared at him. "You always seem to have what you don't want and want what you don't have. You wanted a high-flying high-tech career, but you have a hotel, instead. You wanted a dream life in California, but you have a real life here in Texas. Now you say you want me, but you've got other important responsibilities. I can't possibly displace them, and I don't want to. You can't walk out on them!"

Hands on hips, breath rasping, she waited for his reply. His jaw was clenched; she could almost hear his teeth grinding. And his eyes narrowed with the pain her words caused. But she remained silent.

"Are you finished?" he asked quietly.

She nodded.

"Good," he said.

Molly squirmed as his eyes examined her for what seemed like an eternity. And then he spoke again.

"I have never run away from responsibility in my entire life, and I don't plan on starting now." His voice was low, his words clear. "I faced my employees in person, every single one of them, when my companies went under. I was the last one out, shutting the lights and closing the door behind us."

She hadn't known the details, but she heard the grief as he relived his story.

"Adrienne disappeared so fast I couldn't even

feel her breeze, and she never told me about carrying the baby to term. Never. She was going to get rid of it, Molly. So who walked out on whom?''

Molly tried to draw even breaths. Sam continued to look at her as though she held the keys to the kingdom. Hope warred with wariness. Warmth alternated with fear. Could he really love her? Did he know what love was? It didn't matter. The child came first.

''Adrienne's changed her mind,'' said Molly. ''She needs you. And it's not too late. That baby needs a mother and a father.''

A ghost of a smile appeared on his face. ''Well, that's one thing we agree on.''

Damn! Molly felt her mouth tremble. ''So go back to her,'' she insisted.

''Impossible,'' Sam replied as he approached Molly. ''I don't love her and she doesn't love me.''

Molly moved backward. Short step. ''It doesn't matter,'' she said. ''The baby needs a good home.'' Long step.

She shouldn't have looked into his dark eyes, now filled with hope and heat. But she did and couldn't turn away. Couldn't move at all.

''The baby needs a mom and dad who love each other,'' said Sam, walking closer. ''And then he or she will have a good home.''

He had a point. An important point.

He stood directly in front of her now. ''Adrienne is giving up all custody rights to me. She's returning to France, *without the baby,* as soon as possible after giving birth.''

Molly thought she must have heard wrong. ''What? Say that again. You've got to be mistaken. A woman doesn't—''

''Adrienne does,'' Sam interrupted.

Molly shivered to her toes and wrapped her arms around herself. The whole idea of abandoning a child... She shook her head, tears stinging her eyes. She thought of Amanda's fabulous kids. Rachel. Marc. Molly would protect them with her life if, God forbid, they ever needed it. ''Do you know what I'd give...what I'd give to...'' She faltered. ''Oh, never mind.''

Suddenly Sam's arms were around her, his broad chest beneath her cheek. Little by little, she leaned into him, and warmth began to return to her soul. She rocked in his embrace for a moment and heard him say, ''I love you, Molly. Please marry me and build a life with me.''

SHE'D ALMOST SAID yes.

But the waters had become muddied and she couldn't see clearly—a baby, an ex-girlfriend, a marriage proposal—and she'd said as much to Sam. But first she'd kissed him. And sizzled to her toes. Knew he felt the same. And that was good. But something nagged at her, and until she figured out what it was, she was not making any decision as important as marriage. She needed a little time.

She sat at her desk the next morning, recalling the

ride back to the ranch house. She and Sam, side by side on their mounts, not saying anything, coming to terms with their individual thoughts and actions. A peaceful ride to soothe the turmoil preceding it, and ending with a kiss—the kind of kiss a woman didn't forget quickly—from Sam when he helped her dismount.

"Take as much time as you need, as long as you come up with the right answer." His joke fell slightly flat, and she heard the strain in his voice, but she appreciated his effort to honor her wishes.

"Good morning, Molly," said Sam, coming into her office and closing the door behind him. He walked behind her desk, bent down and kissed her. "I love doing that."

And she loved his kisses. "Good morning."

Sam leaned away and pointed a finger at her. "It's your fault I've had a lousy night, barely slept, because an awful idea came into my head."

She couldn't tell if he was kidding. His mouth smiled, but his eyes…not kidding.

"You've got an active mind," he continued. "An imagination. And it occurred to me that you might take it into your head that I needed you only to be a mother to the baby. A convenience."

"What?"

"But I swear, Molly, it's not true. If you don't want to take care of the child, I'll hire a baby-sitter. You're not a nursemaid."

She jumped from the chair, reached for the hand

pointing at her and clasped it in both of hers. "Sam, Sam. I never thought it, not once."

"Oh." He paused. "Good."

She felt the tension leave his body as she continued to hold his hand.

"And another thing…" he said.

"What?"

"We were supposed to have a date last night."

She raised her brows and smiled. "Right."

"And I was going to propose then. On top of the Ferris wheel. I love you, Molly, more than I want a child—"

"Wait, wait. On top of the Ferris wheel?"

He nodded.

Her laughter turned to tears. Then she wrapped her arms around his neck and hugged him. "I love it. You're my kind of romantic."

His grin said it all—until he nodded in the direction of the hotel lobby. "But complications arrived before my big plan."

"Oh, it wouldn't have worked out, anyway," Molly said, and then could have slapped herself for not choosing her words more carefully when she saw Sam's complexion turn pale.

"No, no," she said. "Not that. It's just that the amusement parks are closed for the season."

"No!"

"Yes." She giggled. His expression was priceless. "Hey, I run a hotel. I know what's going on in the neighborhood."

"You sure do run a hotel," he said. "And I'd never stand in the way of your career."

She held up her hand. "I know that. I just need a little time."

"The operative word is 'little,'" Sam grumbled as he turned to leave. "Oh, I've got to take Adrienne to meet her doctor today. She doesn't know her way around."

Molly winked. "Congratulations, Dad."

"Somehow I don't feel like celebrating." He stared at her. "Not until you're at my side."

A WEEK LATER, Molly sat on the bench overlooking the lily pond, her favorite spot on the property. The green sweep of lawn, dotted with flowering plants, was restful. Early evening in late October provided a welcome coolness, characteristic of the season ahead. Would she be there to experience it?

She sighed deeply. She loved working at the Bluebonnet. She loved living in Oak Creek. But her skills were portable, and she'd be an asset at any hotel in the world.

She loved Sam. He was ambitious, but he was also kind. Loyal, loving. Honorable. Her heart raced as she pictured him in her mind's eye. Tall, broad, with arms that would embrace her for a lifetime. So why was she hesitating?

She rubbed her temples. No more thinking. Just inhale and exhale. Relax. Enjoy the peace.

"Will you put the poor man out of his misery?"

Molly gave a start, then inclined her head. Adrienne Burke stood just to the side and behind her. Amazing how some women could look stylish and svelte even when nine months pregnant.

"Are the accommodations satisfactory, Ms. Burke?" asked Molly. She had no intention of discussing Sam with anyone, especially not with Adrienne. And if Sam had discussed her... She glanced at her hands, now balled into fists.

"Relax," said the other woman. "Sam's been a perfect gentleman." She stepped to the bench. "Mind if I join you?"

Molly leaned her head back and gave her an amused look. "Do I have a choice?"

Adrienne grinned and shook her head. "Not really. I've wanted a chance to talk to you and couldn't resist the opportunity." She slowly scanned the property. "It's beautiful here. Peaceful." She turned to Molly. "You are very good at your job."

Surprised at the turn of conversation, Molly just stared. "Thank you. I've been well trained."

"No," said Adrienne. "It's more than that. I've watched you for a week now. Seen you listening to and chatting with folks. You're a nurturer. This hotel really is a home away from home for your guests."

"But—"

Adrienne cut her off. "I'm a businesswoman, Molly, and I know what I know. I know what I see. But more importantly I see a man so in love with a woman that he almost ran off the road today on the way back from the doctor's."

"What?"

"You're putting him through hell, my dear. And I'll tell you one last thing just in case it's the root of your silence."

Molly stared, clueless as to what to expect from the woman.

Adrienne leaned toward Molly. "Sam Kincaid never looked at me the way he looks at you, as though you and you alone held the secrets to the universe. Sam and I never loved each other the way he loves you. We were…a mutual-admiration society of two people on the way up the career ladder. And that's all." She rose from the bench. "And that's all I have to say."

"Thanks for sharing," said Molly, "but you needn't have bothered. I know exactly how Sam feels about me. No man could feel that way about two woman at the same time."

"You mean I bared my soul for nothing?"

Molly chuckled. "Sam can take care of himself, Adrienne. He doesn't need an advocate." She threw the other woman an assessing glance. "But your baby does. And you're it. And that's really why you're here with me."

Bingo. Adrienne's complexion turned a shade of light green.

"Your child will be in good hands with Sam," said Molly gently.

"I know that."

"But you came here and found an even better scenario. You found Sam in love with a nice woman, and it was like whipped cream on the cake for you. Now your conscience won't have to trouble you at all. Am I right?"

As Molly watched, Adrienne's lips started to tremble and her eyes shone with repressed tears, before she took a breath and regained her composure. "It was Sam's damn miracle," she said. "So it's his baby. I'm just the incubator." She stood up and began walking away.

Molly called to her. "Adrienne."

The woman turned.

"It's okay," said Molly. "I don't quite understand you, but I think you're being as honest as you can. And I appreciate that."

"I'm returning to Paris as soon as this package is delivered," Adrienne replied. "Sam's name will be on the birth certificate. The baby's his."

Molly watched Adrienne's retreating back and started to tremble. She had to find Sam. Immediately.

SHE STOOD UP and plopped back on the bench. Her legs wouldn't hold her. Her cell phone was in her pocket, and she dialed Sam's number. He picked up.

"I'm by the lily pond," she said. "I need to see you."

"Two seconds and I'm there."

The phone went dead, and Molly replaced it in her skirt pocket. When she looked up, Sam was loping toward her through the woods from the new building. She'd called and he'd come. He was everything she wanted, and she was scared to death.

But not too scared to get up and start running toward him. She needed to hold him, to touch him, to feel his solid presence.

She hadn't counted on the slope of the ground. Short step, long step. Short, long. Her feet tangled, her strides melded together, her balance off. Dear God, she couldn't suffer another big fall. What if the rod in her leg came out? What if she couldn't heal again?

Gravity pulled. Her arms whirled at her sides like propellers in her attempt to remain upright. The gentle slope had morphed into a steep mountainside.

The ground rushed up to meet her and she screamed.

"Gotcha!"

Crushed in Sam's arms, snug against his chest, she struggled to breathe. Her heart raced, her arms and legs turned to jelly. If Sam hadn't been holding her, she would have folded like a paper lantern.

She started to cry. "This was why I called you," she said between sobs.

"You knew you were going to fall?"

She smiled and shook her head. His fingers lifted her chin and he kissed her. "Hey, girl. You're fine. Nothing happened."

"But I'm so scared, Sam. That's why I needed you."

"And I'm here, Mol. Always."

She leaned backward to see him better. "You mean that?"

He stared at her. "Of course I do. I love you, Molly. And that's forever."

She believed him, but...

"Once before in my life, I put everything into one basket, and I lost. I lost big time." She put her hands on his arms and squeezed. "Do you know what I mean? I lost everything. And now there's even more at stake."

His expression became incredulous. "Are you saying you're afraid to try for a wonderful future with me? Are you, the intrepid Molly Ann Porter, really a coward? Are you...afraid of failure, Molly, or afraid of success?"

Stunned by his analysis, she could only stare at him. "Afraid of success?" she whispered. "What kind of question is that? I aimed for the Olympics for years! I wanted gold!"

"Then you missed the point."

"The point? Winning was the point."

He shook his head. "Maybe for a medal. But in life, a real winner goes back and keeps on trying. Again and again. Your worth is not measured by a two-minute run down a hill." He kissed her. "And, baby, this time you're not alone on a mountain with only a cold wind at your back. I'm right here beside you."

Tears stung her eyes. *Alone.* That was the problem all along. Before she met Sam, she'd pictured herself alone for the rest of her life. Her career would substitute. Her family would be there for her. She'd convinced herself it would have been sufficient.

But after meeting Sam and loving Sam, how could she go backward, settle for less? She didn't want to. But what if something happened and she lost everything again?

"Love…is…risky," she said.

"Life is risky," Sam replied with a laugh. "But love is everything, Molly, especially between a husband and a wife."

"Yes," she breathed.

"So, will you marry me now?"

"Yes," she breathed again. "Because I love you, Sam Kincaid. And love is worth the risk. I would be honored to take one step at a time through life with you."

Love, strong and heated, shone from his eyes. And then he kissed her, and she knew she'd found her home.

"Sam," she whispered when she could, "you don't have to hire a baby-sitter. Your child will need a mother. I'll love him or her. I promise."

He tightened his embrace again. "*Our* child will need a mother," he corrected. "And he or she will be the luckiest baby in the world to have you as a mom."

"Thank you, Sam." She lifted her hand and stroked his cheek, basking in his loving expression.

Her heart was light. True happiness meant sharing her life, sharing her love. Creating her own piece of heaven on earth.

EPILOGUE

Three years later...

"DON'T YOU THINK he needs poles?"

Molly looked over her shoulder at her husband, who was slowly skiing his way toward her, looking about as stylish as a grizzly bear. His eyes, however, were glued to their son, Jonathan, who knew no fear as he skied down the bunny hill at Diamond Ridge. No question that Sam preferred skiing on water, but he was game for anything that involved the entire family. And Molly loved him for that.

"Hey, Mommy," called Jon. "Look at me!"

Molly waved as the child skied by. "You're doing great, sweetie." She looked at Sam. "And so are you." She raised her face for a kiss and received one. "Jonny's a lot closer to the ground than you are, Sam. Little kids don't need poles. He's finding his balance just fine."

"And how are you doing?" Sam asked.

Molly glanced around. "With a bright sunny sky and a temperature of thirty-eight, my family all around me, how could I complain about anything?"

"Now tell the truth about the rest of it. I can't believe the bunny hill is enough for you."

"As a matter of fact," said Molly, eyeing the mountains surrounding her, "with my special boot, there's technically no reason I can't challenge one of those." She waved at a double-black-diamond trail, the most difficult they had.

Sam gasped, and Molly quickly patted his arm. "But I won't," she reassured him. "I don't need to prove anything anymore." She sighed. "Adrienne didn't know what she gave up when I adopted Jonathan."

"She thinks she does. Remember her visit when Jonny had a stomach virus?"

"Oh, yeah." Molly giggled. "She couldn't wait to leave."

"And she'd never understand why we'd like another child. But from Adrienne, birthday cards are enough."

"Amen."

They watched in companionable silence as their son walked sideways back up the hill.

"It's been a nice visit," said Molly. "But I'm starting to itch. I think the Bluebonnet's calling me."

Sam laughed in agreement. "I know the feeling."

"Oh, cut it out! It's not the hotel that's on your mind. It's the Tech Center and Sam Kincaid, Leading Edge Design, Inc., that has you going."

Sam's grin acknowledged the truth of her words. "When did you get so smart, my love? Between the training component and our own design company—especially the new hotel-system package I'm working on that Zach's so excited about—I have more than I can handle. But, Molly," he whispered, signs of laughter gone, "I'm very happy. Thank you."

"My pleasure." She maneuvered next to him and put her arms around him. She swore their love grew stronger every day. After three years of marriage, of making sweet gorgeous love with him, she couldn't imagine a life without Sam. "Your uncle would be proud, Sam. Very, very proud."

Silence prevailed for a moment. "I hope so. I think about him a lot."

"Yeah. So how about we take his namesake and do the four mile beginner's trail as a family? It'll be fun."

"Four miles?" asked Sam, a frown creasing his forehead.

"Afraid you can't keep up with Jon and me?" Molly teased. "It's an easy trail, small inclines. You can do it."

"Afraid? Me?" Sam protested. "It's you I'm concerned about."

"Don't be," Molly grinned. "It's not a race. It's family time."

She called to their son and started leading both her men toward the appropriate trail when her cell phone rang.

It was her sister. "Get right back to the lodge," Amanda said. "You and Sam. Immediately. You received a phone call, and you'll want to return it without delay.''

Molly looked at her husband. ''Sam,'' she said in a hoarse voice as she returned the phone to her pocket. ''I think this is it.''

''And if it isn't?'' Sam asked, grasping Molly's hand and tipping up her face so he could meet her eyes. ''It's still okay, Mol. We've got our family. We've got each other.''

''You're right.'' Molly breathed slowly, trying to calm down. ''But another child would be...wonderful.''

''Let's go.''

Amanda met them at the door to the lodge, eyes shining. ''Congratulations, you're pregnant! I'm glad I'm your lawyer, because I get to tell you the good news. The embryo transfer worked. Your surrogate is two months along with your biological child. She's healthy and happy to be able to help you.''

Molly froze, unable to believe.

Sam didn't have the same problem. ''Yahoo!'' He whirled Molly around. ''Hey, girl! We're having another baby.''

''Baby!'' Jonny yelled. ''Mommy, I not a baby!''

Noise, voices, sounds of celebration all around her. Molly scooped her son up into her arms. ''You're my big boy, Jonny. Mommy's very big boy.''

The child leaned against her and yawned. His eyes closed and he relaxed, his weight settling against Molly's chest. She kissed his dark wavy hair, inhaling the smell of little boy and outdoors. She cuddled him closer, thankful for this miracle. Unable to believe they'd be blessed again.

It seemed she'd won the gold, after all.

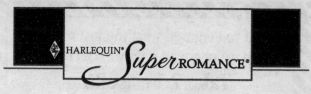

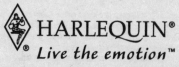

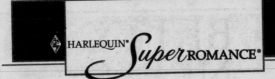

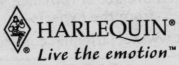

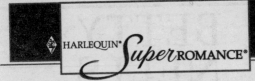

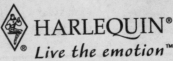